THE OTHER
OREGON

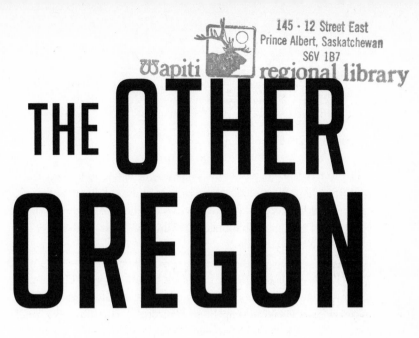

THE OTHER OREGON

A Thriller

STEVE ANDERSON

YUCCA

Yucca Publishing books may be purchased in bulk at special discounts for sales promotion, corporate gifts, fund-raising, or educational purposes. Special editions can also be created to specifications. For details, contact the Special Sales Department, Yucca Publishing, 307 West 36th Street, 11th Floor, New York, NY 10018 or yucca@skyhorsepublishing.com.

Yucca Publishing® is an imprint of Skyhorse Publishing, Inc.®, a Delaware corporation.

Visit our website at www.yuccapub.com.

10 9 8 7 6 5 4 3 2 1

Library of Congress Cataloging-in-Publication Data is available on file.

Cover design by Yucca Publishing

Print ISBN: 978-1-63158-045-1
Ebook ISBN: 978-1-63158-055-0

Printed in the United States of America

THE OTHER OREGON

1

Duct tape had sealed the mouths of the three men. The three were left facing each other, standing in a tight triangle, their wrists bound together to a pole, first crouching, then standing again, two of them shaking their wrists and heads in panic. Their newer sedan was still there, just feet away, parked at the old gas station that stood alone at this rural junction, closed long ago. The car doors were ajar and all the tires flat. The plates read Oregon: Publicly Owned. On the ground, their three wallets lay in a pile. Their business cards had scattered. Whiffs of smoke shifted in the air.

The two men in a panic were state officials, wearing button-downs. Neither would continue in their jobs after a traumatic experience like this. The third man, FBI Special Agent Rich Torres, knew that much just by seeing them quiver and groan under all that duct tape.

All three of them had their pants yanked down, and branded on their buttocks were two Xs, like so: X X.

Their burns were red, though not too deep. Their captors had used a handheld propane torch to get the branding iron hot, but it wasn't heated enough—Torres had noticed that from the iron's weak glow. Yet the state officials had only seen that branding iron coming at them, heard their captors cackling, smelled the smoke.

Now their eyes showed more fear of having the bare skin of their asses branded than of any lasting pain.

Agent Torres stopped looking at them. He breathed through his nose to better regulate his breathing, to keep his heart steady and calm. He was wearing a new khaki suit to show these state guys the FBI always meant business no matter where they were. His angular face was crowned with thick black hair. Colleagues and criminals alike said Rich Torres was handsome in a casual way, like a pro golfer, and he made sure he kept his composure like any pro did, even here with his pants down and his ass raw. He scanned the far-off countryside with eyes that did not blink. The two-lane highway they drove in on ran parallel to a dry and rocky riverbed, a long gray line through the low, rolling landscape of scrubby brown grass and knotty shrubs, well east of the Cascades mountain range—still Central Oregon by name, but it might as well be Eastern from the vast and faded desolation of it all. Beyond, Torres tracked a cloud of gritty Indian summer dust kicked up by the six masked men who had branded them and run off, now just a wisp on the horizon.

2

Greg Simmons loved this cemetery. He hated most of them. Graveyards only reminded him of all that he had buried. He had helped bury a corpse, years ago. Lone Fir Cemetery was different, however. It filled a small old forest in Portland, Oregon, far enough from the Cascade Mountains where they had murdered the man. Greg loved this cemetery because its eternal residents were Portland's first settlers. Pioneers. These people had tried to start over. How many had succeeded? He wished he could ask them. Most of the tombstones were pocked and weathered, dating back to the 1840s. Yet their names and dates and hometowns stood as reminders of what was possible. They had come here, to the Pacific Northwest. They had made a better place.

The pioneer ideal appealed to him. He had helped commit a gruesome act, but he had strived to bury his grim secret forever by becoming a person seemingly incapable of such a deed. He had returned to Portland after ten years as a reporter around the US and abroad, a wannabe vagabond stringer in Eastern Europe and South America, mostly. He had been a journalist, a nonfiction writer, an observer of nasty truths. This had taken his blinders off. This had humbled him. It left him wanting more humbling and gave him some kind of hope. Since returning to Portland, he had made himself into a known authority on the dream of Cascadia— on the prospects of the Pacific Northwest bioregion seceding from the US, what would be called Cascadia if he had anything to do with it.

Earlier, Greg had gotten a phone call while riding his bike on SE Seventh. He had slowed to the curb and pulled his phone from his pocket as cars and trucks rushed by the bike lane. He'd dropped his phone. Picked it out of the wet gravel, wiped it off. Missed his call. But it rang again. Unknown Caller, it read. Usually he ignored unknown callers, but something made him answer.

"Good afternoon," a male voice said. "Are you Greg Simmons?"

"Yes?"

"My name's Rich Torres. I'm with the FBI. I'd like to meet with you."

The FBI? Greg recoiled inside, his stomach churning.

"Is that all right?" Torres added.

"Sure, okay. Why?"

"It's nothing to worry about."

Greg laughed, had made himself laugh. "No, I didn't think it was. Just curious—not every day you get a call from the FBI."

"It's about Donny Wilkie."

The name Donny Wilkie had always weighed on Greg's memory like some deep dark water keeping him under, but hearing it spoken was like filling his lungs with the stuff. He wanted to cough on it and vomit it up. He managed a little chuckle instead. "Now there's a name I haven't heard in a long time," he said.

Torres didn't comment.

"So, where and when?" Greg said.

"Somewhere discreet. As soon as it's convenient."

Greg might love Lone Fir Cemetery, as cemeteries go, but he had picked it because it was secluded and perfect for his discreet meeting. The long block of woods stood between SE Morrison and Stark in the twenties' streets, on what once was the crest of a grand forested hill. He chose the oldest corner. Looking out from this hill long ago, one probably would have been able to see far up the Willamette River south toward Oregon City or even the tall masts of ships traveling the Columbia River up north. Across the Willamette back then, downtown Portland was only a muddy, scrappy little settlement down low along the water's edge. Around Greg the oldest tombstones had faces chiseled on them, likenesses of hardened settlers who glared at him with matted down hair, thick mustaches hiding toothless mouths, and tightly pulled buns as if to say, I fought and scraped my way across this brutal continent to remake myself—you understand that, Greg. You only get one shot at this.

Rich Torres from the FBI would spot him easily. Greg was in his late thirties and still working his half-nerd, half-rebel look with vintage horn-rimmed glasses and western shirt, black tee underneath. His beard growth not too long or short but with some gray creeping in. As he waited inside the cemetery woods, clouds the color of gunmetal passed over the tops of the trees. A mini-mausoleum loomed behind him, its stonework cracking and stained glass windows dulled, the gargoyles all pitted, and a coat of arms illegible. It was no bigger than a backyard shed but had the grandeur of fallen empires. Did his forebears mean for this mock Romantic-Gothic to end up looking so decayed, as a warning to those who dared to think as big as they? Or was it simply from all the rain and sap and pollution dripping down through the branches, from the occasional shifting of the earth below?

Greg heard a shuffle of feet—from inside the mini-mausoleum. A man filled the arched entrance.

"Jesus," Greg muttered, startled. He stepped back.

The man came out, ducking for the archway. "Thanks for coming," he said and held out his hand. "Special Agent Rich Torres."

"Ah, right," Greg said and shook the hand. Special Agent Torres had a helmet of dark hair and was almost good-looking in the way a tennis coach might be, Greg thought. Torres wore a simple hooded rain jacket and those all-purpose shoes made for rain, hiking, and city. He was about fifty, Greg guessed. The gray outdoor light shadowed his features though and lent them bulk, making him look more like a jaded private detective or some stressed-out property developer.

"I didn't expect you here before me," Greg said, as any innocent person with his personality and demographic would in such a situation. He used to have to work at sounding this way, trying out various steady responses, but it had been years since he felt real pressure. Now he felt a little squishy in his knees. His chest tightened. He added a smile for Torres.

"What did you expect?" Torres said.

Greg just shrugged. "I hate to ask, but can I see some ID? It's not like I get a call from the FBI everyday and, well, there are a lot of scammers out there."

"Certainly. You'd be a fool not to ask." Torres produced an FBI ID card, balancing it between fingertips as if ready to do a magic trick with it.

Greg looked at the official FBI photo and words but a slight rattle of panic fogged his eyes and he couldn't have repeated what he saw if asked. He turned the ID card over, then handed it back.

"I'd give you this card but suddenly I'm all out," Torres said.

"That's okay. What can I do for you?"

"Tell me about Donny Wilkie. When did you hear about his death?"

Hearing the name again made Greg straighten up inside like someone shot a hot liquid metal up his ass. This hit him in a half-second blur, in the time it took him to twitch. He wondered if a guy like Torres could notice. He masked it by taking a deep breath, as if having to think about the question. "Oh, years ago. Around the time it happened."

"You sound relieved. Like you were relieved."

"Really? It was so long ago."

"Word is, it happened in Mexico."

"It was a robbery, right?—another robbery. Probably drugs involved, I'm guessing. There was some sort of explosion, I remember. What an idiot. I wasn't relieved or unrelieved. I hadn't seen the guy in years."

"Who told you about it?" Torres said.

Greg cocked his head at Torres in a way that said: Should I be answering these questions? Do I need a lawyer or something?

"We're just talking here," Torres added. "It's okay. You've been a journalist, right? It's like an interview. Off the record."

"All right, let me think." Greg stared at his feet and focused on his retro New Balance runners, using their artifice as his time machine. It must have been ten years ago when he found out, but how much should he say?

"Ten years ago," Torres said for him.

"Right, right. Ten years. I must have looked it up. It must have been the state database. The old LexisNexis maybe? That was when I was a reporter. Is that how you found me? From a database—from the logs?"

"You hadn't returned to Oregon yet."

"No. I was in New York City probably. I traveled a lot."

"You two were friends."

"I wouldn't go that far. We had been friends years earlier. I hadn't seen him in years when he died."

"So, fifteen years?" Torres said. "Maybe more. Wilkie moved here in high school. A country kid, fish out of water. He gets on the wrong path. You don't. Later, you got curious about him.

Maybe you saw a little story in it—one of those sad pieces about dumb criminals but with a name you know."

"That's probably it. I wasn't the best reporter ever, but I was good at following stuff deeper. I would go on these tangents."

"There you go. It's completely natural," Torres said. He turned away a moment, looking in each direction as if on a boulevard heavy with traffic.

That rush of hot liquid metal tightening Greg inside had subsided, and Torres' pause to check their environs helped. Greg only hoped it wasn't some kind of tactic to lull him.

Torres turned back to him. "How we doing so far?"

"Doing? Fine. I'm fine," Greg said.

"Do you know where he's buried?" Torres said.

"Who, Donny? No. That I do not know."

"It was not Mexico. We do know that."

Greg held out his hands, palms out. "Okay, you know what? Let's stop a sec here. This is the part where I have to ask you what you want exactly. No offense."

"No, of course not," Torres said. "Let me ask you something—how's this for a book idea: the true story of a chronic criminal, torn between country and city?"

"'Chronic?' Not the best word choice, but . . ." Greg let his words trail off. He was intrigued and didn't like the feeling, because this was no subject to be liking. He stopped. "Wait, just wait. I just don't understand what this is about. This is all because I kinda knew a guy almost twenty years ago who's been dead for ten?"

Torres and Greg had a staring contest for a good five seconds, but Torres was winning as if Greg was one of these tombstones and Torres was reading it. Cars whooshed by beyond the tree line.

"Come on," Torres said. He walked Greg over to the doorway of the mausoleum, his eyes searching the grounds again even though they were still alone and certainly didn't look suspicious; if anything, they were keeping this cemetery less weird, populated as it could be by various LARPers and mushroom-trippers and wannabe Wiccans.

Torres pulled a few photos from his rain jacket and arranged them like a hand of cards, faces down. Greg's jitters returned and he blurted out a giggle, which only made him feel like some perv seeking dirty photos in the park.

Torres turned one photo over, showing it to Greg.

The man in the photo was wearing a casual suit and a cowboy hat. His lean face had those faint acne scars but also the dimples, and he was still smiling that great smile he'd had. It was definitely Donny Wilkie. The photo was a little grainy, like a blown-up surveillance photo. It was difficult to tell how old Donny was, but Greg figured it must have been right before he died—well after he knew Donny.

"Yeah, that's him," Greg said. "He looks so normal."

Torres showed Greg another photo. Donny was wearing paramilitary clothing with many pockets. The matching camouflage was vibrant and the fabric crisp as if new, less like a hunter and more like a military contractor. Donny grinned in this photo, his teeth clenched in a way Greg didn't recognize, his already dark eyes punctuating the photo like ink blots.

The very ground beneath Greg felt squishy now, though it was an all-concrete path. The jitters had settled low in his stomach, and he needed to say something to fight the sick feeling—to distance himself from this Donny that he may have had a hand in creating.

"He was . . . what, in the Army? I didn't know that."

"No, that he was not," Torres said.

"All I know is, violence was never his deal," Greg said.

"I thought you didn't know him that well."

"I'm just saying, not from what I remember. Not the Donny I knew. Maybe he was hunting in that one photo. He is from rural Oregon. They all hunt out there, don't they?"

"You really don't know what they do, do you? Just so you know: I'm a Special Agent, Field Agent, whatever you want to call it. Also, what they call a Resident Agent. I'm not in Portland much. Been out in Central, Eastern Oregon for years."

"That's your territory."

"It is. I get to do my own thing. Can it get boring? Yes. Then? Something happens and it's all you."

"Not sure if I'd like that," Greg said.

Torres shrugged. He made the photos disappear inside his rain jacket. "We know one thing for certain. Prison got him connected to militia types."

"Militia? You mean like Timothy McVeigh, homegrown terrorist stuff?"

"It doesn't always go that far," Torres said. "A lot of militias out there just run around in the desert with guns and rave about how great the Constitution is, like it's some pastor's daughter who's been raped and they will avenge her, restore her good name so they can finally have her."

"I don't think it works like that," Greg said, keeping calm. A militia was the last thing he expected. A militia just didn't fit into any concept of Cascadia he could imagine. Even the word sounded awkward, as if he was saying it for the first time.

"No, it doesn't work like that. The Constitution is still a living document, one that could leave them hanging any time."

"Okay, but the database I saw didn't have any of this on Donny."

"True. Back then it didn't. His felonies were for robbery, drugs, mail fraud. After, though, Donny had contact with certain people."

And what about well before? Years before? What did this Torres know exactly? Greg had been around long enough to know a guy like Torres always knew more than he let on. It was all about finding leverage and knowing how to tap the power of that leverage.

"So, you want me to write something?" Greg said. "Why you brought up a book idea. That is what we're talking about, right?"

Torres nodded. "What you do with it is up to you. I, we, are looking for someone to look into Donny's last steps, see what he was up to, what he helped create, but someone who doesn't seem like us. Someone who could have their own reasons completely. See what I mean? You'll have to go certain places. The where and who will be what I tell you."

"Wait. You're recruiting me? Like, an informant?" Greg let out another chuckle, but this one was so real it made a squirrel peel off among the branches above them.

Torres only stared back, squinting a little, like a director considering someone for a role. Greg didn't like the feeling this gave him. He kept his smile going, but it wasn't easy.

"When would this happen?"

"As soon as you can."

Greg shook his head. "I got too much going on."

"We would compensate you, of course."

"I have enough to get by. Doing what I love."

"Well, what if I told you that there is one militia group, right now, right here in our State of Oregon, that is a direct and violent threat to all you've written about Cascadia?"

This was the last thing Greg needed. A militia was the drunken uncle at Thanksgiving, peeing on the side of the house and passing out on the sofa, ranting about government takeovers and New World Orders, and shouting out family secrets at the table. Drunken uncle destroyed Thanksgiving just by being there. He said, "And, Donny was involved in this, uh, militia?"

"They could not exist as they are now without him. They talk a big talk and that kind of thing is free speech, as you well know, but here's the thing: They may be stepping over the line now and becoming a verifiable threat. They use X's as their calling card."

"Two X's?"

Torres' phone rang somewhere in his coat. He killed the sound after a few notes. "Two X's," he added.

"I'm just not sure about this," Greg said. "It didn't end great between me and Donny. I can tell you that. We had kind of a falling out."

"Even better," Torres said. "You're just trying to find out what the hell happened to this guy you used to know. That's all it is. You wouldn't even be lying, not that much."

Greg didn't answer. He didn't want to find out what the hell had happened to Donny. They were rid of each other, and Donny would have felt the same. At rare times like this, Greg wished he had a cigarette. He'd quit years ago, before he'd made himself leave Portland—all part of his transformation. He pulled off his horn-rims and polished them with a corner of his pattern shirt and could have just as well pocketed them since he could see well enough without the glasses. But there was a certain posture to maintain. He was a certain kind of guy now.

"You look different without those," Torres said.

"Maybe I don't care what happened to him," Greg said.

"Or his militia?" Torres took a step forward. "Look. You want to make the world a better place? Right? That's what your Cascadia fantasy is all about. So here's your shot."

"It's not a fantasy. I appreciate you don't call it that."

"Sorry. Though, it's probably better I look at it that way. For your sake. I am FBI after all."

"True. Okay. Fine. What else you want me to know?"

"We think they're planning something, these people. We just don't know what," Torres said. "I can tell you that."

"Planning something?" The thought of doom and death made Greg shiver as if a thick drop of rain had splashed on his neck from the branches above.

"It looks like it, yes."

"So, I would be checking into this group, with the pretense being I somehow knew Donny Wilkie had been there once, and he was a guy I used to know?" Greg said.

"Correct."

"And how would I tell them that I knew about them?"

"You wouldn't necessarily. You would just 'discover' them as part of your research. We'll get to that—we'll brief you on everything . . ."

Greg nodded along to Torres' words, but he also went on a little walk. He stepped over to the mausoleum and peeked inside. He saw nothing but darkness and smelled dust and cobwebs and nodded at that. Torres had left him alone. He glanced over to see Torres scratch at his rear end, but softly, touching only with fingertips, not as if adjusting underwear but more like he had an itch but wasn't supposed to scratch it. Which was odd.

Greg gave Torres a moment to himself, then walked back. "So, just by listening to you, it doesn't mean I've accepted anything, right?"

Torres' eyes shifted inward a bit as if he'd taken an imaginary step backward. "That's true. Yes. We're just talking. Like I said, It is up to you."

3

"Afternoon, fellow Cascadians," Greg said at three o'clock on the dot. He made eye contact with his audience and smiled. He held up his book *Rescuing Cascadia*. "One thing before we start. If you haven't read it yet, the price has dropped."

"Is it retroactive?" said a blogger guy up front. This brought a few chuckles, but Greg knew the guy was not kidding.

Greg sat up, making his face taut in his best impression of a serious young professor. "Okay, so, let's talk about the practicalities of founding Cascadia," he began. He was sitting at a fold-up table in a corner of a former warehouse in the Central Eastside, near the train tracks and river and the last remaining produce suppliers that had given this area the name Produce Row. The audience, if you could call it that—ten attendees tops—had taken spots among the four rows of school chairs fanning out from his table, sixteen total, mismatched but all hard. The warehouse was now an event space. The event was the Cascadia Congress, an offshoot of a more mainstream Cascadia conference staged in the Convention Center and attended by the region's top politicians, scholars and wonks, developers talking green. Greg had been an advocate for offering an alternative that resisted riding the bandwagon of co-opting anything and everything Cascadia. The warehouse space had a prime location near food cart pods, brewpubs, bike events, microdistilleries, and a few friendly strip bars. The requisite freight train even ran through the riverside area. It still had a lot of homeless people. As the edgier conference, the Congress stood on its own legs now. It had climbed in attendance every year, and the write-ups in the alternative weeklies said this was the one to attend. It had the true cred in the long run. They had the youth, the sacrifice, and surely, people who would commit to making Cascadia happen one day. Greg got mentions in the weeklies and blogs as one of those—if not the one—who would lead things, or at least inspire others to lead. Some (admittedly minor, local) articles and interviews embarrassed him with their praise, their over-the-top pronouncements. He was the golden boy of Cascadia, their Steve Jobs and Guevara and JFK all rolled into one. Of course, it was exaggerated, but there was no one else to wear the honor. His words and deeds were all theoretical. Years ago, he'd gotten his start on YouTube laying out the idea of Cascadia. His blog began to get hits even when he didn't update it. The book had finally come out the previous year. A stack of the books stood dead center on his table. Hanging from it was the Cascadian "Doug" flag with its blue-white-green horizontal stripes and Douglas fir tree silhouette up the middle. T-shirts and stickers waited in neat stacks bearing images of Cascadian maps and flags of Doug firs and Sasquatches. A tabletop sign read Cascadia Discussion Group. Greg had thought his talks would help the sale of his book, to help cover the sad truth that it hadn't done that well—yet. It didn't help that even Powell's in Portland had shelved his book alongside conspiracy theorists' opuses, off-the-grid handbooks, and ecological manifestos, even though his was serious political, economic, and environmental nonfiction. The Pacific Northwest section would've worked. He wished he would've had more control over that. He should have self-published the book instead of signing up with that small local publisher that was now out of money yet held his rights, including e-rights. He knew it would find its audience one day. Thus, the Cascadia swag. It sold way more than the book.

This was his second day of the four-day event. Many of these attendees he'd seen already, the day before even. Blogger guy up front posted about Cascadian matters but mostly it was the Portland Timbers, which Greg could hardly fault. He wished he'd grown up knowing more about soccer; he'd always sensed he was missing out on something basic, like hiking. A couple anarchist street boys sat in the back row. On one end was that grad student with a neck tattoo he tried to hide with scarves and who used to be in a band and had been working for ages on his MA thesis on Cascadian dialect (the Sasquatch of linguistics niches, Greg joked to himself). Sitting dead center was the über-fellow with a waxed handlebar mustache so long and neat it transcended ironic. More than one of them had coffee going in a mason jar. These were the normal ones. Some people made fun of them, he knew. Said the Cascadia lovers were no less than alternate-reality-slash-future reenactors, only without the costumes. Freaks, really. So be it. Let them laugh. He'd stopped wincing inside a long time ago, stopped hearing the stale *Portlandia* quips. Though sometimes he just wished more girls would come listen, really listen.

He could always be doing more. The ideal could always be improved, he knew. Yet, at the same time, he always had that lurking fear that someone would look too far back into his past. Maybe that was why he both envied the Cascadia bandwagon and feared it so damn much.

Three days had passed since his sudden meeting in Lone Fir Cemetery with Agent Rich Torres of the FBI. He hadn't called Torres. He did not plan to. He was stalling, he could admit it. Yet he hadn't gotten a call from Torres either, and he wondered why. His hesitation at becoming involved must have thrown Torres off, he decided.

Greg continued: "Let's be truthful. Full disclosure here. We are not really talking about a secession when we talk about Cascadia. We're talking about what's called a 'release movement,' meaning, we would use established democratic processes to petition for release from the US and Canada with full consent of their governments. A form of Velvet Revolution, if you will. Breaking away without consent is succession, which could also be seen as a form of treason from many and invite retribution if not civil war. Secession is selfish, self-destructive. Ours is a progressive-thinking, enlightened movement. So, how can such a thing happen without doing harm? How can we rescue ourselves as a people and really get to who we want to be?"

It could sound a little preachy and pretentious at times. But little did they know, he was speaking from experience. He plowed on:

"Granted, it might be difficult without causing pain, but the way this country is self-destructing? The opportunity for a harmonious, even peaceful reinvention could present itself."

A hand raised in the back.

It was FBI Agent Rich Torres.

He had showed up without Greg noticing, stepping out from behind the nearest food cart to stand behind the last row of chairs and raise his hand in one fluid motion. He wore a business casual sport shirt and Dockers-type khakis. The look said suburbs, tourist, or a dad visiting from Ohio, often holding a pink box of Voodoo Donuts. Yet the way that Torres stood, with his feet planted far apart and his hands grasping at a chair back, hinted at something far more threatening. In the movies, a man looking like this was a grieving father who had lost a son in war or a baby daughter to a pharmaceutical company cover-up.

Was Greg supposed to pretend he and Torres didn't know each other? He went with it. "Sorry, I didn't see you there," he said. "You have a question?"

"How far are you willing to go with this?" Torres said.

Heads had turned Torres' way. Greg could see the crackpot alarm ringing in their heads. The normal-looking outsiders often came asking the most abnormal questions as if Greg should seriously consider Cascadia's connections to, say, Nazis in Atlantis or the president's birthdate as a cipher predicting the date of Rapture.

"We can discuss that," Greg said, speaking softly. Why don't you have a seat?"

Torres glared at the hard chair seat as if it bore spikes, and Greg wondered if others saw how Torres' face had darkened.

"I just have the one question," Torres said. "How far are you willing to take this secession thing?"

Was Torres announcing a veiled threat—help us, or we'll come after you? Greg told himself that only happened in movies. Any dreams of Cascadia were protected under free speech. So, could he know about Greg's past? Greg told himself it was impossible.

"It's not really secession, though," Greg said. "We were just talking about that."

"Sorry—'release movement,'" Torres said. "But the question remains."

Hands had gone up. Greg ignored them. "Well, I guess it depends," he said. "Who would we be up against? I think remaining nonviolent is key."

"Nonviolent? In the real world? Come off it," Torres said.

All looked to Greg, hands lowering. This was Greg's deal now. "As I said. In reality? It could never happen without federal consent," he said.

"I'm not talking about Feds. Not talking about democratic processes, even. I'm talking about the rest of Oregon, outside this shining, forward-thinking city you got here, outside the green valley. There will be people and groups who don't want to play along or have their own movement altogether, and it will be nothing like yours."

"I hear you. I do. There are people out there," Greg said.

"Damn right there are. What about a militia, for example?"

Greg heard a ripple of groans. The 'm' word was not something any would-be Cascadian liked to hear. "Well, I would say there's a fundamental difference between any militias out there right now and anything we would have. Theirs are there to take. Ours would be to protect. Theoretically. Though I doubt we would even need anything so martial."

"I see, so you're Costa Rica all the sudden. You have no military. Though you are incorporating hunting country. Speaking of taking—what if they beat you to it? What if they go and secede on their own? What then? They don't have a problem with violence."

"You know what?" Greg said. "You're right. I could do a whole chapter on that."

"How? You already wrote your book."

A rush of adrenalin filled Greg's sinuses, a heat behind his forehead. This Torres really knew how to dig at him. He fought the urge to dismiss Torres as unreasonable—if the man wanted to be a part of the discussion, he could refrain from aggressive argument, that sort of line. Meanwhile, conversations had burst forth. Blogger guy and grad student were arguing about nonviolent crowd control methods and a couple new arrivals about hypothetical forms of taxation while the anarchists just snickered. But Greg and Torres held eye contact.

"You make a good point," Greg said, adding "maybe I should have done more," and only Torres seemed to hear it over the din.

Torres nodded. He loosened his grip on the chair, relaxed his stance. He stuck around for the rest of it but didn't ask another question. Greg got things back on track, keeping it light with jokey hypotheses about employing Sasquatches as Cascadian border patrol or better yet the back line of a Cascadian national soccer team.

By the time his talk was finished, Torres was gone.

Outside, after the day's events had ended, Greg expected to find Torres waiting for him. Torres wasn't there. Relieved, Greg breathed in the cool, moist air and lugged his bag over to the parking lot, a vast line of bicycles. It always gave him a thrill to see so many bikes for this was Cascadia in the making. His was a gem, a locally-made commuter with sprung leather saddle, custom-fit wood fenders, oversized front cargo rack, a vintage refurbished Sturmey-Archer hub, and lots of shining metal, the saddle alone worth more than he could afford. He rode away, the street showing stretches of old cobblestone and lined with old loading docks. He linked up with the Burnside Bridge, to cross the river. On the west side he pedaled through a dense urban mix of condos, bars, and shops—the Pearl District to the right and Old Town at his back and the up-and-coming West End still before him. A slick streetcar whooshed by, just a few meters away—yes, meters; Greg had made a big deal in his book about adopting the metric system and he'd ended up thinking in it. Goofy, sure, but he couldn't help himself. It was all part of remaking himself, of living the day-dream. In his daydream, Portland is the capital of Cascadia. The streetcars run on biofuel. Waves of bike commuters travel main roads and the few cars use the side lanes. At least 53 percent of buildings have green roofs, residential front yards are gardens, and giant rain barrels abound. Water flows and flows. River taxis glide on the broad Willamette River running through the city. On the waterfront, Cascadia flags fly above a riverside auditorium packed with a rapt audience. On stage—and this is the really goofy part, Greg stands before a table stacked with his books. And wild applause kicks in. He couldn't help this last part. The first part of the dream was what actually mattered, he always told himself.

He rode over to Providence Park, the Portland Timbers' soccer-specific stadium, downed two pints with buddies before the game, took two hits off a pipe to boot, and once inside, inserted himself in the North End, the Timbers Army section. He waved a Doug flag and wielded his Timbers scarf like a medieval mace and shouted and sang the songs and yelled at the ref. He didn't really understand the offside rule, so he just screamed when the others did. His Timbers lost in the final seconds despite having the ball all the time. A match wasn't always fair. Life was not. But there was no ref to scream at in real life.

Anything to forget about FBI Special Agent Rich Torres coming to stare him down. Anything to purge the feeling that Torres gave him. He had recreated himself, and he was still free after all these years. All he had to do was keep his dire secret safe.

4

The security guard lay on the oily pavement, next to a dumpster. He was bleeding from his neck and head, a fast growing pool of it. He stared up at them, up at Greg and Donny Wilkie standing over him. He tried to speak but could only get out a gurgle.

"Jesus. All I did was barely hit him," Donny had muttered. "I'm not a fighter. Jesus."

This was how it had happened, about twenty years ago. Greg had just turned eighteen. Donny was still seventeen. It was March. They had been snowboarding all day at Mt. Hood Meadows on the south side of the mountain. Donny had wanted to take a snowboarding lesson, just one lesson, but Greg had insisted he'd show him how instead. As it turned out, Greg wasn't much help and hadn't meant to be. It was just too much fun watching Donny bite it. Donny had laughed too but then it became one bite too many and Donny had sulked off, making Greg go find him and show him a few pointers. Donny ended up tired, beat up, responding to Greg only with grunts.

As always, Greg had made Donny drive. The routine got started because the sight of Greg riding in Donny's country pickup brought laughs from guys and girls Greg knew, not to mention the respectful stares from would-be toughs who had picked on him. Plus, Greg had realized he could save on gas money this way, always promising Donny he'd pitch in but rarely doing it.

On the way back, just a few miles from the mountain, they found a minimart off Highway 35, at one of those little junctions that served as a bridge between highway and some neglected small town further off the beaten path. They sat parked in the far corner of the parking lot, drinking the two cans of Rainier they had stolen from Donny's Uncle Jerrod. Donny lived with his uncle. That's why he came to Portland. His parents had sent him to stay there while they finished off the all-out nuclear war of attrition that had been the last year of their marriage. Donny's dad had worked in logging and had never recovered from the death of the industry. The man's odd jobs as a mechanic and cook all over Southern and Central Oregon did not make him a happy dad. They had spent the longest time in a town called Pineburg. Donny loved it there. His dad didn't care. Donny's Uncle Jerrod in Portland didn't have a better temper, but he was a long-haul trucker so wasn't around much. This new kid Donny, Greg saw, had time, freedom and a certain gullibility. This Donny kid could be a type of project. Let's see how much of the country bumpkin Greg could remove from Donny and replace with something new. He even told Donny his plan, joking about it. Donny grumbled about it but fell in with whatever scheme Greg planned. At the time Greg claimed to be a "neo-punk nihilist" type, even though he dressed like an Abercrombie and Fitch preppy. Punk and anarchism were all about creating something new, Greg told Donny, which demanded having no respect for what came before. It was all about pushing yourself. Clothes didn't mean shit, not really, except as a means. It was what was inside.

Donny was sitting at the wheel of his old Ford pickup, Greg in the passenger seat. They still wore their ski gear—stocking caps, sunglasses, bandannas. "I can't believe I never been snowboarding. Thanks for letting me borrow stuff," Donny said in that tender voice of his that Greg said sounded like the hick stud in that old movie Midnight Cowboy.

"Totally," Greg said. He was smoking a joint. The parking lot of the minimart was packed with cars and people coming and going from skiing, snowboarding. "Bet the only time a shithole like this does any business is when the snow is killer," he added.

He passed the joint to Donny, who took a hit and coughed. Greg chugged the last of his beer and held it up.

"Keep it down, boy," Donny said.

Greg laughed. "You say some funny shit. What the fuck they gonna do? Yours done?"

"Yeah," Donny said.

Greg handed Donny an ID. It was an Oregon Driver's License with Donny's photo on it. The way it worked was: Greg sold pot to this artist guy, who did up the ID in trade.

Donny held the ID with his fingertips. "It's even got my photo on it. How you do all that? You're good at this."

"You can do it. Fucking easy. Now don't look at it. Good. Ready? Tell me, what's your name, son?"

Donny closed his eyes even though Greg hadn't told him to, which the conniver that Greg was back then had loved. Donny said, "Uh, Charles. Charles Adler."

"Nice. Told ya, fucking easy to do."

"But, I don't know if we need any more beers going here."

"Sure we do. They're empty."

They laughed, but Donny's laugh sputtered. "Why's it always me going though?" he said, looking out the window.

"Think about it, dude. You look way older," Greg said. Donny didn't really look much older, but Donny always bought the bluff. As long as Greg didn't have to go in there.

"Okay. Okay," Donny said.

Greg watched from the truck as Donny went inside the min-imart. An elderly security guard followed Donny around inside, a middle-aged guy with a silver-gray ponytail. Donny and the guard exchanged words, each puffing up their chests.

The security guard moved on to another group, and Donny bought beer without any problem. He came out and jogged across the parking lot with the short case tucked under an arm like a football.

Back in the truck, though, Donny's face was different. His mouth hung open a little, and his eyes had gone dark. He stared back at the store as if it was a house fire he'd just escaped. "That tin badge bastard was in my face the whole time," he said in a strange, mechanical voice. "Reminds me of my dad."

"That's fucked up," Greg said.

"Fuck you dad!" Donny shouted.

Greg faked a giggle. Donny's outburst had stunned him. He had never seen Donny act dark, or violent. It was not in his plan for Donny. Greg decided to keep it light. "There you go, McCloud," he said.

"Shut up with that McCloud shit," Donny said.

Greg showed Donny a snicker. "Hey, come on. ID sure worked, didn't it?"

"Yeah, it did. Damn."

They cracked the beers. Greg lit an American Spirit, one for him and one for Donny. The magic of the ID, the way it gave Donny a brave new power, did seem to work for Donny despite the dark stuff. Donny had stayed puffed up, his face shining with intensity. So vanity was the key. Pride. Greg would have to pursue this line further.

"Don't let that tin badge give you any shit," Greg said when their third beers were halfway down. "Just like all those guys in Portland—they live for fucking with outta-town dudes like you."

"Girls try it, too. But then I got em right where I want em," Donny said, smiling, joking now.

"There you go," Greg said. "Next time, you go show that fucking tin badge. You're the cowboy."

"Damn straight there, son."

They laughed, toasted cans.

The parking lot had emptied out, leaving their pickup exposed in the corner. Inside the minimart, the security guard was peering out the window, scanning the parking lot. Greg kept an eye on him. The way the old guy was facing them gave Greg an uncomfortable feeling, a slow-moving shudder inside that made his forearms bristle. It reminded Greg of a forest animal looking out for dangers, but with a sadness, a deliberateness to it. A creature sharing a fate.

"Maybe we should go somewhere else," Greg said. "We could drive back. See who has coke or some shit."

"Okay by me, but I gotta pee." Donny pushed himself out the door and dropped down to the pavement, bending his knees like a paratrooper as he landed. Greg watched him go around the side of the minimart, into darkness.

The security guard headed outside. He went around the side of the building, where it was darker. To where Donny was?

Greg moved to get out, but he couldn't. His fear had become an iron belt on his waist, pressing him to the seat. He shivered from the cold. He felt like some little kid waiting for a parent who'd been in the bar way too long.

Donny had emerged from the darkness, arms bent, hands clamped up. He ran back wheezing, almost hyperventilating. He heaved himself up into the cab, started up the truck, threw it in gear, and drove them around to the back of the building.

"What? What the fuck's going on?" Greg said.

A minute later, in the side alley around the back of the building, Greg and Donny were standing in the darkness looking down on the security guard lying next to that dumpster, the blood from his head leaking on the pavement. Staring up at them, gurgling his words.

Donny muttering about hardly hitting him, he wasn't no fighter, Jesus. Greg didn't console or even answer Donny. He was trying too hard to think.

The security guard didn't carry a gun. Greg told himself that was a good thing, but he wasn't sure why. The pickup stood behind them idling, its lights off.

"Let's get him in the truck," Greg heard himself say. "Donny, listen to me. We have to think about this."

Ten minutes later, Donny was driving them hard and fast on the mountain highway. "I think I know where there's a hospital," Greg had told him. Darkness surrounded them. No other cars on the road. Thick snow hit the windshield and started to flock on the road.

"You get rid of the beers?" Donny shouted now. "Did you?"

"I told you. I told you I did," Greg said.

"Sometimes you say that but then you didn't."

"I'm telling you. Besides, what does it matter?"

"Dammit, where's that hospital around here?" Donny said.

Greg stared back through the cab window, at the pickup bed. The security guard lay still there, half under an old blanket. Blood had soaked into the fabric and seeped out from under and glistened on metal of the truck bed. Snowflakes swirled inside the bed, sticking to the blanket and exploding as swirling steam in the hot blood.

Donny shouted: "Dammit, where is it? You told me. You told me you saw a sign before."

"There wasn't one," Greg said. "I lied. I lied to get you to go. To get out of there."

"You what?"

Five minutes later, Donny was still driving onward. He hadn't spoken to Greg since—ever since glaring at Greg with a hardness Greg had never seen before. Donny's face had fixed into a white mask, and it wasn't from the snow illuminated in the headlights.

"What are we gonna do with him?" Greg muttered, and his voice broke as he did. He didn't care what it sounded like. "Donny? Help me."

Donny drove on. They rode in silence. Donny had both hands on top of the steering wheel, his knuckles white now, but his face had regained color.

"I know this one place," Donny said after a few minutes, his voice monotone and hollow, like a phone recording giving instructions. "Back up in the high mountains, on the old route to Pineburg. My dad took me there once. No one goes there. Doubt it's even on a map."

"Okay, good, okay." Greg stared at the pickup bed again. Skis, a toolbox, and a shovel lay back there too.

A half hour later, the pickup was parked. Donny had driven them to a secluded little lake. The snow was falling heavier. Donny and Greg hauled the security guard's body, wrapped in the blanket, out of the bed. They had thought about it, talked about how. They were careful to hold the blanket by the dry ends and not its blood-sodden center.

The body twitched. The man gasped like a man held underwater. A hand grabbed at Greg.

They dropped him, and the blanket unraveled just enough to show the man's face and blood-soaked neck, chest. Darkness obscured his face, but his eyes glinted, from what Greg wasn't sure. The man clawed at the cold air, at them, and his silver pony-tail unraveled now too and splayed out beneath his head, stretches of it sticky with blood and others shining like corn floss. The man gasped again. Greg started.

"He's just an old man," Donny whispered, his voice breaking, "just doing a job …"

Greg felt something click inside him, a clarity. He said, "Listen: He's just like your dad, that's what he is. You said he was."

They stared at the man, his mouth open. Was he dead? They must have stared a good minute.

The man reached for them, this time in a slow arc as if doing an arm exercise.

"Just like your dad," Greg repeated to Donny.

Donny kicked the man. The man groaned and seemed to shrink up.

Greg stared at Donny in shock. Donny glared back at him.

"You do it," Donny said, his voice strong and set again, stronger than Greg had ever heard it. It sounded military, maybe like his dad or uncle might have sounded.

Greg shook his head. "I don't even know the guy's name," he muttered.

"That's exactly right." Donny stepped closer to Greg and showed teeth, but it wasn't a smile. "Where I come from. You put a wounded animal down. With mercy. That's how you do it."

"No. Wait . . ."

Donny, still grimacing at Greg, grabbed a corner of the blanket and pressed it to the man's face. He held it there, watching Greg gape in horror as the man's features stilled for good.

Greg kept his eyes locked on Donny's for as long as he could. It was all he could do. Later, he would tell himself that he had never looked away.

They dragged the corpse along a trail to the other side of the lake. They took turns shoveling, burned the clothes and blanket, and Donny kicked the charred security badge and metal fittings of the uniform's belt off into the lake. They argued about marking the spot or not like two teens arguing over a video game—like the two teens they were, but Donny had a can of orange marking paint in the back of the truck so they might as well use it. They might want to know where the spot is someday, they both decided.

By the time they finished, the snow was dumping and making it down through the tree branches to help cover the slight earthen bump they had left—the burial spot, marked with the orange-painted rock embedded in dirt.

Back out on the highway, the snow was piling up on the road. Greg felt a new horror, compressing his gut like a steel belt ratcheted, ratcheting tighter. Could they even make it through this weather? He looked to Donny.

Donny drove with one hand on the wheel, nice and easy, and his grip had relaxed.

"The passes go one way, that's what we always say," Donny said, shaking his head.

"What?"

"When it snows, you city people always expect us to come over the mountains to you."

"We don't know how to drive in it."

"That's right. You sure don't."

As Donny drove on, he smoked one of Greg's smokes and drank a beer. "Good thing you didn't throw out them beers," he said.

At that point, at three in the morning it must have been, Greg had no energy left to speak. He sat slumped against the cold passenger door and window and felt like he had lost ten pounds and a foot in height. Even the cab's bench seat had seemed double the size. For the first time in years, he had felt far younger than his age. He was just a boy. Unformed. Squishy like a soft fruit.

"We gotta be smarter next time," Donny had said. His voice sounded even fuller, hardened, more adult. And he cracked another beer.

His words had made Greg sit up. "Next time?"

"I don't mean killing. Just mean, in general. None of that rough stuff, no sir. So that killing like that don't happen again. Never again. Smarter. Like you do it. With words, all friendly like. Using my head. You know, smarter. That's the way I aim to be."

5

After the always disturbing shock of seeing the Portland Timbers lose, Greg rode back over the Burnside Bridge to his apartment close-in on the Eastside. To a guy like Greg, Eastside was the alternative to the Westside's manufactured, too-clean, and new Pearl District that had risen up from a similar graveyard of warehouses and grimy workshops. Skaters and punks still lived here, day laborers could stand on a corner without getting harassed, and a few workshops and repair garages lived on, dying hard and proud. But don't let it fool you, Greg thought. The change was already coming. The warehouses, garages, print and machine shops were becoming galleries, small presses, pop-up cabarets, local meat purveyors and butchers, small-batch distilleries—a Russian doll of do-it-yourself urbanism. Greg was another aging poster boy for it, he knew. He could crow, if need be, that he was one of the few actually from Portland. But the reality was still damning: Everything gets found out and then it's damned.

He reached the crest of the bridge, the downtown bank's lights twinkling at his back, and for a moment no traffic rumbled past—he could almost hear the Willamette River lapping below. He loved when that happened. At this moment he had the strange sense that he was seeing and feeling this for the last time. He shook it off, picked up the pace.

As he pedaled down into the Central Eastside, as the silhouettes of squat old buildings enveloped him, he couldn't help thinking about the ghost of Donny Wilkie. What would Donny have thought of him now? Would Donny even recognize the new Greg—a Greg that worked hard, knew what he wanted, and treated people with fairness? Greg had come back for a reporting job at the *Oregonian*, but they cut staffers six months later and the newcomers had lost out. Fleeting, low-paying stints followed, mostly for magazines or content sites that started up fast and went under faster. He did some freelancing and got a few articles published to support the book, none of them paying. He could have earned more pouring beers in a brewpub. His money was running out. He had emptied his meager 401k. He told himself he was no worse off than half the country with their overpriced mortgages that they had no jobs for. Besides, he had resolved to become who he wanted to be instead of masquerading—hiding—in New York and on the road as something he wasn't. There he was always boasting about how great the Pacific Northwest was. People had no idea. So why didn't he live there?

He climbed the slight rise of East Burnside. A parked car's door swung open; he swerved, almost went down into traffic, and passed through a yellow light, cursing not the car door but himself for giving his fellow bikers a bad name by running a yellow.

Ten minutes later, he was sitting on his sofa—his girlfriend Emily's sofa to be exact. Considering his financial situation alone, being able to live with a catch like Emily was a blessing. It was a nice setup. Emily had the first-floor apartment in a brick, townhouse-style building near her job at a small boutique that carried local clothing lines. The street wasn't prime but close-in, and she somehow had three bedrooms, one as her workspace. He could hear her finishing something down the hall in her workspace—a mix of vintage and carefully selected IKEA-style pieces arranged so well even her savvy friends had a hard time telling what was old and what was new. The right lighting helped. Emily was all about correct lighting.

Greg choked down another swig of his dry-hopped triple IPA. The window was open and he heard bicycles whizzing by, clattering away from lots of good fun usage. Laughter echoed as they passed, probably hitting the next cheap bar. Emily should be out there with the twenty-somethings, he thought, not in here with me and my thirty-seven years.

He heard a puff he recognized as her iron—one last shot of steam. "Here I come," she said from the workroom.

"Okay-ee," he said.

Emily pranced out swaying her small hips to help hide the blouse she was holding behind her back. She was a waif with big blue eyes and short hair that only a waif could pull off, but she didn't look skinny. She had curves. Her smile stretched wide.

"Organic cotton, all local. Carbon footprint of like, a hummingbird," she said.

The blouse had both lacy details and shiny fabric, both cute and elegant, just different enough from the ones her friends and peers were wearing. On them it might look like an old woman's blouse but on her it looked like, well, Emily. Emily was into clothes, yes, but it was like a science and an art to her. It flowed from her personality, from the way she approached any subject, often with a raised eyebrow. She wasn't materialistic but did like "pleasant" things, she said—an odd word choice, but that was Emily. She'd say a word like that and soon people would be trying it out themselves. She had told him there was a difference between acquisitive and appreciative, and she was definitely the latter. If anyone could make a trendy nerd girl in her late twenties appealing, it was she. She was grinning. Her teeth were a little crooked in two spots like a stereotypical country girl's, which, she had joked with Greg, should in itself give away that she was part of the constant migration to Portland from the Midwest. She was from the rural Iowa contingent. Yet most assumed she had switched coasts straight from Brooklyn.

She kept grinning. He grinned back. This time she was going to need a better reaction from him.

"That's great. They'll want it for sure," he said—they being the small fashion line that sometimes contracted her for designs.

Emily hopped up and down. "They already do. They called."

"I'm so proud of you, Em. Everyone talks. You just go and do it."

She came close and wrapped her arms around him, swathing him with the heat of the sewing machine and work light that was still in her hair and skin and sweater. She kissed him. He kissed her. She pulled back showing damp eyes.

What was she tearing up about?

"Hey, what is it?" he muttered. "You should be happy."

She went into the kitchen and fetched a beer for herself, one of his IPAs. She drank wine normally, so this made him feel a tad territorial, and her eyebrow raised at him. She toasted him. He toasted her. They drank. Greg had to look away. Thoughts of Donny and his past, of Torres and his mocking of Cascadia, made him feel heavy, weary. Torpid. Sinking. It was weighing on him like sandbags on his shoulders and this, his sixth hoppy beer, was not helping.

"How was the conference?" Emily said.

"Good. It will be fine."

"Something happen?" Emily said.

"No. It's okay," Greg said, though he'd slurred it a little.

Emily gave him a little rub on his knee. She drank, eyeing him. Her damp eyes had dried up. She stayed on the sofa with him, knees tucked under her, watching him. Her eyes had a different shine now. A sharpness, like glass.

"So, I was thinking," she said. "Ready?"

"Yup. Sure."

"What if we . . . had a kid?"

Greg did not flinch, not even inside. He turned to her. He showed an open and supportive smile that hinted at surprise in the way his mouth curled on one end. It was the same face he used whenever he was doing an interview and the interviewee was gushing that they had something truly important for the story, but Greg doubted he could use it. He wasn't proud of the face. It had belonged to his old self before he had left Portland. It was one of his few fake faces left. The problem was, he couldn't find words to match. He said:

"Honey. We don't even sleep in the same bed half the time."

"Says the guy who wanted his own room." She glanced away, took a chug of her beer, and set it down.

"You thought it was a good idea, too. The way I am."

"A place just for you—I get it. I do. If we're going to live together. I'm the same way. We like doing our stuff alone. Look. I know what you're thinking. I don't mean marriage, silly. I just mean, it might give us sort of a structure. Some focus or something."

At some point, Greg wasn't sure when, Emily had untwisted her legs out from under her and was sitting upright, her back straight like a contestant on a reality show waiting to hear the judges' decision. She kept her chin up. She'd given it her best shot.

He reached out for her narrow yet soft hand and held this rare piece of art in both of his hands, cradling it. "It could be a good idea, Em," he said. "We'll see. We'll talk about it."

The next morning, as Emily nestled back into her workspace, Greg pedaled off to another long day at the Cascadia Congress. At the end of the block, he turned a corner, stopped, and called a number. It rang once, and he heard: "You've reached Special Agent Richard Torres of the FBI. Please leave a detailed message."

After the beep, Greg announced himself and said: "Thanks for contacting me, Agent Torres, but, I have to decline your proposal. It's just not my thing. I don't feel comfortable with it. Oh, also, I appreciate your coming to our event and offering your thoughts. Best of luck to you."

6

In one photo, Greg saw a kid of about eighteen, his chin up and one corner of his mouth curled in a smirk, his eyes glaring as if daring the shooter to take another, and another—he'll just keep doing this shit till you run out of film. This kid was Greg. Others could laugh at themselves after so many years. Seeing himself like that still made Greg wince.

He had pulled out three old photos from twenty-plus years ago. They were so well hidden and for so long that it took him a few long minutes to find them—inside a fading manila envelope buried deep within his compact box of childhood drawings and stories, with school awards for both, and report cards, and certificates.

In another photo, Greg was posing with another kid of eighteen, a wide-eyed young man who had the kind of open, happy smile that came from the heart and was not put on for the shot. This kid held his wiry frame rigid for the shooter and didn't blink as if he were so courteous he wanted to help avoid any blurring, any eyes shut. This kid was Donny Wilkie. Donny was still the new arrival in Portland when the photo was taken. He had on a western shirt that Greg had been horrified to be seen anywhere near in those days—today Greg had at least six shirts like that. In the third photo (from about six months later, Greg guessed), they shared the same smirky smile. Both were dressed in an awkward, post-preppie style that made them look like a cross between private-school frat boy and what most kids were already ridiculing as "grunge" by then. Thrift store flannel and stocking caps mixed with cuffed chinos and plaid ties and collars up was not a good combo. It could have been called "dick wear" and been right on, because Greg just wanted to be contrary. He didn't give a shit, not back then. He was smoking in the photo. His other hand flipped off the camera.

In the same photo was a girl wearing a black leather jacket and smoking, doing her best impersonation of Joan Jett. Deep eye sockets highlighted with thick mascara, cheekbones like river stones, and a full mouth with plump lips. This was Leeann Holt. She must have been seventeen still. She looked older than her age, and the way she often dated older guys helped keep that going. Leeann Holt was the one who told Greg about some artist guy who did a fake ID for her and would do one for them. Leeann was able to get Greg and Donny coke. Leeann had that rare mix of tough, sexy, and innocent—but how long could it have lasted? Looking back, Greg was never certain why Leeann bothered to hang out with him or Donny. She had preferred older guys, especially the ones who seemed darkly enigmatic. She must have found that same quality in Donny. Greg had started out seeing her, but he had dumped her. After, when it all fell apart between them, Donny was all too happy to step in. For a long time, Greg used to wonder if Leeann was able to find her way. Surely, it didn't last with Donny? She could not have still been with him there at the end, could she? He had Googled and Facebooked her once or twice, but nothing had come up.

It was the following night. Greg had gone late at the Cascadia Congress that day, after he'd declined FBI Agent Torres' offer first thing in the morning, and he just wanted to be alone in his room like he sometimes did. His oversized bedroom was also his office. It connected to the main hall that led to Emily's bedroom and her separate workspace, close and yet livable. Greg couldn't help himself. His need for space had come with his effort to shed his young self and had never left him. Emily had always said she respected his needs.

He hauled out a box of old papers and research. He fished out specific wire service and computer printouts from ten years before and piled them on his desk. Small local news items and database queries mostly that had chronicled Donny's descent into sordid crimes, from misdemeanor to felony.

He heard Emily come home. She passed down the hall and into her workroom. She was working on a new leggings sample and could be a while, but who knew? He placed the photos under the printouts. He got an Oregon map open, covering the pile. He stared at the Cascade Mountains between the Willamette Valley and Central Oregon. The Cascades region was the darkest on the map, the topographer making little color distinction between dense coniferous forest and the dim, rain-soaked earth and rocks beneath the branches. The valley and coast had a friendly light green, while expansive Central and Eastern Oregon were all browns and reds—there, in the remote center-right of Oregon, stood the town of Pineburg. Here was where young Donny Wilkie had lived longest before Portland.

Emily was coming down the hall. She cracked his door open and peeked in.

"You could say hi-ee," Greg said, raising the last syllable to show he was joking.

"You could be dead," she said—their other joke. She was smiling until she saw the pile of docs and map on his desk.

"Remember that one loser guy I told you about one time?" he said. "We were friends end of high school. Newcomer."

"Danny something?" she said. "That the one who died?"

40

Greg nodded. He always did this somberly, slowly. He showed it on his face. A sad story. "Donny," he said.

"He wasn't a loser then," Emily said.

"What do you mean?"

"He was hanging out with you."

"Right. Funny. I don't mean loser. Bad word choice. I just meant, it's weird how people end up. It kinda sucked for him here in Portland. He didn't really fit in."

"Kinda like *Footloose*, but backwards. It's not your fault. It wasn't like you went and enrolled him in the state pen."

"No. You're right. That's true," Greg said, looking her in the eye, showing her that somber mood he had always employed when Donny had come up. It had been years and he'd used it for other situations, but it was always a little creepy to Greg how easily it came back.

Emily left the doorway and drifted into the middle of the room without even stepping, it seemed—as if carried along by the power of her curiosity. She peered at the map.

"So, I might be working on a new project," Greg said. "This Donny guy is one angle. It's a follow-up to the Cascadia book." It wasn't a bad book idea, he told himself. He could cover the influence of the Posse Comitatus movement and go beyond militias to include the Rajneeshees and Jefferson Staters. Separating itself from the bad strains was something any Cascadian society would have to deal with, so why not get started on it? "Past-Overcoming," the Germans called it. Differentiating, marketing people called it. Show how Cascadia was the opposite, wasn't all about the will to power over people. Besides, Donny was dead. They couldn't threaten each other anymore. "I'm thinking of it as the threat-to-Cascadia book," he added.

"It's about the brown part of the map."

"More or less. Green parts can be a threat too."

"Huh," Emily said and walked out, her hands on her hips.

Once Emily had removed herself to her workspace, Greg spread out the photos and printouts in front of him.

His phone rang. The screen read Unknown Caller. He answered.

"Mr. Simmons, Rich Torres here."

"Hello there. Look, thank you again, you really got me thinking, but—"

"We should meet," Torres said.

"Now? I . . . I'm in bed."

"You really can't meet? You've made up your mind. Is that what you're saying?"

"Yes. I thought I did."

"So you think."

"No, I know."

Torres sighed, deep enough to crackle in Greg's tiny speaker. Then Torres paused, and Greg imagined him looking around so that no one could hear him. Greg waited for him. Torres said:

"I have some news for you. We have reason to believe, that Donny Wilkie is still alive."

7

Greg's blood quickened, his heart thumping. He felt like his feet were spiked to the floor and his hands drained of blood. All of him drained of blood. He didn't speak for what seemed like minutes, almost forgot he was on the phone. Torres let him dangle like that.

"What are you saying?" Greg muttered at one point.

"Just what I said."

"Why didn't you tell me before?" Greg said.

"Maybe we're just now finding out. Everything all right there?"

"Yes. I'm okay."

"Well, does this change your mind?"

"Where is he?"

"Last seen in Central Oregon. We're guessing Pineburg area. You know it?"

"No. I mean, I've heard of it."

"Well? Interested?"

Greg could have filled Torres' tiny speaker with his own groaning sigh, but he didn't let himself. He raised his voice in gratitude, adding a hint of levity: "You know what? It doesn't. I'm still not. I appreciate your telling me, I do, it's definitely a weird scenario, but if anything it makes me want to do this even less."

"I see. Too uncomfortable? Dredging up the past and all."

"Yes. That's part of it."

The rest of the call had been a blur because Greg started to spin ever faster inside, from the panic, from the anxiety rattling and squeezing him. Torres offered the few details he had, hoping to convince Greg, but it wasn't much. Greg held firm. He wanted no part of it, he restated. He thanked Torres again, promised to be in touch should anything come his way, and hung up. It had seemed too easy. But he told himself Torres was used to rejection. It had to be one tough gig getting a private citizen to inform, especially without ample leverage, which Torres luckily didn't seem to have. This is what Greg told himself. He hoped he hadn't missed any hint of a threat.

Two hours later, around midnight, Greg had a packed bag out in the middle of his bedroom floor. The next morning at the Cascadia Congress, before it opened, he found his handlebar-mustachioed-fan-fellow, who was also the assistant organizer of the conference. Fellow was checking on this and that, opening boxes, and restocking flyers, the tips of his mustache threatening to brush everything.

"I have a favor to ask," Greg told him. "I'm going to cancel."

"Cancel? There's two days left. What about your booth?"

"It's just a table." Greg added a smile and hoped it didn't look like the sober and urgent rictus of determination it had become. "I'm sorry. I hope it's not a problem."

"Is something wrong?"

"Nope," Greg said, making sure not to raise his voice, keeping it light. "Just going to cancel."

"We can't give you a refund," assistant organizer snapped.

"I know. It's okay."

Assistant organizer eyed him. Fingertips found sharp end of mustache.

"Everything was great, really," Greg said. "I'm not switching to that other convention, I promise. I mean, this one was my idea in the first place."

"Okay. That's good to know."

"Thanks for everything. You can give my spot to someone else," Greg added as if that were possible.

"Fine, okay," assistant organizer said, but Greg was already marching off. He could feel assistant organizer watching him all the way, those tentacles still probing him.

Outside, two teens walked up to face him—they were the two anarchist street boys who had been coming to his table and listening to his talks each day. One was a girl, Greg now noticed. Hoodies and black denim and leather covered with paint and patches can hide a lot.

"You're that Cascadia guy. We like what you're saying," said the boy one.

"Your book sounds good," said the girl one.

"Thanks," Greg said, truly touched. He had expected them to ask him for money, or at least snicker at him as he passed on by. He reached in his bag, and handed them one of his books. He gave them a second book, one for each of them, like a religious canvasser might do with pamphlets. "Happy reading," he said and headed off.

"We will, thanks!" he heard them say.

That afternoon, back in his apartment, he heard Emily coming down the hall. She pushed open his door, stepped in, and saw his bag.

"You weren't there today?" Emily said. "You quit going?"

Of course, she would have found out. Portland was still that small, though most of her friends would no sooner attend the congress than visit a suburban mall.

"I skipped out on it," Greg said.

"But, that's the only thing you care about," Emily said. "I mean—you know what I mean."

"It's okay. It's true."

"You could have told me," she said. Her eyes had darkened and lost all shine.

"I care about you," he added, though it was too late. At least he'd said it.

She gave a sad little roll of her eyes.

"I'm going there. To the brown part on the map," he said. "Well, it's mostly brown."

"Now? How? You're crossing mountains. You don't even have a car."

"I'm renting one."

"You don't have the money."

"It'll be an expense."

Emily had stepped back. Her arms had crossed her chest. This was how she did her thinking. He waited it out, staring into his bag.

"I could go along," she said.

"That's a nice gesture, but you hate sitting in the car," Greg said. She hated when he said this even more, but he needed to deflect her. He'd had the response prepared.

"You're taking your bike, I bet," she said.

"Yes."

"But not me."

"I can save on gas that way," he added. "With the bike, I mean."

Emily glared. "A nice gesture?"

"I didn't mean it like that. Plus, I don't even know if there's good cell reception." Greg tried a smile. "So, it's all yours, make yourself at home," he added as a wisecrack, take the heat off a little.

Emily blurted, "It's my fucking apartment."

"I was joking. It was a joke. Come on." Greg opened his arms and, having to step over his bag, went in for a hug. Emily backed up to the door, shrugging off his embrace, but he followed her. She let him touch her upper arms only. "Look, I got to get something going," he said.

"You do have something going."

Normally, this would have been the point where Emily leaned into his chest, and they had that nice hug, a make-out, maybe get naked eventually. But she held her ground, kept her back pressed up against the doorframe.

"We're not even going to talk about it?" she said. "About, what I talked about?"

"I can't. I just—I have to go. We will though. After, we will."

8

Donny could be alive, Torres had said. They had reason to believe it. Finding Donny was a long shot, but Greg had to pursue the possibility. And he had to do it without the FBI. He didn't have any choice. Special Agent Torres could never know what he and Donny knew.

Cruising in the right lane, lost in thought, he worried about worst-case scenarios. What if Torres knew about Donny being alive all along and was only using Greg's curiosity to snag him? His last phone call with Torres had been so easy. Was Torres simply testing his reactions?

Greg had picked up a silver Toyota Corolla from a car rental agency tucked into a small downtown lot. He was waiting there when they opened in the morning. He had mounted his bicycle rack on the trunk, pulling the straps tight, then set his bike on the rack, fastened that with bungee cords, and secured it with a U-lock. His long bike had protruded from both sides of the car and made the rack sag under its weight. So he cinched everything tighter, leaving the rear wheel higher than the front, all lopsided and out there like from some hunter's big kill for all in his path to see. You will know me by the trail of chain grease and bungees, he had joked to himself, trying to find some amusement in any of this. He hadn't slept much, so he got a coffee for the road, making do with a non-local roaster. He had driven south and connected with the I-5 freeway, trying to wake up and divert his thoughts by wondering why more rental cars weren't hybrid or electric and why bicyclists didn't have insurance. Missed opportunities like these usually came to him when his nerves were being tested, reminding him that a person could never anticipate every little failure no matter how hard they tried.

Soon I-5 South shed its city exits and connecting highways. The last malls and subdivisions gave way to open farmland as I-5 continued on as one long trim path along the floor of the Willamette Valley. Greg passed through Portland's urban growth boundary, the croplands stretching out on both sides for miles, reaching all the way to the hills rimming the horizon. This would be the heartland of Cascadia, he had written in his book, where everything from hemp to sugar beets would flourish and keep them autonomous, dependent on no foreign entity.

Right now, though, he could give a shit. He mulled over how his secret mission could play out, the same penetrating analysis he used for research and writing now creating a world of infinite possible missteps to consider. He had to assume Torres might know something of what he and Donny had been up to, or at least he surmised it. All those years ago, Donny had come into town a fresh face. He fled from it a confident criminal only after getting to know Greg. That was a fact.

From the capital—luckless, neglected Salem—Greg headed east on Highway 22 and passed more vast farmlands. Soon the dark contours rimming the horizon swelled before him, rising up as forest and mountains, and the land around seemed to darken to match it. Greg still found it hard to believe that Donny, dead or alive, could have been involved in a militia movement— basically, a violent-minded form of fantasy reenacting but with real bullets and homemade bombs. Donny hadn't been political, had held few grudges, and he hadn't worshipped money that much, all of which muted the need to play with guns or bombs or threats to society. Force just wasn't his brand of persuasion. Reenacting wasn't Donny's style, not the Donny he knew. Role-playing was, though. Acting. By the time Greg had cut all ties with Donny, Donny was far surpassing Greg's aspirations for him. He could already talk a guy or girl out of or into anything. Greg didn't doubt that Donny might have known sketchy people, but it was probably just to survive.

As the miles behind him mounted, keeping him sheltered, the anxiety smothering his chest gave way to an open buzz of curiosity. How could they have found out about Donny being alive? Someone must have told them, and it was probably someone close to Donny, or someone who had been. Greg knew of only one such person. Could it have been someone like Leeann Holt, wherever she was?

So now here comes Greg, asking around, feeling things out. What would Donny be like now, and how would Donny treat him? How would he face Donny? Greg wondered what he would find out about Donny and what that would tell him about himself. He didn't want to rediscover those things he had tried so hard to suppress. He had been conniving. He had cheated, cold-heartedly. He had taken a dear life like others kill a spider.

But, what if Donny had told one of these people he knew—just one—about the things he and Donny had done years ago? What then? He wondered how he could keep Donny quiet.

Near Sublimity, he turned off for a used tool store that he'd Googled then erased from his browsing history. There he bought a shovel, a pick, a cheap headband flashlight, and gloves. Paid in cash.

After Sublimity, after Stayton, the dark contours rising up ahead consumed him as he followed Highway 22, driving alone for miles. Thick tall pines and firs walled both sides of the road, the low gray clouds obscuring their true height, the light dim like a permanent dusk. He was driving deeper and ever higher into the forested Cascade Range halfway to Pineburg.

On the passenger seat, he had a detailed map of this area containing precise topography and all forest roads and actual names for every tiny lake. He'd bought it at REI along with their cheapest high-top hiking boots, with cash, wearing sunglasses and a bucket hat like a casual bank robber. On the map, he thought he'd already found that little road from so many years ago. He'd know the spot when he saw it. How could he forget it?

As he climbed into the mountains, patches of defiant snow lined the route. Was it some freak new early-October snow, or left over from last winter? He had no clue. He drove on, trusting his phone map more than the paper map. Then his phone was losing network coverage fast, first down to 4G, then barely on Edge. The network dropped away. Phone service cut out. But he didn't need any map now. He felt a sharp twitch in his stomach, and the muscles in his neck began contracting as if he had a GPS built right into his chest. He was close. He just knew it.

He turned into the narrow forest road, the lane dim as if muddy but with just enough gravel to give him some hope that he wouldn't get stuck. More splotches of snow showed along the underbrush among the dark tree trunks. The trees cleared ahead, revealing a lake so small some would call it a pond. The clearing could barely fit a couple cars the size of Greg's or, as he recalled, one large pickup truck.

He parked, got out, and looked back toward the highway. He couldn't see it or hear it. So that was good. He stepped over to the bank, looking out. The opposite bank was no farther away than the length of a soccer field. The water looked murky, darker than the trees' shadows themselves and got little daylight with so much tree line crowding its banks. A draft from the trees made little ripples on the surface and gave him a shiver. Sticks and stems and soggy bushes rose from the water's edge, looking skeletal like the carcass of some unknown lagoon creature.

This little lake was probably ignored on regular maps because it bore few fish. Greg hoped so. Because it wasn't looking as deep and smothering as he'd expected despite all the murk. He turned to his left and saw a trail—that trail, narrow and close to the bank. He heaved the shovel and pick onto his shoulders and headed off down the path. He wore the headband flashlight just in case and flicked it on at first, but then his eyes adjusted and he didn't need it. He probably should have waited for dark, but that could take hours—and what if someone else came?

At times the trail took him deeper into the woods where the moss fought for every inch of underbrush and fallen log. To him, a city kid, it smelled something like a suburban Christmas tree farm, but it was all musty with mold and moss as if slowly rotting from some invasive bug. He stopped once or twice, to listen, but not sure what for, and only found silence except for a faint, muffled trickle that seemed to come from everywhere. He imagined this was what the inside of a sponge sounded like to an insect that had found its way inside the soggy maze, through fear or flight or just inbred stubbornness. Something about that made him snicker, and he didn't like the malice he was feeling.

Less than twenty minutes later, he was standing on the opposite bank of the lake. He could make out the silver of his Corolla just inside the trees and told himself that was a good sign since he could see from here if anyone was coming, though what he would do with such information, he didn't want to know. Pretend he was a lost lake buff? He was wearing dark jeans and a faux-vintage army jacket and told himself that his trendy camouflage was better than none. He did have the hiking boots on. But so what. He tried not to think about what he would do if a person came and got suspicious. His mind went there anyway, like an elevator on free fall, and only when he saw himself bashing a man's head in with a rock and holding his unconscious head under water and snickering about it did he shake himself out of it with a jolting shiver.

He stepped back inside the tree line. He stared at underbrush. This, here, it had to be the spot.

He kicked away at underbrush, working in a circle. This didn't seem to dig up much dirt and it jammed his toes inside his boots, but it didn't take long until he hit something. He kicked some more and used a fir branch to brush away the loose dirt.

A rock appeared, embedded in the dark earth, about the size of a football. He brushed at the rock and could see bits of neon orange that had once had the brightness of highlighter, faint and fading fast now, just enough left to leave a spot no bigger than his fist. It was the spray paint from Donny's truck—construction marker paint.

He wondered if Donny had ever been back here. The underbrush gave no clues, but wouldn't Donny have scraped off the orange if so?

Less than a half hour later, he was digging away. He had dug out the rock with the orange markings, and he was sweating, panting.

A half hour after that, he was sitting on the edge of the shallow pit he'd dug, still holding the fir branch he had used to brush away at the dirt, like that archeologist he'd briefly dreamed of becoming when he was eleven. His sweat had cooled, he shivered a little, but he didn't care. He stared down into the pit.

Just enough light made its way down through the layers and layers of branches to illume the white contours of bone that protruded from the dirt in relief. A face, half of a skeletal face, stared up at Greg, its mouth open. Other contours showed that the body was curled up as if sleeping—the arms bent upward with the hands at the chin and the legs pulled up high, the thick knee bones meeting the elbows. He and Donny hadn't placed the body like that thinking it was somehow more comfortable, or even respectful. It was the only way it fit in the hole they dug.

Greg had come to make sure it was still there. That no one knew. He stared a minute longer. Then he shoveled the dirt back in, stomped it down. He replaced the rock, heaved on some more dirt, stomped that down, and brushed it smooth. He gathered all the underbrush and set it all back over, brushing that out too. He carried over handfuls of wet snow, his palms stinging from it, and laid it around so that the snow would melt leaving the spot looking more natural. All he could see of the spot was three splotches of snow. It would do. He warmed his hands inside his pockets, then pulled out his phone and used the flashlight to survey his work in one, two bursts of light to make extra sure.

On the way back he sensed a warm surge of pride in his efforts and forced himself to instead feel something pensive, something wistful, anything. He gazed up at the sky where the trees gave way above the lake. The clouds had broken, and he saw a smear of blue. This only gave him relief.

At the car he banged his cheap boots together to get the mud off, slid them inside a plastic shopping bag. He placed this in the car. As he slipped his retro running shoes back on, he gazed again at the sky, but the clouds were back already. He pulled away, screwing up his eyes for the highway.

Only after he was back on the road a few miles did he realize: He hadn't even thought of scraping off the last of the paint.

Sometime later he pulled over next to a dense stretch of forest, pulled out the shovel, pick, gloves, and headband flashlight and tossed them high and deep into the trees, the handles knocking at tree trunks like so many discarded bones. He drove on. He drove miles of dim, wet Cascade Range highway, way up high. It snaked through dense forest before delivering him downhill.

He hadn't meant to dig it up, not all of it. He was just going to check on it. But he could not help himself.

His phone coverage returned. Emily had called. Her message said she was just checking in to see how far he'd gotten.

Greg called her back. Her voice had that quiet calm it always had when she'd been alone in her workroom with her designs and sewing machine.

"Where are you now?" she asked him.

"Way out here," Greg said, trying to imagine how far he had gotten if he hadn't stopped. "Highway names keep changing, all two-laners. It's starting to look more like desert, at least to me. Few hills. Brown. Not much green. It's another world. Definitely the other Oregon."

"Iowa can get like that," she said. "Know what you should do once it's dark? Check out the stars."

"I will. You okay? You seem quiet."

"I'm okay. Just reading. Started a new novel."

He imagined she had been talking with her friends about him and so seriously that they had tea at home instead of drinks out. He being *the* issue to be discussed. He had always thought he could be a form of parent and guide for a younger girlfriend like Emily, but with Emily he could see that it was and always would be the other way around.

"Sure you okay?" he said.

"Yes. I'm sure. You know me."

This was not the best conversation to be planting the seeds of lies to come. And yet Greg found himself welcoming the intrigue of it. This was that part people didn't know about him, not these days, the part he had tried so long to shake. He liked to double down and didn't give a shit about what it could bring. Screw it. In breaking this compulsion, or trying to, he had wondered long and hard if maybe it was just the doubling down itself that he liked. The risk of utter destruction could be as much of a high as the prospect of total happiness. He'd read that about gamblers somewhere. It had nothing to do with winning. It was all about the rush of pushing it.

All he knew was that the best lies had kernels of truth in them.

"Listen, I might not get much cell reception where I'm going," he said.

"So you told me. Where is this place?"

"Central Oregon, practically Eastern. It's called Pineburg. There aren't too many pines there, I'm guessing."

"We got the pines," she said.

"That's right."

"Your bike okay?"

"Yep. Still there."

A silence crept in. He added:

"Listen, Em, I'm sorry. I just don't think I'm ready."

"I've been thinking about it too," she said. "I don't think you are either."

He didn't know what to say. She was right, of course, but to declare it like that? It initiated the threat of closure, and he wasn't ready for that either.

Mumbled cross talk followed, each promising to check in soon.

After he hung up, Greg realized he hadn't even asked her what the novel was. And why would he? He had only called her back to give himself an alibi, to use her for an alibi. She would remember he hadn't asked. It would have been a better alibi if he had asked, he realized too.

The other Oregon beyond the valley began to reveal itself: The mountain highway delivered him down into that very flatland he had fabricated to Emily. He thought of tossing out his boots along the road and assured himself some hitchhiker or poor vagabond would find them and put them to good use. But it might also be littering. At the first roadside minimart, he parked on the secluded side of the store, went inside, and bought a pepperoni stick and was glad to buy it from a tired-looking Korean man who, he told himself, hadn't even looked at him and would never identify him. People like that didn't want trouble from anyone, not even cops. He assured himself this wasn't racist. He dumped his boots in their bag into the garbage can by his car. And he drove on, thinking, sure, this was all overkill, worrying about covering his tracks from twenty years ago, but he had to be wary. It felt good again, too, like uncovering a secret but in reverse, and he let it warm him. The pepperoni stick was a nice meaty treat he never would have picked out back home.

It was nearly six in the evening. He didn't want to drive into Pineburg when it was getting dark. Best to start fresh in the morning. At a remote highway turnoff, he passed a roadside motel standing alone. He turned around to stay the night there. The motel had little bungalows, each with a parking spot for a car, chipped pink tiles in the tiny bathroom, barely five channels on TV. Once it was dark out, he walked outside to the edge of the parking lot and stepped onto the dry, flat, and barren red earth that was so unlike the Willamette Valley. He shined his phone flashlight on it. It really was a Mars-scape compared to what he knew. It was colder out here at night than he expected. He looked up and could see that all the stars were back. Emily was right, of course. And he was keeping things sensible—by doing just what she had told him to do on the phone—he had one less thing to ever have to lie about. He looked down. Something was crawling past his feet, long legs, fat body, maybe a spider or a beetle or even a cockroach. He jumped back. It turned for him, came at him. He jumped on the thing with both feet, smashing it with a squirt and leaving an ooze, and headed back to his bungalow shaking his head. That was what he got for looking up.

9

Out in a brown field, a homemade billboard read Defend Our Water! It had an image of a trapper bearing a musket but distorted as if someone had tried to reproduce a sketch from a napkin.

Greg had no clue what that was supposed to be about. It was the next morning. He had driven the two-lane highway heading east, eyeing the vast land around him of scrubby pale grass and knotty shrubs with defiant woods here and there. Highway signs had told him he was in Oregon, but he might as well have been in New Mexico or even Australia. It looked like a set from a western. He had checked his phone: No Coverage. He had tried the radio but got static mostly. The traffic was so sparse that he had hauled ass, not worrying as much about his bike coming loose or a random truck-trailer clipping his protruding, spinning wheels. Here, closer to Pineburg, the highway was running along a dry riverbed. This barren trench was once the Redpine River.

Defend what water exactly, and whose? Torres was right. He should have had more of a clue. He hadn't bothered to write about this part of Oregon, of Cascadia possibly, and the truth was it hadn't even occurred to him. When most people thought of Oregon, they thought of rain and moss and rust, not their opposites. Out here any strike of lightning could cause a wildfire, he did know that much. He also realized that out here most conflicts were contaminated by a critical wound that had been gaping and festering for so long in Oregon—the downturn in the logging industry. He had read up on this quickly before leaving. The loss afflicted everyone, even here. Despite the look of the land around him, there had been logging on the green stretches and mountains of Pineburg's county. Many Oregon counties were practically founded on timber sales. The decline wasn't overnight, though, and it had a safety net. For decades, federal timber purchases from within county lands had helped pay for police, prosecutors, health clinics, roads, and other services—they had cut a deal in which the Feds got to share in harvest revenue. But the end of logging in federal forests did come eventually, and it was a slow bloodletting. Congress had approved payments to replace the money and extended it twice, but the bandage could only stop so much hemorrhaging. The later do-nothing, corrupt, partisan Congresses of the 2000s could never agree on a solution, which left many counties facing hundreds of millions in lost revenue and up to fifty percent reductions in budgets and funds. Not to be outdone, many local citizens, feeling particularly maverick and self-destructive, militantly voted down any new taxes that could help and heal the situation while blaming only those outside the region for their troubles. So, Greg figured, the death of logging must have stored up reservoirs full of bad blood for any coming plight such as water. Lines had been drawn, sides taken, feuds fixed. And to certain locals, any outsider from an urban region would always be a living and reviled specter of those Feds and state administrators who had stabbed them—and their ways—in the back, between the ribs, twisting ever deeper to puncture more vital organs, unleashing more and more bloody hatred. Greg could understand their grievances. Some of these people had been in logging for generations. It was all they knew. If someone from outside could have explained it all more clearly, maybe they would have seen what was coming. It was all about education, about learning together. And the chance had been lost.

A low, old fence lined the road. Dusty cows stood here and there watching Greg's car whiz by. He honked at a group of them and could have sworn he heard them moo back. Was this their grazing land? It didn't look very green to him. But, what did he know about cows? They probably knew more about him.

An old gas station stood at a junction. Long closed, the station had rusting pumps and fading, chipping paint and the usual broken windows, straight out of some clichéd roadside thriller. A newer sedan was parked at an odd angle, all four tires flat, gathering dust, waiting for a tow that might never come. It had government plates. Strange. Greg could only image that predicament.

After the gas station, the road winded through low hills and straightened out, heading for what looked like the cliff edge of a massive, horizon-wide butte. This revealed itself to be multiple, interconnected buttes forming a rim, and the road descended between two of them. He slowed to take in what he saw before him below. The town of Pineburg was tucked in a canyon. The side closest to Greg was browner like the country he'd just passed through while the other side, beyond the town, was more lush, green, and certainly farmland. The riverbed Greg's route had followed passed one edge of town along some woods, and Greg saw it reappear on the other side of town as a line of sparkles—over there it had enough water to live on as a stream if not a river. In the middle of town, grand old trees stood in clusters, most near a main street of brick and stone buildings and, standing nearby, a few Victorian houses. This place had probably hit its peak about 1910, Greg thought. Somewhere in town, old iron rails could certainly be found—half-buried and leading nowhere—from the railroad that made this town and left it stranded. Current population: 1,900.

The road delivered Greg into town. A street sign read Callum Street. This was the main drag. Greg had his pick of so many parking spots that it was hard to choose. He first rolled up in front of a mid-last century storefront with a 1950s brick facade, plate glass, and a fading For Lease sign in the window—surely once a Woolworth's or J.C. Penney. The spot was in full sunlight though, so he rolled ahead a few spaces under the shade of an oak tree, before a used bookstore with paperbacks out front for a quarter. They were even selling used magazines. How quaint, Greg thought and imagined he already sounded like a pretentious prick-nerd from Portland.

He checked his phone coverage: barely a bar. He stayed seated in the car to eye this scene, focusing and refocusing as if he had just set down a landing craft on some untraveled planet. The pavement carried little drifts of brown-red dust that exploded into the air as the tiniest funnel clouds. On the other side of the street, he saw an elderly man shuffle along and felt a little disappointed the man wasn't wearing a cowboy hat.

Greg mulled over what little he'd learned from his last blur of a phone call with Torres in which the FBI agent had hoped to change his mind. Torres had reported: Ten years ago, before supposedly heading off to Mexico, Donny had arrived in Pineburg with a couple losers he'd known from prison. The two had militia ties from Idaho and had since moved on (one now dead, the other back in jail). But Donny had stuck around. Mexico being some kind of ruse. Donny had become something of a recluse. Meanwhile, the local militia types had come to respect him.

"Why?" Greg had muttered to Torres.

"You tell me," Torres had said, adding before Greg could guess, "He's recreating himself, that's what I think. Wouldn't you if you were him? It's not about the respect, but what you do with it. For guys like this, it's all about seeing if you can get people to do what you want."

Torres had not told Greg why they believed Donny could still be near Pineburg ten years later, which was just as well. Greg would find that out himself. He could act on it himself, in his own way.

The longer he sat here in his car, the harder it was to get out. He was nervous, he realized. He took a deep breath, gathered his notepad and voice recorder, pulled on a thin blazer that he hoped made him look more professional or at least more reputable since the rest of his outfit showed a sense of irony that might be lost on some here. He had on skinny jeans, green-and-yellow soccer shoes, and a faux-vintage fitted western shirt like a flashy rodeo rider might have worn thirty plus years ago. Underneath his unbuttoned western shirt was a tee shirt that read People's Republic of Portland, which he had thought could provide a jokey conversation piece, but now he decided could also get him sucker-punched. Plus, attracting too much attention could shut mouths. He buttoned up his shirt under his blazer, then the blazer. He thought about riding his bike, but left it locked to his rack. Pedaling the strip would make him a one-man main-street parade.

He locked the car and walked the strip. He hit a hardware store and asked the only salesperson, who told Greg he'd never heard of a man named Donny Wilkie. He entered a dress shop, and the kind woman stared at him with his question as if he had four heads. He tried an antique shop where the frail old couple running things from behind a heavy wooden desk only shrugged, no, though they added that they had voted for Wendell Wilkie. That made Greg smile and reconsider the word "quaint" until he noticed that they turned their sign to Closed right after he left.

Economy aside, he could see why the older ones in town would be wary of outsiders. North of Pineburg, about thirty years ago, that international New Agey cult called the Rajneeshees had set up shop on harsh land bordering the near-ghost town of Antelope and tried to take over the county for their own. When influence got them nowhere, they attempted to spread salmonella to poison officials and voters so they couldn't vote against them. Few Americans knew this was the largest biological terror attack in US history. Yet Greg still hadn't bothered to put it in his book. His Cascadia could never plunge into such an abyss.

He found a coffee shop. A couple suburban-looking woman were in there and a group of boys with soft faces. The teenage girl holding the fort was eager to help but knew nothing, adding a sorry and a sigh. She was pretty new here herself. He got a coffee, which was better than he expected, which made him feel that twinge of prick-nerdishness again. Why shouldn't it be good? Outside the wind had picked up, clogging his nostrils with the aroma of the trees and that grit of the brown earth edging the town. But his spirit was winning. So much for getting his ass kicked, he thought as he walked along, feeling looser now, the last of the fall heat helping to relax his muscles. Then again, he would need to get more ballsy and try a bar.

As he walked along Callum Street, he noticed a pickup truck that wasn't parked there before. It had two rifles in the cab window. Two rifles! He slowed his pace to stare, wondering if they might just be heavy fishing poles. Nope, rifles. Fighting a nervous grin of awe, he pushed on, making a mental note that the words Carver Farm Supply were painted on the pickup's door.

At the next corner stood a chunky sandstone building that looked like a bank from the robber-baron era. A street window sign read Office Space for Lease—Callum Properties, and etched in a cornerstone: Callum Building. City hall was in the building on the second floor. Greg jotted the Callum connections down in his notebook.

He moved on. At the end of the street, he could see where the town more or less ended, giving way to that rugged and dry brown earth. He sensed something, out of the corner of his eye, and turned to face the brick wall of a building. The bricks had been sprayed over with white primer, to cover something. Under the dull white, Greg could make out, in black: X X.

Two Xs. Just as Torres had said. Look out for the two Xs. Greg took one step back, unknowingly. Was this just a coincidence? Some sort of random graffiti or even construction markings? In any case, he shouldn't be seen writing it down. He slid his notepad into his pocket and pretended to rock on his heels, just looking around, checking things out.

He started back toward the central strip of Callum Street to hit the other end beyond his car. As he passed a vacant lot, he saw a man strutting toward him, a large figure but not tall. Greg kept going. This man was surely just aiming to cross the street. But as the man strutted closer, his hands as squared fists, he corrected his path to track alongside Greg's. Greg picked up his pace but subtly, hoping it didn't show. He pretended to gaze around so he could steal a look. The man's body depicted an epic battle between stout and chubby. He wore tan work wear, but the shirt and pants were too clean, like a uniform. The man stared, his small mouth a hard line. He was maybe ten yards away and strutting parallel with Greg now, like a dog behind a chain-link fence stalking a passerby. Like this the man resembled an overgrown fifth grader looking for someone to beat up on recess, but that stare was showing something far darker. His heavy brow looked like an armor plate, those eyes like dark stones shoved into dough.

Greg chuckled to himself. This was silly. His imagination was just playing tricks. The man might even be mentally challenged.

Greg slowed down. Let the guy come at him if he wanted. They could talk.

Then Greg noticed: The man had a semi-automatic rifle slung on his shoulder.

Greg jumped back a step, squinted. It was so surreal to him, he hadn't even noticed.

"You looking for something?" said a voice—a female voice.

Greg whipped around to see a woman of about fifty in a black tee shirt, denim skirt, and cowboy boots—her long, pulled-back hair was darker than the shirt, apart from streaks of gray.

"Said, can I help you?" the woman said, louder now. "You . . . understand?" She nodded for him like a good actor in a bad play helping an understudy with his lines.

Greg realized he hadn't said anything. He had crouched down, one eye on the man, one eye at her. "That man, he has a weapon," he muttered.

"Ah, don't mind him."

"Shouldn't we do something, call someone?"

"Who? No one to call. He's just an open carry—just wants the attention."

Greg had only seen open-carry advocates in stories on the Internet. He'd always clicked them away in disgust. The man kept staring back at him as if daring Greg to make one of the five snide remarks that had entered his head.

"Oh. All right, then," Greg said, facing the woman. "Hi. Yes. I'm okay, but thanks." He stood up straight. He smiled for her.

She smiled. "Good, okay, hi. Way you're dressed, thought maybe you were one of those Euro tourists who come through. They get lost. Usually wanting the ghost towns up north or turquoise this or that. You looking?"

"Turquoise? No, thanks." Greg saw her eyes shift back in the direction of his big new shadow. Was she helping him despite her calm? She might be. "But, I do need a good place to eat," he added.

"There you go. The tavern's good. Just go on back that way, way you're heading. Go on. Only one this side of the street. That way. That's it."

"Thanks." Greg started walking that way, and she practically shooed him along like a lost cat. He looked over his shoulder to see her march off down a side street. A few steps further on, he dared to look over his other shoulder.

The man stood tall at the edge of the vacant lot, holding his ground, one of his fists tight around his gun strap, still eyeing him.

10

"Hello? Anyone here?" Greg said, just below a shout. He stood in the middle of the bar, sensing the chilled stillness of the dim and empty watering hole. The sign outside read Tam's Tavern in blue letters hand-painted over bumps that were once mounts for grander neon letters. The walls had real wood paneling and ghost-town decor with wagon wheels and settlers' tintype photos. The bar had chromium trim and cracking leather stools.

"Hello? Anyone here?" Greg repeated, but no one came out the swinging door to the right of the bar. He had a wicked thought like the kind he always used to have. No one seemed to be here. He could go behind the bar, make himself a drink, pocket a bottle or two, even open up the register. Who would know? He would go in back first and make sure no one was in the kitchen. It was only too bad some greenhorn like the young Donny wasn't here so he could talk him into it. That was even better. That was the way he used to operate. Many people entertained such thoughts, but they denied them. They used to rule Greg's life, not entertain it. He hadn't felt them so strong for years. Why now? He wondered if it was nerves. The shock to that order he had so carefully created? Maybe it went along with his rejecting Torres' authority. Seeing that open-carry guy just now hadn't helped matters; what was more terrorizing than a stranger strutting around in public bearing a rifle? He shut his eyes a moment, fighting it, took a deep breath.

"Be right there!" someone shouted from beyond the swinging door.

The door flung open and the woman from the street came out behind the bar. Greg grinned, and she showed him a grin to match. "Hi again. Want a menu?" she said.

She introduced herself. She was the Tam on the sign. She was Native American, just as Greg had guessed. To him, it was in the way she spoke as much as her looks. It reminded him of Hawaiians, the words rising and falling in subtly different ways. Tam made him a good ham sandwich with a great house-made pickle. She disappeared in back, leaving him alone to eat. At precisely ten o'clock she came out, placed four bottles of beer and two wrapped sandwiches in a sack, and set them on the counter. Then she went in back again. Soon two guys came in, looking like ex-hippies to Greg, grabbed the bag and shouted, "Thanks!" Tam shouted from the back, "Welcome, boys—eat the sandwiches or I'm cutting you off," and the two giggled and tumbled out the door like teens busted for leaving the toilet seat up. Greg wanted to follow them and buy them more beers, maybe smoke a joint even. Get them talking.

Now Tam was back out behind the bar, on her haunches, wiping something down. Greg hadn't noticed the door swing open. He really needed to be more aware, he told himself.

"So, just where are you from?" Tam asked him.

"Portland," he said. "I'm a native." It was an awkward way of putting it, at best. His face had heated up, all red. "I just meant, I'm from there."

Tam stared at him, waiting for more.

"That guy outside on the street? You can't open carry like that in Portland," Greg blurted instead.

"That so? Well, you sure can here."

"At least, I don't think you can," he added. He told himself to look it up. He checked his phone and saw no bars.

"No coverage?" Tam said.

"No, but, it's okay. I could use the isolation."

"Sometimes you do get coverage. It depends." She took his plate.

"Great sandwich, thanks," Greg said, looking around the empty room. "Though I sort of feel like I'm *The Prisoner*," he added, trying a joke.

Tam didn't smile. "I wouldn't call it the state pen, though it can be like that for some."

"No, I just meant—dumb joke. TV reference."

"I get it. Patrick McGoohan—he was the lead guy in *The Prisoner*, right?" She showed him the smile he'd wanted, her teeth healthy squares.

"Good one. I was going to look it up."

"If you had coverage."

"Totally."

Tam went back to wiping down. He emptied his beer. He waited a good half-minute, practically counting off the seconds.

"I have a question," he said. "You ever hear of the name Donny Wilkie?"

"I sure haven't." She reached the end of the bar and stood. Her face was a little flushed, which brought out the gray in her hair. "I take it you're not on vacation."

"I'm a writer, researching a book," he said. He told her that the book, if the research panned out, would be about the urban-rural split in Oregon and focus on people's stories over the history, the wonkish policies, the politics. This Donny Wilkie person fit one example. Donny Wilkie had come from rural Oregon and ended up in the city as a teen. Greg had known him, so he figured he should start with what he knew. The last Greg had heard,

Donny had become a criminal. What had caused that? Did the city help, or was it already ingrained in this Donny?

"Not sure about your whole city-versus-country deal," Tam said. "People are just people. A guy like that, he might have been simply wired that way to explode at some point. Then again, as a teen you're hardly fully formed. Any bad influence could bring out what might not explode otherwise."

"I suppose you're right. All I know is, I got a lot of digging to do," Greg said and paused. He'd probably told this Tam too much, but he couldn't just hang around and hope for a clue. "In any case," he added, "there's an issue in all this I'm trying to nail—what does this idea of two Oregons do to Oregon as a whole?"

"Good luck with that, professor."

Greg didn't know if that was a joke. He smiled anyway.

Tam smiled back. "You know I took you for one of those movie location scouts at first?—once I figured out you weren't a Euro looking for turquoise. Scouts come through sometimes, but never choose us. Shows how much I know. Anyway, you find anything out?"

What could that mean? Was she talking about the XXs? What if she was pushing him? "Like what?" he said.

"You know, anything. Maybe just being here gives you ideas."

"No, not yet."

"You'll figure it out, I'm sure." Tam grabbed her rag and started wiping the taps.

"Let me ask you something," Greg said. "Were you protecting me from that guy back there? Helping me, I mean."

"I told you. Don't let open-carry guy worry you."

"He's not. He isn't. It's just that, how do you even know if it's loaded, or on safety even?"

"Who's the good guy?"

"That's what I'm saying."

"You don't know. And that's just one part of the problem."

Greg wanted to joke about gun fanatics, but for all he knew she was packing a Glock under that skirt. "Man," he tried anyway, "I guess I know what it's like to be under an occupation."

Tam stopped wiping. She stared at him, stone-faced. "Mister, you got no goddamn idea."

"Oh!" Greg waved hands at her. "No, I didn't mean . . . No, you're right, I don't at all." His face flushed again.

Tam laughed. She started wiping again, faster. "Just riding ya, take it easy. But, yes, I was helping out a stranger if that's what you mean. You looked hungry."

"Okay. Thanks."

"What makes you think he was here?" Tam said. "Your friend, I mean."

"Someone told me. Plus, Donny had lived in Pineburg as a kid and when I knew him he used to talk about going back one day."

"Uh, and that's it?"

"Also, legal records have this as his last destination in the US."

"His last?"

"About ten years ago. He'd fled to Mexico. But I had this wild idea that maybe he came back." Greg stopped there, let Tam finish her wiping. He didn't have much cover story left. He didn't need to lie any more than this. And yet something about the possibility of making up more, of completely recreating himself, appealed to him in one warm, pulsating moment deep inside him. Why not say he was a movie scout? Why not the director even? He could probably get Tam and others to do all kinds of things that way. And then the moment was gone, leaving him feeling refreshed, breathing clearly. He guessed that was what heroin or maybe a women's orgasm felt like. He got what the con man felt. He could go there in a place like this, where no one knew him. Why hadn't he thought of it before? He had striven to be a better person, but if he had taken it in the other direction and simply become someone else entirely, maybe he would have ended up with no demons.

Tam was staring at him with a curious half smile like someone watching a cat clean itself in weird places. He shifted in his chair. "Those pickles of yours?" he said. "You could sell those from a cart in Portland and rake it in." Going with the first thing he could think of.

"Nah. I'd have to dress them up. Deep fry them in batter, wrap them in pork belly or whatever. I been to Portland, seen your food carts that are all the rage. Why bother? It's just a pickle."

"Yeah. I guess so."

She stared at him again, then at her bleach rag, and back at him as if she was thinking of wiping him down with it. "Ten years, that's a long time. People come and go," she said.

"I know. I was thinking, though, maybe there are still people here that knew him, or who are still getting into trouble doing what he was doing."

He hadn't mentioned a militia, and yet Tam was nodding her head.

"Oh, there are still the same people, all right," she said. "Only they think they're all grown up now, and in a way that's never any good. Thinking everyone else owes them. Like they deserve it."

"Like their time is ripe," Greg added. He shook his head. He did understand that. He had felt that way once. The entitlement of the non-entitled could be a scary fucking thing. Infectious.

Tam sighed and set down her rag. "Let me give you a tip, writer guy. If you're looking for someone, especially for the story of someone like that, there's a whole 'nother part of town you probably haven't tried."

11

On the side of the road, sitting in fold-up chairs under a large umbrella fixed to the hood of their old Chevy Blazer, a young Native American couple was trying to sell fresh fish from a cooler. They eyed Greg passing in his car, he being the closest thing to an actual tourist. This edge of Pineburg was looking to him like yet another rural two-lane highway with a strip mall. Depressed, if not discontinued. Most shops were out of business, their windows browned with road dust and last winter's snow dirt and still bearing ads for cell phone deals, local artists, investment property, Your New Outdoor Paradise! Something called the Food Stamp Info Office was open and had people coming and going. A small chain market next door looked busy too, its windows papered over with posters announcing low prices in huge numbers and the products in tiny letters. One poster exclaimed that they always accept those same food stamps, which nowadays came as a barcoded plastic card called, with no irony intended, the Oregon Trail Card. American Dream or Oregon Dream, it sure was looking like the end of the road to Greg.

The strip had roadside angle parking. Greg pulled in facing an empty, unleased storefront. It had a banner in the window: It's Us or Salmon! Don't Let Them Kill the Dam!

Greg wondered what kind of property owner would allow a militant message like that on a space for lease. He noticed the For Lease sign was from the company called Callum Properties.

At the end of the strip stood a former barn, low and squat without windows. It was now a flea market. Greg sat on a bench outside to get his bearings. Across the dusty road from the strip was a line of trees. To the right of the woods stood an abandoned diner. Its look was an odd mix of country cabin and mid-century roadside spot. The faux log walls and plank doors clashed with aluminum trim and windows that were boarded up—yet another relic from a time when, Greg imagined, this place could still let itself expect great things to come.

Deep, clomping footsteps sounded from the side of the flea market. They rounded the corner. It was the man from the parking lot who had watched Greg. Without looking at Greg, he sat at the far end of the bench, which made it creak and seem to sink an inch, and for a second Greg grasped at the bench thinking he'd get flipped off his end like the smaller kid on a seesaw. He saw no rifle on the man. Then Greg saw he was wearing a holster of brown leather, the butt of a chunky black pistol sticking out. The man leaned forward, his forearms across his knees as if he wanted to spit out tobacco. All he needed was a badge.

"Afternoon," the man said.

"Hey there," Greg said.

"Wayne Carver."

"I'm Greg. Greg Simmons."

Only now did this Wayne Carver look at Greg—he snapped his head sideways with such force he could have pulled a muscle.

Greg offered his hand. Wayne studied it a moment, his dim eyes receding under his thick brow. He shook Greg's hand and held it, squeezing for an uncomfortably long time. It wasn't like a vise grip but rather a steady, moist smothering.

"You a writer, Simmons? Reporter? What?" Wayne's voice had an accusatory whine to it.

"Both." Greg showed a smile. "You the sheriff?" he added, trying to make a joke.

Wayne grinned, and Greg felt the relief. The quip could have gone really wrong. In Wayne's case it appeared to be flattery.

"You got a place to stay?" Wayne said.

"No. Not yet. I wasn't sure where I'd end up."

With that, without a word, Wayne stood, smoothed the tuck of his neat and clean brown work shirt into his matching pants, and walked off. Greg watched him get into a pickup—the same one he had seen in town with the two rifles in the window and Carver Farm Supply on the doors. Wayne Carver was his name so he must be the son since Wayne wasn't any older than him. And something about that made Greg wipe his hand on his pant leg.

As Wayne's pickup drove off, he noticed that far more people appeared, coming out from doorways and onto the street and sidewalk. An elderly couple hobbled past, each with canes and plastic bags hanging from their free hands. Each bag held a few cans and bottles. They approached a garbage can, and Greg looked away so they could poke around in peace. In the other direction, a kid was running circles around a primered, mold-splotched Yugo as the boy's teenage mom popped the hood and fed the thing oil.

Greg heard frantic whispers. Three teens stumbled out from a side alley, two guys in their late teens and a girl, their outfits of baggy jeans and hoodies, baseball hats and mud-caked high tops interchangeable. Greg pulled back to watch them as they passed. Their skin was pale, their pupils dilated, movements jerky. Sharp, stale smells like mildew and charred firewood followed them, passing over Greg. Meth tweakers were the same anywhere, he thought. Zombies.

They headed off across the street for the line of trees.

Greg followed, keeping his distance. Long before he was a reporter, he had learned that if you were after a secret, you didn't ask those holding it but rather those on the fringes—the artists, cabbies, restaurant workers, and the users—those with lives little understood by others.

The three kept up the same fast pace entering the woods as if having tread this route many times, traversing the same holes and logs. Greg would have stuck out inside the woods so he kept to the edge of the trees, skirting the three. He ended up at a riverbank lacking a real river. The bank lined a wide and rocky riverbed, but only a rope of water trickled on through—this was the Redpine River he'd seen coming into town.

He crouched at the feeble stream. To his left, he could see into the woods. To his right and just yards away, stood the dead diner—what was once quite the riverside spot, he imagined.

Inside the woods, the three teens were meeting with two guys who looked like would-be cowboys from a bad country rock band, their getups garnished with touches of leather and fur. One of the teen tweakers, a boy, passed the two country wannabes a small bundle.

The girl tweaker had turned her head Greg's way. The two wannabes turned and started for Greg, charging through the trees for him.

Greg stayed at the bank. What else could he do? He wasn't doing anything. He was just checking out the water.

The two got in Greg's face. "What you doing?" said one, and the other said, "Fuck you doing?" Their arms had cocked back for fighting but their gaunt, crooked faces made them look like they'd been beat on more than they'd beaten. They were sweating. One was shaking. Greg caught a sour smell.

He stepped back, trying to smile. "Guys, come on. I wasn't doing a thing—"

"Listen up," boomed another voice. "You two go and leave this here man alone."

The voice had come from behind them.

Greg and the two turned to see a man. The man had stepped out of the dead diner and stood tall, wearing a crisp button-down shirt and new jeans.

It was Donny Wilkie.

Greg's insides tensed up, his organs pressing together.

It was Donny, but a bizarro version, a Donny who had gone to West Point, had nine awesome lives, later wrote a best-selling book, and could retire off his inspiring speaking engagements alone. This was what the figure of this man standing before him was saying, if not flaunting. His erect stance and hard-set look showed he was ready for anything, for more than even Greg had seen the man handle.

One of the two said to Donny, "This guy here was following us."

"He is not your problem," Donny said.

Greg had frozen up as if the straps inside him were cutting off blood flow, numbing all.

Donny handed the one who spoke a twenty. "You two need grub. Get some protein. If I find you didn't eat, I'll send Wayne Carver come looking for you."

The two straightened up.

"They'll have food coupons at the school tomorrow," Donny said. "Right down the street. Best you two get in line there."

The two nodded and backed up, moving along. "Yes, sir, thank you," they said as one.

Greg was still frozen, but his neck could move and he could shake his head, and shake he did as Donny Wilkie turned to face him. Was it really him? Donny confirmed it by smiling, then grinning. He still had those faint acne scars and dimples, but it was all deeper, more etched now. His grin might have gone all wrong by now, yet it still brought out that sparkle Greg remembered—that charm Greg had urged Donny to use so they could get girls.

"Here I am," Donny said.

Greg looked around, to make sure all had gone. The woods were empty and the street clear.

"Coast is clear," Donny added. "Well? You were going to find me anyway. Right?"

Greg didn't know what to say. "I don't know what to say," he said.

Donny's smile had fallen away, revealing those sandpaper cheeks, sharp lines, and peering dark eyes. "You could say it's good to see me, but if you did I'd really want to go and bust your jaw," he said. He turned and started marching up to the road.

Greg sighed, which seemed to relax the straps inside him. He caught up with Donny, who whispered: "This here's the way we play it. My name is Charles now. Charlie Adler, people call me. They have for a long time."

Greg walked in step, trying to make this fit in his head.

"You got that?" Donny said. "Tell me you got that."

"Yes. Okay. I got it."

12

Greg's whole face felt numb, unable to make proper reactions. He couldn't sort his colliding thoughts or figure out a next move. Which was probably a good thing. Because it could show on his face. Because Donny was eyeing him with his face so hard and set.

It was ten minutes later. Donny drove Greg in a new king cab pickup on a narrow old road that skirted Pineburg. Donny kept eyeing Greg as he drove, knowing the road so well he didn't need eyes on it—as if the pickup rode fixed on rails, Donny only needing eyes on Greg.

"I should thank you for saving my ass," Greg said finally.

"Those two weren't going to do anything."

"Who were they?"

"Casey, Damon. Couple Darwin Awards candidates, but they mean well. Just need someone to tell 'em what is what."

"Darwin Awards? You sound like a cop," Greg said.

Donny chuckled. "I am definitely not that. As you well know."

"And those kids? In the woods."

"Jamie and Rory. April's their little sidekick."

"They were doing something. It looked like a drug deal."

"That right?" Donny said. "Wait, don't tell me—meth use is getting big in rural areas, you read it in *Willamette Week*, or maybe it was the *New Yorker* even?" He had locked his eyes on Greg. Was this just a ploy to find out where Greg lived now, where he was coming from? Greg had to consider everything a tactic, a maneuver. For a moment he froze up again and had to look away, out the window at the landscape that seemed to be turning greener by the yard. Crops lined the road now, sprinklers and sparkling green on one side, neatly stacked hay blocks on the other. The brown Pineburg was behind them. They were going uphill.

Screw it. It was no secret where he lived. "I see it on Portland streets all the time," he said.

"Touché," Donny said.

Greg had probably first read about it in something more like the *Atlantic* or *Mother Jones*, though the *Oregonian* often had articles about the onslaught of meth, especially on how it had hit rural Oregon. Some called it cliché now, yet the epidemic would not die. Authorities had been fighting back against local meth labs by getting those over-the-counter cold medicines that meth cookers used changed to be prescription only; that and an increase in raids, awareness programs, and counseling had helped. But in the last few years Mexican drug gangs, seeing a market opportunity, had moved in more pure and potent crystals to build on the demand that the amateurs had created. Yet Greg dropped the subject, refrained from talking too much. He should let Donny do the talking and let him reveal himself.

Donny had one hand on top of the steering wheel, his sinewy, bony fingers hanging off it. His lips shifted back and forth. And Greg felt like a kid the parent had to pick up from school after being sent home for the day.

"We're not going back into town?" Greg began.

"You don't have a place to stay," Donny said almost before Greg finished asking as if thinking the same thought. "Your car will be safe. I'll make sure no one touches it."

"Thanks. I'm not worried." Of course he was, but what could he do about it?

"Or your bike," Donny said.

Did Donny really have such power? Was it just a bluff? "You know I can't help having questions," Greg said.

Donny stared at Greg, his lips pressing together like he wanted to spit. Greg's face had lost the numbness, but he did his best to pretend he still had not lost his shock.

Donny put one eye back on the road. "You come over the mountains?" he said.

Greg nodded. "Only way."

"You stop there? At the lake spot?"

Greg showed a blank face as if he didn't get it at first. "Nah."

"Don't gimme that shit, boy," Donny said.

"All right, yes. I did. I was there. Just for a minute though. I couldn't even find the exact spot. It looks like it's never been touched."

"You're damn right there."

"It was my first time," Greg said.

"I went once. Long time ago. And that was enough."

The road headed uphill. Donny slowed for a broad gate constructed of thick logs so nicely stained they looked just finished; ironwork framed the logs with designs of horseshoes and saws and, along the horizontal log above, the words Old Callum Ranch. Signs to the side read No Access, Private Road, and No Trespassing. They passed through. The entry road, lined with trees, ended at a grand old restored Victorian house. It looked like a high-end B&B or something out of the Old South. Greg didn't ask questions, and Donny offered nothing. He parked at the front steps, barked, "Come on," and went inside. Greg followed. He found Donny in a study. Donny was closing the thick wood blinds, making it so dark he had to turn on a desk lamp. In the middle of the room stood two broad chairs upholstered in a soft piebald cowhide. Lining the walls were bookshelves showing trophies and art pieces that looked, to Greg, like those corporate inspirational awards he always laughed at in in-flight catalogs, while other shelves had photos of vast landscapes or horses or bulls. Donny poured a whiskey for them, C.W. Irwin, sighing with each pour.

"Charles Adler doesn't drink," Donny said as he handed Greg his whiskey. He added a smile. "That's what they say. He's reclusive. Few see him or would know if they saw him. You don't even remember the name, do you?"

Greg didn't. Maybe it was someone they used to joke about. "Back in Portland? I drink the same stuff," he said. "Here's to Oregon whiskey."

Eyeing Greg again, Donny pressed his glass to his mouth as if by a mechanical arm and drank. "Why the hell are you here?" he said. "You tell me exactly."

Greg gave a long sigh, like Donny's. "I'm not going to lie to you. I was looking to do an article, maybe a book."

"A book? You?" Donny's eyes sparkled a moment, then dimmed.

"About how city and country conflict. Ready? It was going to include this guy named Donny Wilkie, talk about what led him on the path he took."

"Why he done what he did, how he ended up where he was? That kinda deal?"

"Something like that."

"Bullshit. You came here to make sure I didn't tell anyone about the lake. Or won't."

"That would be true. I would admit it," Greg said. "Except that I thought you were dead."

"You had to have a hunch. It's the real reason you come. Just admit it."

"I just told you, I'd admit it if I had any idea."

"You are looking after your own skin though," Donny said. "Just like always."

Greg nodded. "You're probably right about that."

"Well, I didn't tell anyone, and I won't," Donny said. "But, you? You have to be sure. I know that about you. Maybe you came here to kill me. Maybe that's it."

A laugh burst from Greg. "That's absurd. I didn't even know you're alive. Besides, I could say the same about you."

"I guess you could, couldn't you?" Donny burst out laughing, but it was affected, a mock of Greg's laugh. His mouth snapped shut.

Greg didn't like the shiver this gave him. "I could," he said.

"Okay. Okay. Well, did you?"

"Tell? Fuck, no. I never told a soul, and I never will."

Donny sighed again, this one long enough to leave a whiskey aroma in the air. "I didn't even tell Leeann. Don't eye me like that. Leeann Holt. Of course you were wondering about her."

"That's good to know," Greg said.

"We were together a long time, you know, me and Leeann."

"Oh? How is she?"

"I wouldn't know. She left me."

"Oh. So, about the time you died? In Mexico?"

"It was around then, yes. How did you know?"

"I was a reporter then. I read it was in Mexico. Must have been on the wire."

"Okay, all right," Donny said, nodding. "I didn't tell her though, Greg. I never did."

"Okay. Thanks."

They drank. Donny stared at Greg, his fingers tight around the whiskey glass. "Now. What about this book bullshit?"

Greg shrugged. "Sounds like a bad idea now, considering."

"Little close to home, isn't it? You'd have to leave out some real good parts."

"I guess so. Of course." Ideally, the book was now an ever better idea, considering the latest revelations. But it could never be told, not with Donny alive and able to talk. Finding Donny had changed everything. A part of Greg had not yet accepted that he would ever actually locate Donny, and especially not so easily. He took a quick drink, and another. What the hell had Torres led him to? And was Donny right? Had he really been prepared to kill Donny if need be? He told himself that he wouldn't even know how.

"Don't look mad at me. It was your idea," Donny said.

"I'm not mad. It was just research, Donny—"

"Charlie. It's Charlie."

"I could easily not have found you here. You could have avoided me no problem. I would've just moved on. You know that, right? You could have stayed hidden."

"I know," Donny began to say, but he had turned to face the window as if hearing something outside. "Turn that off," he barked.

Greg switched off the desk lamp, bringing darkness. Donny bounded over and raised a wood blind a little, about an inch. Greg expected light to stream in, but it only brought the purple dusk. Donny knelt there and peered out, his eyes just above the windowsill. He closed the blind.

"False alarm," Donny said and stomped out. "Come on."

Greg followed Donny out to a long back porch that stretched to either end of the house. Dusk had thinned out fast. Donny kept the porch light off. They stood looking out at the dark, the darkness pure out here. As his eyes adjusted, Greg could make out the contours of a barn-like building beyond. It looked tidy and organized with none of the farm machinery or junk or goods left out like he'd seen driving past other ranches.

"I always feel better outside," Donny said. "Got a smoke?"

"Quit years ago, or I would."

Donny turned to Greg, a black silhouette imprinting even the darkness. "I don't think you understand the spot I'm in. No, I know you don't. It's only a matter of time before they're on to me."

"Before who is?"

"County Mountie, state, Feds, who knows?"

Feds. Greg faced a choice here. He could tell Donny the FBI had approached him, gain his trust that way. His gut told him not to—not yet. It might only have the opposite effect, make Donny mistrust him more, or worse. He needed Donny's trust to make sure that Donny would never tell. "For what, exactly?" Greg said.

"It's not about the lake. Don't worry."

Not yet it wasn't. But after they caught him? Who knew? "Okay, that's good—I mean, you know what I mean," Greg said, stalling. He calculated a response, one that would sound logical coming from a former reporter: "What about the city police?" he said.

Donny shook his head. "Pineburg PD? No more. Not since last budget cuts. Which people voted for, by the way." He smiled and shook his head again but this time on a perfect swivel. "Oh, sure, there's a county Mountie on a string who makes the rounds, but he don't know the score as much, not nearly. Made it easier for me. Why you think I'm still here?"

The darkness, it amplified every nuance of their voices. Any hesitation hinted at deception. Every assurance suggested worse.

"Whose house is this?" Greg said.

"Whose you think? Mine? A woman named Karen Callum."

"I've heard that name."

"If you haven't around here, you're deaf or Chinese."

"I'm not sure what you're telling me."

"We're not married, but we might as well be," Donny said, looking out into the darkness. "We partnered up, see." He didn't say it like congrats were in order.

"So, let's back up a second. How do you know they're on to you?"

Donny took his time. He leaned on the railing, and he rocked forward and back, the floorboards and balusters under his weight so sturdy they did not creak, not even out here where it was so silent. He looked to Greg, his face a compact black monolith, but Greg could see the glints of his eyeballs. "This is between you and me. There was this group of officials come snooping around a little while ago. Because of our dam. Her dam."

"There's a dam somewhere on this side of town. I saw it on a map."

"Yep. Pineburg Dam."

"I saw billboards about water. Homemade ones or something. Wait—*her* dam?"

"It's privately owned. Callum Utility Company owns most of it."

"It's for power?"

"A little, but mostly for irrigation—that's water for farmland. Ranching."

"I know what irrigation means."

"Well, those officials, they done come around, and they bring their enviro cronies of theirs. The relicensing is coming up, but I don't think they aim to give it. They're all looking to remove the Pineburg Dam, you see . . ."

Donny paused. He went into a crouch, grasping at the railing balusters. The Greg of twenty years ago would have stood there smirking and told Donny: "Dude, you look like you're already in jail"—maybe just to see how Donny would react. But the Greg of today only waited it out. Appearing respectful. He needed to show Donny that he wasn't going to make Donny say anything he did not want to say.

Donny said, "Some fellers I know, they went and played a little trick on those people. I don't think those people liked it too much." He stared up at Greg, and the glints in his eyes looked softer, wetter.

"What kind of little trick? Who are these fellers—guys—you know?" Greg said.

"The deal is, they really fucked up." Donny shook his head, and he stood. He paced the porch, passing right by Greg and then back again, his thumbs tucked into his pockets and his elbows out. Greg couldn't help being reminded of a gunslinger before a big draw, waiting for sunrise outside the saloon. Donny reached the end of the porch again. He pivoted, faced Greg. He said: "Only reason I'm telling you this? I'm thinking you can help me. Both God and the Devil know you do owe me that."

13

Greg woke up in the dark startled, then paranoid, anxiety squeezing at his chest, hot and cold and hotter. He was exposed, both he and Donny were, just by being together. And what was next? He canceled out the nonstarters. If Donny wanted to blackmail him, he would have tried it already. If Donny wanted to kill him, he would have buried him by now. Donny could have revenge in his head, sure, but Greg couldn't sense it, couldn't see how. So, why was Donny confiding in him? Did he really think Greg could help him after what they had done together, done to each other?

Donny had put up Greg in an upstairs bedroom with a huge four-poster bed and decor that Greg would've described to Emily as country foofy. All that was missing were the stuffed old bunny rabbit dolls wearing prairie dresses. The bed was too high off the ground and the mattress so soft it wanted to pull Greg down, submerging him, and he just couldn't sleep, not with Donny somewhere below him lurking. Donny had a bedroom upstairs, but he had never gone up, claiming he preferred to sleep in his den downstairs. As Greg lay there, he kept feeling twinges of an alternate reality in which he would do whatever it took to keep Donny from destroying him. But was it alternate or just what loomed?

He fought the urge to call Agent Torres, tell him he'd come to Pineburg on his own. But it was too late for that. He'd already rejected that route. It would only make Torres wonder why he'd suddenly come around. Torres might start asking tough questions.

Out on the porch earlier, Donny had never said how he thought Greg might help him. He needed to think some shit out first, he had said. They had shared another whiskey and tried to talk up the good times of twenty years ago like when Greg had Donny do his rural Western thing to confuse and lure Portland chicks—working their own brand of Midnight Cowboy scam. They had laughed about it. But now Greg thought: If Donny was playing the bumpkin babe magnet, what had that made him? The wannabe Ratso? Some third-rate pimp and con man?

It was near five in the morning. It would be light before long. He needed sleep or at least something to help it along. He had a little pot in his car, a baggie that was mostly shake and had to be below the legal amount. But it was still stupid of him. This was all so fucking stupid.

The next morning the big old house was full of light, its tall windows getting lots of it despite the large shadowing trees that stood at precisely the same distance from each corner of the house, more like giant sentries than sturdy old friends. Greg couldn't take it anymore and was up by seven and downstairs by eight, roaming the living room, looking at photos of what had to be a young Karen Callum—the sole remaining child of one Loren Callum. Donny had told him: Once there were three great families in Pineburg; but the other families' children sold off the ranches, moved away, or died, and only the Callums remained standing. A first-born son, Ben, had died in an auto accident on a twisting road outside Pineburg, hitting a utility pole so hard that it knocked out electricity for miles. Loren Callum had been sitting at the kitchen table at the time, mulling over how best to pass on the ranch to Ben. After the loss of Ben, the Callums might have died out too. Loren Callum had already lost his wife too early, to cancer. Then young Karen stepped in to keep her father going. They were quite the partnership until Loren died a few years ago. None of the photos Greg saw included Ben, though he imagined there had once been many. He saw Karen looking like a tomboy in western riding gear, then posing with her father in multiple photos, the man always wearing a western suit and a Stetson. Greg wasn't surprised to see the similarity to Donny's new self, Charlie Adler.

Donny came in and sat Greg at the dining room table by the window looking out on one of the big sentry trees. In the daylight, coming back to his senses, Greg felt all the more relieved that he didn't come here as an informant for the FBI. This way made his questions all his own, thus all the more credible. For the answers, he might have to go places that a guy like Torres could never know about.

Donny sucked from his coffee mug. "That bad, huh?" he said.

"What?" Greg had forgotten to drink his coffee. He took a quick sip.

"I know it's not your Stumpville brand or whatever from Portland," Donny said, grinning. He still had those bright and healthy teeth, still all white. How had he kept them like that all these years, after all he'd done and seen? While on the run, had he paid off dentists to clean and whiten his teeth at midnight? Or maybe a guy like Charlie Adler could simply afford dental care.

"Coffee's fine," Greg said.

They heard the stairs creak from footsteps. Donny sat upright and tried on a smile as if for an interview, which Greg thought odd. He did the same.

Karen Callum strode in. She had long, wavy brown hair and a Barbie figure, but she also wore little makeup and a simple outfit of dark slacks with a button-down shirt.

"Morning," Greg said. "You must be Karen."

"Right you are, sir. Pleasure." Her firm voice matched her firm handshake.

Greg kept a smile on. "Your name's all over this area. I'm impressed."

"Yeah, and so is cheatgrass, mister." Karen stood over the table like a mom wondering just what two boys were up to. "Charlie here told me you were friends as teens?"

"God, that was years ago. But, yes, it's true," Greg said. "Thanks for putting me up."

"You're quite welcome. Anyways, I gotta be off."

"Nice meeting you," Greg said.

"Bye, honey," Donny said and rose to give her a kiss. As he did, Karen kept one eye on Greg. He didn't look away. She didn't blink. The soft contours of her face would stun with a little make-up, he realized, surprised to find himself thinking so old-fashioned. Maybe she was sick of guys after her all the time. He knew that Emily purposely dialed it back when she didn't want to be bothered.

Karen marched out. Only when the front door shut behind her did Greg and Donny share that wide-eyed, almost-busted look they used to share years ago when telling a lie together.

Donny's smile dropped away. "That there's about as close as we get half the time," he muttered.

When had Karen come home? Greg wondered. The middle of the night? Or had she been here all the time? Greg never heard anyone come upstairs to the bedrooms. He was about to ask but held back. Donny had always been touchy about girls. He had never wanted to hear Greg's stories about sex with Leeann Holt, most of which were embellished, of course, and the recollection made Greg want to sigh. He looked out the window. He couldn't get over how green it was here. In the distance, he saw white oval puffs moving along the green. Sheep.

"Pretty, huh?" Donny said. "Now, how about I show you the rest of my ranch?"

"Your ranch?"

"Sure. It's just an expression, ain't it?"

Less than an hour later, Greg and Donny stood at the top of a hill overlooking the sweeping expanses of Callum Ranch. The march up was nothing like riding a bicycle. Greg had to catch his breath, sweat trickling under his shirt. They had taken shade under a cluster of trees.

"This out here? It's all Karen's, technically," Donny said. "And a lot more."

"How much more?"

Donny smiled. "Back in the old days, even the biggest rancher was still a rancher. He was out mending fences, putting down a calf if need be. Karen's late father Loren Callum was that rancher. Karen, she's the new breed. She doesn't do any ranching. It's all hired out. That's why the property around the house is so spic and span. The trucks and trailers, machines, and whatnot get parked elsewhere. She's the inheritor. She just oversees. And I don't mean that in a bad way. Not t'all. She's looking to do great things, building for the future that's coming here."

The expanses of ranch looked to Greg more like farmland, with vast crop plots irrigated by a network of wheeled line sprinklers spraying, each spout its own mighty fountain. Other stretches had large cows and those puffy sheep. Ranching sheep was rare anymore, Donny had told him on the way up, a dying art that had given way to cattle many decades ago; but the Callums had stayed diversified. Widening his view, Greg saw a vast, elevated valley contained in a massive bowl. Hills and buttes ringed the horizon, and a narrow but sparkling irrigation waterway ran through the landscape, too evenly shaped to be a natural river. Donny pointed to a gap between two buttes. "Over yonder, between there? That's your Pineburg Dam I told you about. Listen: Don't you worry about Karen. She won't ask questions."

Greg barely heard. His cooling sweat had heated back up, a slow burn rising up in him. Something about his silly, doily-smothered bedroom and now this grind of a hike had made him remember Wayne Carver and just how Donny knew that Greg was in town. "She's not who I'm worried about," he said.

Donny smiled. "I have to be careful. I told you, feller."

"So this Wayne Carver guy is your friend?"

"I wouldn't call him that. Ole Wayne, he's not anyone's friend. We've worked together. Man, you gotta calm down."

"I'm all right," Greg said.

"What's eating you?" Donny said.

"You said Charlie Adler is reclusive. Said you don't want to be known."

"You're right, I did. Some folks aren't even sure where I live. I didn't say I was crazy. I have to know people, and some of those people look out for me."

"Because other people might be after you."

"That's it."

"Okay, so why don't the ones after you just arrest you or whatever they're going to do?"

Donny glared at Greg but in a forced way as if he was trying to bite down on something tough. He went for a walk around the tree, with his hands on his hips, and ended up looking out toward the gap in the hills where the dam was. Greg followed him over. Donny, staring out, said: "You see, they want more. That's what they do. Always take more, these people. It's especially like that with your successful men, self-made men like me. They suck our good blood. Oh, they'll come for me when they're good and ready and be sneaky about it, too, just like goddamn rustlers. Which means I gotta be sneakier." He turned to Greg. "Just like you taught me."

"Me?"

"You heard me" Donny's head had cocked sideways. "Hey, you okay?"

"I told you, I'm good."

"Okay, feller."

"Don't call me feller," Greg snapped. He didn't mean to. It just came out. Donny had pulled back. Greg grinned to pretend he was joking. "I'm fine, it's fine."

Greg's bike was hanging differently on his car, all crooked, the rear wheel up high. His lock was on differently too. It had been unlocked, put back on. But not stolen? Seeing it like that made his stomach shift and twinge as if he'd swallowed vitamins without eating something. He eyed Callum Street. It looked as empty as usual. He checked that his tires were full, and he pulled his bike straight and re-locked his lock. He went to unlock his car doors. They were already open; they had been opened. A pang of paranoia hit him now. One of the rear seats had been pulled down, to reveal access to the trunk. He climbed in and went through his things, but all seemed to be where they had been. His little baggie of pot was even there.

After their hike to see Callum country, Donny had driven Greg into town and dropped him off in a side street near his car, Donny saying he had "some things to see about." Greg could go tool around a while. He had patted Greg on the shoulder. "You're not leaving, are you? Just because of little ole me?"

"No, man. I just got here."

"Good. We'll see ya later then at the house."

As they had pulled up, Donny had chuckled about something. But Greg had only seen things were not right after Donny drove away. Had Donny been snickering about his locked bike, his locked rental car being fucked with?

He would show Donny tooling around. He would find out things on his own. He drove outside of town, out beyond Callum Ranch, down twisting roads along a high canyon that took him to the base of a rock-rimmed ridge. He found the little turnoff that served as a viewpoint for Pineburg Dam. He stood against the car's warm front fender and looked out at the concrete barrier filling the gap between the two buttes. He spread a county map out on the hood and followed the line of the Redpine River running through town. The river ended way up here at the dam. He had expected the dam to be bigger, like the ones in panoramic IMAX movies. Bonneville. Grand Coulee. This one was no wider than a small-town bridge, shaped more like a funnel than some great high mass of wall. The two buttes dwarfed it. A compact lake—Pineburg Reservoir on the map—pressed up to the dam, and a couple small boats floated on the dark, deep water. Guys fishing. A water skier. Still, it was impressive. This sole, narrow, stopped-up bottleneck probably controlled the flow for a whole county if not more.

He drove past the green and vast Callum lands, heading downward, then skirted town on a side road that followed the river where the land was brown again. The Redpine had once been far broader, even he could see that—the depression of the almost dry riverbed wider than his road at points. He drove on to the opposite, far side of town, with central Pineburg at his back and those two buttes just bumps on the horizon behind him. Here the road left its riverbed companion, sending Greg into barren land that looked like the set of an apocalyptic western, the earth tan and pale, laden with rocks and faded drier shrubs or gnarled trees that were barely trees. The dry grasses wishing they were cacti. Greg expected to see tumbleweed or a steer's skull bleached by the sun. Some barns still stood, their siding wood kept alive with dark oils and tars rubbed into them, but every half-mile or so he'd see another abandoned shack or a barn leaning, ready to fall, showing more light running through it than gray siding on its withering frame bones.

A store-bought sign stood close to the road. It read Farm for Sale. Greg pulled over. The land had some fencing, but there were gaps and the posts leaned in every direction. He wondered if this no-man's land could have once been ranchland like the Callums'; and when a few scrawny and dusty cows appeared and wobbled in his direction, he realized it was probably true. He had seen more of these dead and dying ranches than barely working ones out here. He got out and stood by his hood. The air had the grit of dust and had an acrid smell—like dried-out insect carcasses, he thought. A usually clichéd comparison to a moonscape would actually do this place justice.

The cows lumbered closer. One dropped down as if from exhaustion, letting a hoof get lodged underneath itself. He heard a thumping at his back from the other direction across the road. A cow stumbled its way through a gap in the fence and came right for him, and he jumped out of the way as it crossed the road. Slobbering, swaying, the cow clip-clopped and pushed through a hole in the fence opposite. It dropped down in the barren field there and lay on its side. Greg walked over and stood at the fence. The cow let out a nervous moo as if to say, *I'm still alive, so there, but please don't fuck with me anymore than I'm already being fucked with.*

"You thirsty, buddy?" Greg muttered.

The cow lifted its chin high, held it there, and released a resounding blare of a snort.

14

Donny Wilkie didn't do much hating, but he really hated this god-damn room of Wayne Carver's. Wayne called it his den. Donny usually liked dens, a man cave some called them, but not one like this all done up in the style of Wayne Carver. Wayne always kept his shades drawn and his drapes to boot, so that it always seemed like they were huddling in some dark underground bunker after the Armageddon. The guy didn't even have a reason like Donny did. What had Wayne done except fake a half-ass job at his dad-dy's farm store and prance around with his open carry and his militia shit in his head all the time like some war reenactor going berserk? The man was not right in the head. Plus it smelled damp stale in here, like a fridge going warm. Donny really did not know how long he could put up with this charade, his acting like he gave a shit just so he could go on being called Charlie Adler. There was one plus to the darkness though. It made it harder to make out all of Wayne's weird and antique guns on racks, all the animal heads, the loads of military collectibles—medals and plates and spiked helmets—from who knew where, probably some other creepy dog's creepy-ass den. Donny had expected more Nazi crap from Wayne, but those were probably in an actual underground bunker Wayne had locked up tight somewhere along with the real high-speed advanced weaponry. Donny didn't want to know about it. He just wanted to do this meeting and be done with it, get back to living and getting by, and staying free.

"Why you so riled up?" Wayne said, his voice giving off that little squeak it got—and a smell like mothballs.

"I'm not," Donny said. He was. Of course he was. He sat across from Wayne, just the two of them with a small desk between them. Wayne had slid him a bourbon but it was the shitty stuff and gave Donny more burn in his chest than buzz in his brain. He needed a way better high for whatever they were sure to talk about.

It had to be about Greg Simmons. So, good ole Greggy shows up after so many years, and he's poking around. Of course Wayne would have his suspicions. The man didn't even trust a tired old cow crossing his path.

The desk lamp light was bright on their hands and faces, and Donny had to pull his eyes back out of the light or he was going to need his sunglasses in here. He had mastered a way of keeping a mask on no matter what, but a freak like Wayne could still tell. Wayne smirked at him, his bourbon shot almost hidden inside his fat fist, his face weighed down with so much shadow it looked like someone had dumped a bucket of clay on his head and patted it onto his forehead, cheeks, big jaw, and chin—a freaky mask of himself. Hell, Wayne looked like some psycho carny gone apeshit in a midway food truck and couldn't stop eating. Donny knew a skunk like that once, in prison. Skunk didn't last long. That wasn't Donny's fault then either, no sir. He had tried to warn that guy, too.

Donny sat up straighter. "I just want to know why you got me here," he added.

Wayne, smirking again, slid a business card across the desk with one thick finger and left the card in the middle of the desk lamp light between them. Donny leaned forward.

FBI, it read, and had a picture of a black-haired dude looking like a cross between Charlie Sheen and Emilio Estevez. The name was Torres. It had an address out of Bend, which gave Donny a little prick in his chest. FBI had a field office there. This Torres was no short-timer.

Yet Wayne was holding on to that stupid smirk he got when something was not good, not too good at all.

And then it hit Donny. It hit him as if Wayne himself had plunged his fat fingers right down his throat and squeezed his heart tight, tighter.

"Jesus fucking Christ," Donny blurted. "This Fed was there too? At the gas station?"

Wayne nodded, once. "We didn't know. He was wearing a khaki suit, like some preppy. FBI wear dark suits."

"Sure, on TV they do. Fuck."

"Any case, we'd already up and started by the time we saw one of them cards."

"Aw, fuck," Donny muttered, shaking his head. The shit was already weighing him down and this, this right there, was loads more of it dumped all over him. He pushed himself up from the table. "So they're coming for us, then. That's what this means."

"They haven't yet. I don't think they know exactly who did it. We had masks on. Besides, that brand couldn't have hurt too much anyways."

"Stop. Please."

"We couldn't get them hot enough," Wayne continued, "on account of the propane."

Donny threw back the bourbon and wished he had a hit of kind bud and a snort to round it out, but Wayne was no good for those. "You branded them," he muttered. "Degrees don't matter."

"Oh, no? Ask a calf?"

"No. Look: Why didn't you tell me this before?"

Wayne's smirk had wilted, and Donny thought he saw a rare glint of anxiety in Wayne's eyes. "I guess I didn't want to concern you," he said.

Concern him? Jesus Christ, this guy was messed up. *Misplaced emotion*, a smart guy like Greg would probably call it. All of them should be on edge if not holing up, Wayne especially, but Wayne was just going along acting like business as usual? Wayne was so damn cold about it. The man was either a sociopath or a psychopath, Donny didn't know which. He said nothing.

"If we go acting all strange, then they're going to know it was us," Wayne added as if he could read Donny's mind. Which only reminded Donny: Whatever Wayne was becoming, Donny had to keep an even keel in front of him.

"All right, that's true. Well, I can't say you didn't concern me a little," Donny said, sighing, calming himself, getting back into his best Charlie Adler mode. "Pulling a cruel stunt like you did, it's just not right."

"You can't call it a stunt," Wayne said. "You're the one who gave us the idea."

If Wayne wanted to talk like a ten-year old, Donny would speak to him like one: "No-oh, oh no, what I suggested was, 'you go and play a little trick on them, show them you're *not* goddamn idiots.' That's what I said."

Wayne's face seemed to gain even more of that heavy clay. "You shouldn't make fun of us," he said. "The regular guys, they look up to you."

Donny was in a tough spot here. Wayne needed to see that Donny was a leader, but he also needed a little caressing. Donny sat back down. He showed Wayne a softer face and would have even held his hand if he were a woman. "And you? What about you? Do you still look up to me?"

Wayne leaned toward Donny, blocking the light. "That depends. You have to earn it. That means, you got to be loyal as leather."

Jamie, Rory and April sold Donny the usual baggie. Sitting in his new king cab, Donny watched the three disappear back inside the riverside woods. After meeting with Wayne, he had driven across town and, making sure he was on his own, steered into his secret spot tucked away on the back side of the old diner along the Redpine River. He fingered the baggie between his legs, soft, warming, waiting. Making sure those three were long gone. He had to shake his head. And to think that he used to like going to Wayne's place, to the rest of the house at least. Wayne had a newer ranch house on the nicer side of town. The house belonged to his daddy, the mayor. The mayor who no one saw. The mayor who people voted in just because there wasn't anyone else. Donny always figured that situation would work to his favor, and it had—the mayor doing less now than hardly lifting a finger. By throwing his hat in with Charlie Adler and the Callum name backing him, Wayne had more power than his daddy ever would. The freak used to be fun when he could have a beer, relax, throw a dip in. But Wayne had stopped chewing and never did drink much. He was nothing like the guys Donny hung out with before Mexico. They were all dead or running or in jail, a couple of them over in Iraq or Afghanistan; and he could just imagine what kind of rackets they were running over there using their shiny-ass uniforms.

He never went home at times like this. He wanted to be inside that old diner next to him. He had a date with his dear baggie. He resisted the cravings by switching on the oldies station that was almost out of range but always came in clear here for some reason. The Byrds were playing. Or was it the Animals? Turn, Turn, Turn.

Wayne used to be Pineburg Police. Some in town said that after the police department was defunded, Wayne had changed. A person would think Wayne would lobby for the PD to return for the power he would have, but Wayne also believed that government always had too much power. He was one of those free-market, government-is-the-enemy types who think practically everything but a fire department (and probably that too) should be privatized. So Wayne was getting the world he wanted. He had been shaping the Double Cross along those lines too, and Donny had never felt comfortable about it. Wayne and the militia were always boasting about staying true to the Constitution, always claiming to use it as their guide to power. Donny chuckled at that. Who knew what a Constitution of a couple hundred years ago was supposed to mean nowadays?

All he knew was, Wayne hadn't been gobbling up what he had been feeding him lately. It had been so easy before. But then Wayne probably knew that. Wayne had really gotten to him today. Wayne hadn't brought up Greg Simmons, but as Donny was driving to the old diner, he got to thinking that maybe Wayne had meant Greg when he talked about being loyal.

Whatever the hell Wayne meant, Donny was going to have to step up his efforts. He didn't have a choice. Certain people looked to Charlie Adler for leadership, looked to him as an independent maverick, and that was the deal he done cut. He would have to roll with it.

Meanwhile, he was going to need that little boost of confidence. No one could see his truck from the road and barely from the woods. He stepped out, found the back kitchen door hidden below the river balcony, and into the old diner he went, reemerging up in the dining room. It was clean enough inside, despite the dust and mold. They just didn't get the break-ins here that they got in the city. In Portland this place would be laced with graffiti and wrecked with debris, but the people with a mind to do such a thing here rampaged in the riverside woods instead. And the ones with nowhere to live? They camped farther inside the woods, or they ended up in some abandoned place well far out, such was their shame. Many, they just left. He almost left too before things started looking up, before the Callums. Besides, most knew Wayne would come hunting for them if they ever touched this place. Wayne said it held his favorite childhood memories.

If Wayne only knew, Donny thought. He sat in his usual booth by the boarded-up window that he could just see out, peering between a crack in the boards. This was the very same spot where he had watched Greg approach the river.

He fingered open the baggie and poured out a couple big pinches and crushed it up on a small mirror he had set out on the table. He made two lines.

He snorted up one, then two, and let it tingle and burn.

It fucking wrapped around his head and squeezed and shook like a motherfucker. This hard-as-glass shit coming in from Mexico was stronger, sure, but it wasn't anything he couldn't handle. When he came out the other end, he was raring to go. Minutes later he was up and pacing and dancing a little—if only there was a good jukebox in here. Then he had one in his head, rocking out. Telling himself, boy, someday you're going to buy this place and with cash too, sure—something of his own that his dear Karen and not even Wayne could fuck with. Maybe he could give Jamie, Rory, and April jobs, and everybody, too. Bring in the folks living in trailers and barns and woods 'cause they got nothing. Sure, Jamie, Rory, and April were dealing meth, but what the hell were they supposed to do? Go get killed in Afghanistan? Move to Bend or Grants Pass, get a job working the drive-thru in the Arctic Circle? No, they were doing what they could with what they had, and that was just as he had done. He may be dead in Mexico, but he was alive and kicking right here.

Run if he had to. Do anything he had to. Go right to the fucking Feds maybe even, though he couldn't imagine that. That would be his Afghanistan.

He set his escape shit out on the table, had it in a fanny pack he'd hidden. Couple passports there he could use, at least to get him out of the country. On a note pad he'd written incriminating things about Wayne Carver and even Karen Callum, even had the combination to her safe, told how she was looking to grab up land by any means possible. He had it all right here.

Hell, he'd even kept the business card of that FBI man that Wayne had handed over to him.

The meth was kicking in now and he popped back up, feeling the dancing in his toes, feet, steel springs. Who needed that fucking jukebox when you had one in your head, man? He was dancing to speed metal now, Pantera and Megadeath, which was not so much dancing as rocking it out hard, back and forth like a bad boy, but the point was he was pumped, really pumped.

What if he just called the number on that card?

He got out his phone, turned off his caller ID.

He danced a little more, checked the diner windows.

Screw it, he thought, and dumped all his escape shit back into the fanny pack and into his coat pocket, not forgetting the meth and the FBI card.

He headed on out. He had to stay fired up. Had so much to juggle, between what Wayne was up to and what Greg would soon see of it, not to mention those Feds who were sure to come around again. Everyone was feeling the goddamn pressure. Fucking earthquakes happen. And when the ground split open, he had to be sure he had his good foot planted on the right side of that gaping crevice.

15

Greg had to consider the possibility of killing Donny. Of course he did. It had to belong to his calculations, to his various scenarios. He had to make sure that Donny never told anyone about what they had done, and, with the way Donny was? Donny was volatile. Greg could sense it. He would have to tiptoe. He was on a slackening tightrope. He had rejected Torres, and he came out here on his own with his thin cover story of writing a book. Of course it was really to find Donny, to make sure. But he hadn't expected to find Donny—or Donny to find him—so quickly. If at all. A more cutthroat person in his position would have to kill Donny. Call it good. Greg worked out the morality of it in his head. The tradeoffs. One big problem was, Torres could come around eventually and figure things out.

Greg had Tam's all to himself again after his visit to Pineburg Dam and beyond. He was hungry. He'd had another delicious sandwich at the bar. Now he sat there fighting boredom like the child of a food server waiting for his parent to get off work. Tam was restocking the bar. Whenever she passed, her pleasant aroma canceled out the sour smells of empty booze bottles and bleach. The woman smelled like some kind of aromatic wood, Greg decided. She kept glancing and smiling at him. He wanted to tell her about how someone had messed with his bike and car but decided to let it go. He didn't want too much connected to him, just in case. The less people remembered, the better. Still, he had to know things.

"Can I ask you something?" he said.

"Sure, Portland. I could use a break." Tam set her elbows on the bar.

"How long has Charles Adler been here?"

"What, giving up on your other guy?"

Greg told himself it was a good thing she hadn't repeated the name Donny Wilkie. Maybe she had forgotten it. "Well, he is dead."

"Good point. Oh, about seven years. Eight maybe. No one knows for sure." Tam's eyes had drifted off as if looking for cobwebs in the corners of the tavern.

"He seems like a nice guy."

Tam's eyes locked back on Greg. "You met him?"

"Sure. And, what's Karen Callum's deal?"

"Her deal?" Tam pulled her elbows from the bar.

"I just mean, there's a slight chill there. A little distance."

Tam smiled. "You met her too? You are good. All I know about Karen Callum is, she is one tireless land agent."

"Land agent?"

"Like a realtor but for ranch and farmlands. Large tracts, the big properties."

"I saw a lot of For Sale signs today."

"That you would."

"A lot of those lands weren't looking so good."

"No. Part of the problem is—among all the others, they get their irrigation from wells. There are water rights to wells. And the wells aren't doing so well around here. Ranchers, farmers relied on them for too long."

"Who would want land like that?—don't tell me. Callums."

"Half of it, she ends up buying for herself. I used to not believe it. But then I used to not believe a lot of things were possible." Tam took his plate and made it disappear in a tub below. She popped up smiling and said, "So, something sweet? I got cookies or I got pound bread."

Greg chose an oatmeal cookie, best one he ever had, chewing away and wondering how people could ever let the Callums' benefit so much from the dam. Then he realized: The Callums owned it after all. Donny had said so. So what could they do about it?

Back out on Callum Street, Greg pulled his bike from his rental car and put on his bike helmet covered with stickers, Free Cascadia and Zero Miles Per Gallon among them.

He'd already decided: Someone wanted to screw with his bike, wanted to send him a message. So he'd send one back. He would roam as freely as he wanted, find out whatever he needed to know. Making sure regular people remembered little about him was a decent strategy. Giving the guy who screwed with his bike something to worry about was another.

He pedaled on over to the poor side of town, near the strip mall and drying riverbed and abandoned diner where he'd first met the man named Charlie Adler. The modest new Silver Feathers Casino was near there, set back from the main road and inside a newer line of trees, giving the impression that it was squared away in the woods—one with nature. It was built on the site of Pineburg's onetime timber mill, once owned by one of the town's other great families and linked by a rail line that hadn't been used in decades, rusting, sinking into the earth. Tam had told him: Logging had once been so pervasive that even here, where no true forest could be seen from the highest hilltop, the people had felt its downfall like a punch to the heart. Now, a vast and mostly empty parking lot led to a hanger-like building dressed up with the obvious Native American and Americana designs—eagles and dream catchers, wild horses, and a smiling Native American baby in its own suede leather pouch, all of it kind of spooky to Greg like a Quonset hut on steroids sporting giant roach clips. Greg locked up and went inside. With its jingling and jangling of slots and carpet of neon geometrics, the place could have been any smalltime casino. Despite the lack of cars in the parking lot, it had more people inside than any one place he'd seen in Pineburg, most of them elderly. On his way out, he was almost hit by an older woman riding a motorized wheelchair mounted with a breathing device. Depressing. And yet it gave Greg a strange feeling of inspiration, a rush to his head that left him breathing more clearly. There weren't many Native-Americans left in Pineburg proper, but they had found a way to do something with what little they had left. If their one-time invaders suffered a little along the way, so be it.

He got back on his saddle and rode on, down past the other side of the strip mall, along Redpine River Road. Just in from the road stood an old block of a building with fading, chipping paint. It was the high school. A banner outside read: Food Parcels Today: Apply Within.

Around the side Greg found a long line of locals, about the same amount as in the casino, but many middle-aged or younger. He saw the two from the drug deal incident, Casey and Damon, standing with their heads hanging but looking cleaned up. The whole line of them watched him on his urban bicycle, showing a mix of glares and snickers and even a few smiles of wonder. He might as well have arrived in a hot air balloon. He wondered if someone in this very line could have messed with his car and bike.

It took him a few minutes to find the rickety bike rack behind the school and lock up. He returned to the line and found a young couple to interview and then noticed that a few of those in line glared at him harder as he did so. He ignored it. The interviewee couple were named Sam and Carmel. Their clothes hung loose and smelled a little stale, needing a washing. They faced Greg and kept their faces taut, Carmel with her arms folded as if holding an imaginary baby. Greg had seen couples like this in Portland at intersections or on the street. Sometimes he gave them a dollar or two.

"Things would be even worse without Charlie Adler," Sam was saying.

"You mean Mr. Adler gets you these food parcels?" Greg said.

"No, that there's from the state," Carmel said. "Sam's mostly talking about the casino. The tribe couldn't a done it without Mr. Adler. He'd teamed up with Mrs. Callum like he always does to help them get it done." She nodded to make it true.

"That's what we heard anyways—that they went and kicked in a bunch," Sam said.

"They give me a few hours a week," Carmel added.

Someone laughed behind them—a man wearing a sweat-shirt with US flags on each shoulder, like oversized epaulettes. He shouted: "What does state government do for us? They're all incompetents. All of em. Screw them."

Greg ignored that too and started to ask Sam and Carmel another question, but a second shout rang out:

"And the Feds? They might as well take over. Nothing left anyway. I had to sell my farm—my family's farmstead!"

It was almost as if they had been told that he was a reporter from a city and, worse yet, Portland and Multnomah County where millions of city people would always have more votes than the country. He wondered if Wayne Carver had told them to heckle him. A blaze of frustration smothered his paranoia as he tried to ask more questions and they kept at it.

He turned to the angry ones in line.

The man with American flag shoulders swiped at air with his hand. "Ah, what do you care?" he barked at Greg. "You just want to see the Callums go down, want to see Charlie Adler go down with them."

The Callums? Charlie Adler? Who said anything about them? It was all Greg could do not to lecture them. He wanted to shout: *You're acting against your best interests!* It was as if they thought they would somehow, someday become like one of those three grand families of Pineburg and would have to protect their well-won gain to the death so they might as well start now—despite their sorry situation. It wasn't ever going to happen. *They do not care about you except as a tool! It's a sham. You're all getting bamboozled! Come together, people. We're all Cascadians*, he wanted to scream. But he told himself to take the middle ground if only because a guy like Wayne would want him to lash out.

"Listen. I'm an Oregonian. I pay taxes," was all he could come up with.

A fourth person stepped forward, a woman wearing a leather cowboy hat and a sweat suit. "Screw you and your taxes. You want our dam. You want to take our water. We're better off without you!"

Some cheered her on but most lowered their faces. There were mostly good, friendly, well-meaning people in Pineburg. Greg knew that. He had met so many of them walking around. Why was it always the shrill few who got to speak for a community?

He shrugged, shaking his head. His interview was over. He thanked Sam and Carmel and turned away. Then he saw:

Wayne Carver watched him from the far end of the parking lot, standing at his pickup.

Greg turned back to Carmel and Sam, getting closer so he could speak softly. "Hey, you two know Wayne Carver?"

"Who don't? He used to be City PD," Carmel said. Sam added: "His dad and him had some kind of falling out, I heard."

Wayne kept watching. *Why don't you just use binoculars?* Greg thought. The angry ones in line had calmed down, but some were nodding in Wayne's direction now.

"I hate to say this," Carmel said, "but it kinda looks like he's waiting for you."

Greg's heart pumped faster. He felt like the junior high kid forced into a confrontation. But he had asked for it, hadn't he? What he really came here for.

He marched across the parking lot. Wayne's face showed nothing. Greg eyed Wayne for signs of an open carry, but he saw no weapon. Wayne backed up to the farthest end of his pickup, putting the truck between them and the crowd across the lot. Greg kept coming. He threw a glance in the truck bed in case Wayne had a gun stashed there. It was spotless.

This did not have to be a confrontation, Greg told himself—he would use this opportunity to ask harmless questions, to try to find a way to like Wayne and Wayne him. He showed Wayne a half smile.

"I'm guessing you want to talk to me?" Greg said.

"Talk?" Wayne said.

Wayne patted Greg down low, on the gut.

"What are you doing?" Greg blurted.

Wayne grabbed him by the fat of his hip and squeezed and twisted.

"Ow, fuck." It felt like a power drill plunged into Greg's side.

Wayne let go. He slammed Greg against the pickup bed.

Greg, panting from the pain, stood tall to fight, letting his hip burn. He shouted:

"I know it was you! You fucked with my car—with my bike."

Wayne grinned. And that was it. He stepped up into his pickup and drove away, leaving Greg to face the line across the lot. The line had moved along, and Sam and Carmel were already inside. Somehow, that much lessened the burn a little.

Greg made it back to his bicycle behind the school. Both tires were flat. "Fuck. Fucking freak," he muttered. Quick shots of air at the nearby gas station told him the tires hadn't been punctured—the air had only been let out. He pedaled off, back to his car. He heaved his bike on the rack and drove up to the Callum house.

Donny's pickup was gone. No one home. Out back, Greg wandered the yard, his thoughts racing, seeking answers and signs. He neared the barn-like outbuilding. He thought he heard a pounding sound coming from inside, muffled but clear.

Two large sliding doors were cracked open. He slid one door open and slipped inside. The building was dark, stocked with farm equipment, and had a faint but not repulsive whiff of manure or mulch. He saw light at the far end, coming, he saw as his eyes adjusted, from a finished room built inside. Maybe it was an office. He tiptoed on through toward it and heard the muffled rhythm again. It was metal music.

"Freeze!" someone shouted.

16

"You're dead, you're so dead," the voice said, mixed with giggling.

Greg's arms had shot up as if pulled by cables. He lowered his arms and turned around to see a teenager about his size but with a piercing stare, like Donny's. He wore military-style paintball gear. He aimed a paintball gun at Greg.

The boy was grinning too, so Greg thrust his arms back up.

"It's just paint, right? Go for it," he said, playing along.

The boy aimed and splattered Greg with yellow liquid. It stung but didn't hurt that bad. Greg let out a fake yelp, dropped to his knees, pretended to die.

The boy laughed. "You're so toast," he said.

"Totally. I thought it would hurt more." Greg stood back up, shaking off some of the yellow.

"It washes right off. Karen can get it out," the boy said.

He talked younger than his probable age. His piercing stare had relaxed, revealing one of those broad and soft oval faces that would either stay boyish or grow ugly in middle life. It could go either way. Greg hung around boys like this when he was this kid's age. They had always listened to what he had to say, did what he suggested.

"And, Karen, she's your mom?" Greg said.

"No way. You don't know my mom."

"But, Charlie Adler, he's your dad. Right?"

It was pushing evening by the time Donny showed. Greg was waiting it out in Donny's study. Donny came in singing some song Greg didn't know and made his way down the hall to the study. He was dancing with himself, all tiptoes. He danced through the doorway into the den. He turned on vintage country music. George Jones. He kept dancing, produced a can of chew, and took a dip so strong it smelled like paving tar. He faced Greg and put out his arms pretending to dance with Greg even though Greg had stayed down in the chair.

"Tune like this? Get you through anything," Donny said. "Man."

"I'd like to leave my bike here if that's all right."

"All right," Donny said, dancing away and humming, just him and The Possum.

Greg waited for a break between songs. It took at least a minute, in which time Donny spun his imaginary Greg five times. Donny had always had a lot of energy, liked to get fired up, but this? People were supposed to mellow as they got older. He didn't smell drunk either, and Greg hoped maybe he was just a little high. Greg could do with some of that right now.

"Someone screwed with my bike," Greg said. "It's not cool."

"What's that you say, feller?"

"Someone's fucking with me. Undid the locks to my car and bike, let the air out of my tires. I'm guessing it's your buddy Wayne Carver."

Donny kept on dancing for about thirty seconds. He slowed, sighing, but kept rocking on his heels as if ready to dance some more. "That sounds like him. I'm sorry. Don't know who else it could be. You know what? I'll talk to him."

"Also, I met Gunnar," Greg said.

Donny stopped. He went over, turned down the music. He nodded to something going on in his head and stood before Greg.

"When?" Donny said. His smile fading away.

"This afternoon. Out in the barn or whatever you call it."

"I have a boy. Now you know. Why you looking at me like that? It's not like it's some kind of secret."

"How old is he?"

"Eighteen. Just about nineteen. Good kid, ain't he? Don't worry, I was going to tell you."

"Who's his mother?" Greg said.

Donny scowled. "Like you give a shit."

That stung, but Greg would have to take it. "Leeann Holt?" he said.

"Well, that's a real fine fucking guess, ain't it?"

Oddly, the revelation stung less. Greg stood. He did his best to stand tall, feet wide and shoulders squared, better than he had done with Wayne. "What did you tell Gunnar?" he said. "I mean, about the new you?"

George Jones was doing a real slow song now, practically spoken word as if The Possum himself was telling the story of one Donny Wilkie. Donny took a moment, his eyes bulging and bare and shiny white. He said:

"It was more like, how. I told little Gunnar, okay, little feller, if anyone found out? His dear daddy would go away. Never to return. That's all you need to tell a child. 'Course I didn't like it, but it was the only way to keep us together. Without my Gunnar, why try and make myself something better?"

That night in bed a panic consumed Greg, just like the anxiety attacks he used to have years ago, episodes that, he had learned to see, had everything to do with what started with Donny and ended up at the lake. They returned in the morning as he drove

116

into town, even though his bike and rack were safe in Donny's garage. He parked and stomped down Callum Street, cursing the sun in his eyes. Now he knew why people wore big hats around here. It wasn't for style.

He hadn't called Emily, he realized. Maybe that would help. He had a hard time getting the signal on Callum Street, so he wandered a side street holding up his phone. He ended up in a small town park with barely three bars of coverage. He called and got her message:

"It's Em. You know what to do. Cheers."

He said, "Look, I'm, uh, sorry I haven't called, or texted even. It's just that it's hard to get coverage here. Okay, bye."

Emily had probably seen his call and not answered. The thought made hot blood rush to his brain. It embarrassed him, being denied like that, even though he did it too. She could have been working. Or, as he now imagined, she was sitting at an outdoor table at one of Portland's most precious coffee purveyors with a younger, better-looking version of him. This version had lived abroad, somewhere like Budapest, and had multiple degrees and a trust fund from a family with a long history in the textile business. They would get drinks and go back to his place, but she wouldn't let him do anything. Not this time. She really didn't think she should. This time.

This alone should have made him jump right back in his rental car and head to Portland, or at least make him call or text, but it only made him slump down on a park bench, the anger replaced by a squeezing of his heart.

He shot up and found Callum Street and marched along the main drag, intent on confronting Wayne Carver if he had to.

The streets were oddly empty, even for here. Many stores had signs saying they were closed or would be back later. He saw Tam outside Tam's Tavern, sweeping the sidewalk. She leaned on her broom and raised her eyebrows at him. "That bad, huh?" she said. Apparently she could read his mind as well as make a kick-ass bar sandwich.

"I'm okay," he said.

"You didn't stay?"

"What? Stay where?" Donny wasn't there when he'd got up. "Why? What's happening?"

Tam's eyes widened, and she took a deep breath. "Oh, you don't know about it, do you? No one told you. I thought you knew."

17

Greg's chest had filled with a sickening pressure. His unease was different from that nighttime panic that had returned. This was more like loathing. He stood along a crop field, staring out at the crowd. The people swarming out in the field wore a mix of Americana garb and Teabagger fashions, the flags and eagles on them massive and making their clothes look like drapes cut into outfits. He saw 1776-era three pointed hats, nooses for vengeance, Don't Tread on Me drawings and a couple muskets. It looked to be one of those faux-populist protests of the Tea Party variety or whatever they were calling themselves now, like a July Fourth picnic colliding with an American Revolution reenactment and channeling the mood of a lynch party. It was a phenomenon that Portlanders feared and mocked and thought only happened in the Midwest or South (and future Cascadians would never have to see, according to his book). Yet here they were, so proudly staking their ground in a brown field in rural Oregon. And why not? Greg thought, appealing to reason to help calm himself. If this place could have a secretive militia movement, according to Agent Torres, then why not this? Portland had them. Portland even had Neo-Nazis. He was only surprised not to see more camouflage gear like the militia wannabes sported on the Internet. But, why exactly here? On this very spot?

It was about a half hour after he'd left Tam's. Tam had told him this was Callum property. Yet this part was not green. It was all brown and barren more like those dry lands he had seen on the other side of town. This road had surely never carried so many vehicles. Parked TV trucks from both regional and national networks blocked half the way. Greg had steered around the TV trucks, parked, and got out his reporter's notebook and voice recorder.

He wondered why TV news had bothered to come out here. Any elections were far off, and politicians never visited a place like this unless there appeared a sure reason to benefit.

Greg straightened his posture, chin up, and marched out into the field. TV camera crews stood on the fringes of the crowd, their crews and hosts chatting. He passed them, heading into the crowd. People glared at him with his reporter tools, so he slid his notebook and recorder into his coat pocket. The assholes from the food stamps line were here. He started a moment because more of the open-carry terrorists were here, showing off holstered side arms mostly but a few hunting and assault rifles—and even what looked to be a couple semi-automatics made into fully automatic machine guns, all it took was a conversion kit bought on the Internet. Again this was so surreal that he hadn't noticed at first. He'd seen just one county sheriff's car on the edge of the field, and now he questioned whose side they were on. It was paranoid of him, sure, but he had to consider it. Signs bobbed above the heads:

Dam the Feds.

Stop the Flood!

Live Free or Die.

Secession Now!

Secession? Greg recoiled this time, his knees jerking. Secession was against the Cascadian way. He wanted to shout it out. Any reinvention was to be peaceful, not like this. He'd always known that militias and their brood wanted to break away, but he never took it seriously. Now he saw proof of it right here. Now he got one reason why those assholes in the food stamp line had been so fired up—they'd been waiting for this event, chomping and provoking like tailgaters on the eve of a big game.

Just beyond the crowd, a small stage was being set up. Some men mingled behind it, half-hidden behind equipment. A few would-be toughs stood around as if on guard. Casey and Damon were among them and were looking cleaned up.

A TV reporter approached the front edge of the stage, a little man with the happy little round face of a mediocre comedian—he was grinning, waving at the crowd, then aiming his mike like a pistol. It appeared everyone knew who this man was except Greg. The crowd hollered and cheered, swinging and pumping their signs about the dam and the water, but the signs damning the Feds and calling for secession had vanished as if on command. A producer calmed the crowd, the cameraman leaned into his camera, and the TV reporter gave his live remote report. Greg couldn't hear it from where he was. The reporter spoke low, almost whispering. His face had turned downward, laden with gravitas, nodding with import.

Donny stood farther backstage, behind stacked equipment and a couple tall speakers. Charlie Adler, rather. He wore a cowboy hat and sunglasses, looking to Greg like some country music star waiting to go on. Donny moved in place, doing his version of a jig.

Greg didn't flinch this time. He moved closer. He had to show himself, let Donny see him.

Donny's sunglasses locked on Greg from across the way. His jig slowed. He nodded and grinned. Greg nodded back.

Gunnar appeared next to Donny. Gunnar saw what his dad saw. He dared a smile for Greg.

The crowd began in again, this time for real and with furor. All the protest signs were back, Feds this, secession that. Was Donny really this stupid? Greg thought. Was he going to take the stage as Charlie Adler? Expose himself to the world? Endanger their secret? Surely Donny was not that naive. He had lost such naiveté years ago, Greg knew, because Greg had been there on the very day that he had.

At that moment, Wayne Carver appeared backstage. Standing tall. He wore pressed jeans and a baby blue button-down and looked surprisingly respectable this way, like the manager of a family restaurant where people went after church. Wayne began rolling up the sleeves of his respectable button-down. He didn't so much as nod at Donny. He passed right on by him and strode up onto the stage.

18

Donny Wilkie watched Greg's face pale to bone-white stone as the crowd kicked in and Wayne Carver took the stage. This here show was on. Greg was about to see what he, Donny Wilkie aka Charlie Adler, was really made of. What his real game was about.

Onstage Wayne Carver nodded and grinned, just like Donny had shown him. The crowd roared with more hurrahs, more applause.

Donny could see Greg wilt down in front, actually sagging, a shriveling petal. How funny would it be, Donny thought, to send Casey or Damon on over with a protest sign to hold, compliments of Wayne Carver?

Up on the stage Wayne, still waving to the whooping crowd, pushed up his sleeves even further like he was going to get down to work and right here. Nice touch, Donny thought. Wayne tried to quiet the crowd, but his big grin wouldn't let them. What a grin that kid had. No one had seen it, because Wayne had rarely smiled. Donny had seen it, just once was all it took. Donny had told Wayne, if he had smiled more as a kid, maybe he wouldn't be such a wet blanket now. Which did not make Wayne smile in itself. But now? With a purpose behind it? It was as if Wayne had a twin brought up separately by a happy family in some happy suburb somewhere, his talents in sports and theater helping him to become a beloved salesman. This newly public Wayne was pretty much the opposite of the real ole Wayne.

Donny stomped the ground in delight at his creation. He made sure Greg saw him do it.

"Well, well! Thanks all! Thanks much, much appreciated," Wayne began.

Wayne turned his fancy grin into a straight face. Only this could calm the crowd. Wayne waited for them, for every last eye. He switched to the voice Donny had told him about—start in low, so they can barely hear you, so they need to hear you. Make it intimate. Then rise it right up.

"So, it seems they want to go and flood half the Callum family's land too. Flood out the very family that made this town. Our town. Our water! And all for some measly salmon?!"

The crowd's roar had a growl to it that made the meth surge in Donny. The dose was getting on top of him a little bit—again—so he moved in place to keep his shit together, shaking his legs but not jumping around. He couldn't help feeling inspired and the meth couldn't help helping him. Inspired for Wayne Carver, for following through. Donny had been trying to get Wayne to take a less violent, less confrontational route in public and here he was, playing it cool and populist. No need for Nazi shit or blocking roads or branding people. Wayne would always have his creepy den, that being the real Wayne, but Donny had found a way to draw him out of it. This had gone down over months, had taken a few drinking sessions (Donny with whiskey, Wayne with cream soda). He'd gotten Wayne to realize things—that he hated his father the mayor not because his daddy had ignored him, but because daddy wouldn't let Wayne be like him. But better. A better leader. Wayne's father, Bill was his name, was scared of that. So why not show daddy how much better than daddy you can be? Later, last time in the den, Donny had reminded Wayne: You go around threatening people and branding them and acting the big bully then you're not getting back at your daddy, you're just living up to his expectations for you. That's how you got back at old man Bill, how you got even for everything. For making Wayne's mother kill herself, she was so depressed with that man—hung herself from a tree outside Wayne's bus stop. That's how you do it, Donny had told Wayne, and for a moment thought he had produced the glisten of a tear in Wayne's eye. Wayne had resisted at first. Told Donny, he would try, but it didn't come naturally to him. Nothing comes naturally, Donny had reminded Wayne. There would be setbacks. The mean streaks would want to bust out, sure they would, but they had to be roped in. The more he did it, the better the reward and the better he'd get at it until a person couldn't tell one man from the other—until Wayne barely could himself.

Now look at him! Them! Wayne up there speaking, the people listening as if Elvis himself had returned to earth, one man with his hands clasped together tight with hope and a couple of the women nodding along like in some prairie preacher's tent. Just like Donny had told him. You don't have to sell them who you are. You sell them their idealized version of themselves. Speak as you are they, through you. They are what you are becoming.

Wayne said to them: "You here are a good, hard-working people, farmers many of you, some of you been here for generations. And now look what's happened. Just another example of state, federal governments sticking it to us. Well, maybe it's about time we go about sticking it to them!"

"It's about time!" someone shouted.

"Damn right it's about time, son," Wayne said, pumping his fist, and the crowd erupted.

The crowd chanted, "Stick it to them!" and Wayne pumped his fist and Donny couldn't stop the rush surging through him like rapids cold and hot at the same time. He grasped a speaker with both hands and leaned into it to stop him from striding right up there and making it a goddamn duet with ole Wayne. A wince of regret shot through him: It should have been him up there, but it just couldn't be risked, not even as Charlie Adler. He squeezed his eyes shut and he dug his toes into the ground, his head whirling. And a vision kicked in, wild and glorious, all in a split second:

Armed Double Cross militia, led by Wayne, hoist the two Xs Double Cross flag atop Pineburg dam.

Donny rides a horse across vast green ranch land that surrounds all the town. All cattle are stamped with the two Xs.

Donny marches out of Pineburg City Hall and into a convertible limo. Gunnar sits in the limo, smiling.

The limo travels Callum Street and people line it to cheer. The limo turns a corner into, suddenly: Downtown Portland. The big city.

The limo rolls down Broadway. Greg Simmons rides with Donny now.

In a palace, Greg and Donny dine on lavish meals. They party with hot models. Fat cats and suck-ups offer them stacks of money.

And in an opulent marble courtroom, Donny watches as Greg, now a judge, pronounces a verdict: Guilty! The defendant: Also Greg.

"It's about time, oh, you bet it is. It's about damn time we thought about taking this all back!" Wayne was shouting now. "State Capital can have its green valley! Portland, keep your Socialist People's Republic! Go on! Go on git! We'll be just fine here without ya!"

Hearing this last part, Donny felt his surge getting sucked away . . .

Wayne was taking it too far. Sure, any talk of secession was protected by free speech, but it had to remain idle talk. Donny jerked back to reality in fits and starts, like he'd slipped on a carpeted stairway in socks and was plummeting down. Wayne's harsh, provoking proclamations blurred as one with the roaring crowd. Donny couldn't stop any of it. He had helped to create this, and now he was going to have to ride it out. He might have to fend for himself after all. Scenarios flashed in his head. One involved calling that man at the FBI. Another involved Greg Simmons.

People were clapping again. Donny made himself clap. He looked out across the hollering crowd.

Casey and Damon were moving through the crowd bearing flags—flags with two Xs on them. That was no good either. That was no good at all.

Donny looked to Greg. He just had to.

Greg only stared back, slack-jawed, his mouth stuck open.

19

After the rally, Greg drove back to the Callum house. He took his time, sticking to the speed limit as if his life depended on it—like a man who'd narrowly missed getting in a horrific accident and was still in shock. He wrestled with his anger. He told himself not to take what he'd just seen personally. The biases he had witnessed out in that field reached far beyond him and Donny and had been a long time coming. Before he had left for the rally, Tam had made sure he understood: It was no accident that some in rural Oregon had turned so bitter, so repelled. The logging downturn of the 1970s had blackened hearts and minds by sending rural economies into a decline from which they never recovered. The 1980s brought a recession to urban areas, while rural communities that only knew logging got a full-blown depression. People in Portland and the valley had no idea. Neither the timber industry nor the government had seen it coming—or planned for it. As the remaining lumber and paper mills shut down, tens of thousands of high-paying union jobs vanished, small businesses went under, and once shiny main streets faded out. The prosperous small town had become a term of nostalgia. Those hit hardest never got a good explanation of what was happening to their world. All they knew was, they'd trusted the man they never should've trusted and that goddamn man turned out to be the last man they ever should have trusted. People needed someone to blame. To out-of-work loggers and mill workers, the easy scapegoats were the environmentalists and their lawsuits that halted old growth logging to protect the last ancient forests and defend endangered species like the spotted owl. A coalition of timber corporations, chambers of commerce, conservative politicians, and unions did their manipulative best to incite people, organizing log truck convoys and rallies to protest Federal Court rulings on the spotted owl and the environmentalists' efforts. All the while, any outsiders with green tendencies, who were henceforth known as city-loving, latte-drinking elitists—a caricature that became the enemy when the bitter truth was that corporate forces beyond local control had destroyed the good old order. Meanwhile, to soothe the hard-hit, the angry, and the lost, large new non-denominational churches and right-wing movements stepped in, wrapping the cross in the flag. Pineburg had one of these churches, Tam said, on the clean side of town and indiscreet, like a small Costco and bearing a modest cross on its corrugated roof. Somehow, a seemingly caring church complemented a paranoid political worldview, whether it meant to or not. Feminism, gays, "liberalism" and silly threats of socialism were to blame for all. People passed the good word: Society had to return to a simpler, better time with values that matched those in the small town. And with that groundwork set, in stepped the national political machinery with sophisticated campaigns that delivered the wackos to the center and gave even a militia movement credibility among those who had never known anything but an unjust world that only wanted to destroy them and only them. Now it was their time to fight back.

Greg had let Tam lecture him. People like him deserved it. They all did, for dismissing what had been coming for so long. Federal crackdowns after the Waco siege, the Oklahoma City bombing, and then 9/11 especially had kept the Oregon militias low-key, but episodes like the Klamath River controversy of 2002 started showing them new paradigms, prototypes, role models. That year had brought a severe drought, and yet the Feds went ahead and shut off dam water that fed the quarter-million acres of farmland in the Klamath basin, so that what was left of the suckerfish and the Coho salmon runs could survive. It was all to the letter, all according to the Endangered Species Act. Longtime farmers were enraged, confused, feeling like their futures had been stolen from them. They formed a symbolic 10,000-person bucket brigade. They took saws and blowtorches to dam gates and fought with US marshals. The water was turned on and off, on and off, as various national interests found a way to make this serve them; and the whole process fell into vicious litigation involving farmers and ranchers, environmental concerns, Native American groups. At the same time, the farmers' rallies and protests became a recruiting ground for those believing themselves the true patriots. Anyone else became the enemy, if not the devil. Anyone else never should have been trusted in the first place. The sentiment trickled north to Pineburg. Ranching and farming had become tougher than ever, and water issues weren't helping. Water meant everything. Water would be the new logging. In Pineburg, water came from a complicated network of wells, irrigation canals, reservoirs. It was all about water rights. About who controlled the water. That crucial person ran not just the economy but determined survival itself.

"There is some salmon here," Tam had told Greg. "Just bones found mostly. We've never had much of it, but the rumor now is that the Feds are looking at calling it endangered here. It makes relicensing a lot tougher for the Callums."

"Pineburg is a different deal though," Greg had countered. "These people want a private dam to remain as is, never demolished, want it protected like Fort Knox and think it's entitled to relicensing no matter what—even though letting it flood out would give everyone far more water than the irrigation flow from the dam ever would."

"True. The problem is, it would flood some of the Callum land."

"But, it would bring way more to those wells and canals on the other side of town. Wouldn't it? Am I missing something here?"

"No, you're not. Probably, yes." Tam had shaken her head. "It doesn't matter. All that matters is power. The ones in power got people here thinking they're allies, always had been. Power flows faster and stronger than any water. Every land's different, but the result's always the same."

"It's against their best interests," Greg muttered.

"And yet they fight all the harder for it."

And the upshot was sickening, Greg thought. All of it—the logging troubles, the bad blood, the Feds' missteps, other groups' stubbornness, the water issue, and the militia—in the end it led straight to that meth that sucked out kids' brains.

Greg was glad he'd seen that rally. He was grateful he had to witness Wayne up there. He knew better now why he was here. It wasn't just about getting Donny not to talk. It wasn't even about keeping Donny and his disciple Wayne from doing something stupid. It was about keeping a dark past from persisting forever. Greg was partly to blame. Years ago, the juvenile version of himself had been the one egging on Donny, pushing Donny to become the ultimate expression of himself, acting like some Nietzschean Dr. Frankenstein looking to put the superman principle into practice in real life. He hadn't ever put it to Donny this way, but that was what it was. It had started with one stupid twenty-five cent paperback Greg had read when he was fourteen, *Mastering the Will to Power* or some such bullshit, basically 1970s self-help on acid but gone rancid, tainted neofascist. One's raw ego could be unleashed with no compassion for the weak. Greg had attempted to create something unstoppable out of the unformed clay that had been Donny Wilkie, his very own Golem. Their Übermensch ways could rise above all the shit that kept others down, simply because normal human nature was so fallible. Then Greg gave it up, and early, like a brooding college sophomore chucks his sudden contrarian devotion to Ayn Rand, so much mental masturbation and callousness preached to others only making life worse. The incident at the lake had made him give it up. He had come to see that all he was doing was just being an asshole, a juvenile one at that. So, he had grown up. This was really the whole point of Cascadia. Stop being an asshole. Look after one another as equals. Learn to adapt to the world and your place in it.

Donny now stood on the wrong side, the doomed side. Greg had a duty, he realized. He had to try to persuade Donny to come around and help impede what Donny had conjured from his very own golem, Wayne Carver. He knew Donny wasn't idealistic, probably never would have even bought some bullshit self-help paperback. He didn't get his methods from Nietzsche or Golem lore but simply from the need to survive. To cut deals. Donny was more pragmatic.

Greg hoped. He wasn't stupid. If he couldn't convince Donny to control Wayne, then the real threat could become Wayne. Greg might even have to deal with Wayne in a way that Wayne incited, asked for, deserved. There were no empirical rules for this. There were morals and then there was survival. No one could know about the lake, Wayne especially. Greg would do anything. He didn't want to think about the Nietzschean implications of that. Screw that. An unformed, unreal version of him had done that deed at the lake a long time ago—an altogether different person really, so why should his real self suffer now?

The sun was going down, leaving the Callum house in purple twilight. Donny's king cab was parked out front. Greg didn't know if Karen was there; he realized he had never seen her car, she was gone so much. He parked along the side of the driveway, hoping he wasn't blocking her way, and went inside without knocking.

He found Donny in the study, sitting in a cowhide chair. Donny cradled a whiskey in his lap and had one poured out for Greg on the desk, having heard Greg coming no doubt. Greg ignored the offering. He could already see this was going to be harder than he thought. Donny sat slumped and even showed Greg a pout. As if he could be penitent. Greg considered just strolling right back out and leaving.

Donny held up one hand flat as if to testify in court. "Okay, call me guilty," he said. "It's true. Charlie Adler supports the idea of secession."

An incredulous grunt escaped from Greg. Not the way he wanted to sound right now, but Donny had fired the first shot. "Secession from what?" Greg said. "Tell me that."

"From the state. From the Feds. You know."

"As put forth by Wayne Carver."

Donny sat up. "And how's that so different from your pie-in-the-sky Cascadia deal?"

"Where should I start? It's not a militia. We don't condone violence. We, it—"

"Who says it has to get violent?" Donny stared a beat, holding Greg's gaze. "Who? Who?" Donny repeated the words, jabbing at air with his index finger.

Greg sighed. "I just want to know one thing. Did they give Charlie Adler support first? Or did Charlie Adler bring them the idea?"

"I guess I don't know what you mean there, Greg."

"When you first got here. I'm just thinking of the whole chicken or egg scenario. That was some years ago, right?"

"Boy, come on. They're just letting off steam. Like they're reenactors, you know? In any case, I talked to Wayne about your car and bike and he admits it. Says he'll leave you alone."

"Whatever. I heard better bullshit at that rally today."

"What's that supposed to mean?"

Greg grabbed his waiting whiskey and gulped, his lips stinging, wet. He wiped his mouth and Donny watched him, a sick, snickering smile growing on his face.

The smile made Greg realize something. He blurted: "You were the one. You recruited those two guys from the woods."

"Hey, hold on. 'They' recruited Casey and Damon, not me," Donny said.

"'They' meaning Wayne?"

"If you want to put a face on it, yes."

"So, were 'they' the ones who played your little trick on the Feds or whoever?"

Donny didn't answer. He looked cold, his shoulders drawn in.

"Were you with them? No? You weren't with them?"

"No. Hell, no."

"And Gunnar?"

"Fuck, no!" Donny slumped down and shrunk, seeming to lose ten pounds in seconds.

Greg sat on the edge of the desk.

Donny snorted. He shook his head.

"It all goes back to Loren Callum," he said finally. "The man was a big supporter of this. Them. Always had been, going back decades. I promised him that I would stay true to it."

"He's dead."

"Yeah, he's dead and from all kinds of shit—so don't go and think what you're thinking. He had kidney, blood, heart issues well before I got here."

"I wasn't thinking it, Donny."

"Well, that's all it was. A promise. And, okay, a little survival luck to boot. It's a damn cliché, but he always wanted a living son no matter what Karen did for him. But it's not like I'm their damn Führer or something. You saw Wayne up there."

"And I saw you back there behind him." Greg drank up the last of his whiskey, directed it straight down his throat without spill, warm and charging, straight to his belly and heart.

"Yeah, so?"

"You do want me to help you, somehow, right? That's what you said."

"Did I?" Donny said. "Well, what the fuck do I know?"

Why should Donny trust him? What could he do for Donny? Greg thought it out. He could go to Torres, hat in hand, and plea for some kind of arrangement for Donny. But would Donny ever consider becoming an informant or some kind of special witness? Greg wondered if Torres would only go after him for doing this his own way.

He stayed at the Callum house that night. He was in bed when he heard what had to be Karen coming home late so he lay still, listening for any sign of argument, laughter, something. All he heard were the crickets outside. He couldn't sleep now, again, so he clicked on the nightstand lamp and stared at the old photo of him, Donny and Leeann Holt at seventeen. Studying Leeann's defiant yet feminine charm. He wondered what Leeann would make of all this. He might have been the one influencing Donny back then, but she had been the one spurring on both him and Donny. Her ability to walk and talk and party like a fully-formed, badass adult had been something every late teen aspired to. So why didn't he stick with her? Why did he leave her to Donny? He lay in bed going over it, but he never got the answer.

The next morning Greg slept late, till nine. Donny and Karen had already left, each leaving separately, Greg guessed. He wandered the house, made sure no one was home. Then he went outside, out back. Laying awake, he had realized one thing: Since Donny was connected to the Double Cross, his son Gunnar could be implicated too when they acted up again. That was not fair. It also left Greg with other questions about Gunnar. Gunnar was almost nineteen, which meant he was born not too long after Greg and Donny had gone their own ways—not long after Leeann went running to Donny.

Greg entered the ranch outbuilding and approached Gunnar's finished room inside. He knocked. No one home? He tried the door. It opened.

Gunnar's room was the usual mess of posters for metal bands Greg had never heard of, paintball equipment, video game setup, computers. Drop this into any house in the Portland suburbs and you'd never know it was in a glorified barn in rural Oregon. Greg turned a lamp on. He looked around for photos but found little indication of Gunnar's past, of course. He meant to leave the closets and dresser drawers alone—he was only going to snoop a little. But, turning to leave, he spotted something protruding from behind the dresser.

A narrow black handle and rod. He thought it might be a fireplace poker.

He tiptoed over to it.

He grabbed the handle and pulled out the thing, which was iron and heavy.

A branding iron? It had to be. At the end were the two Xs of Double Cross. He held it up to the light to be sure and set it back in its place behind the dresser.

Once outside, Greg settled on the back porch in a rocking chair and went over his notes, making sure he still had enough to make it look like he was doing research should anyone come asking. He rocked and rocked in the chair, wondering why Gunnar had a Double Cross branding iron. What the hell were they going to do with that?

He sensed something, to his right.

Gunnar stood at the end of the porch watching Greg. For how long, Greg didn't know. It gave him a jitter, but he fought it with a smile and waved Gunnar on over. Gunnar, his shoulders set, took measured steps to reach Greg. He stopped before Greg and stood so rigidly that Greg felt like he should tell him to stand at ease.

"Thanks for taking care of that paint on my clothes," Greg said.

"Well, I was the one who shot you."

"True. Whoever washed them did a good job. Left them folded on my bed too. Was that Karen?"

Gunnar shook his head.

"You did it? I don't see a maid around here."

Gunnar nodded. "We used to have one, but Karen didn't think we needed one since dad's around so much."

"You do most of the laundry, I bet."

Gunnar nodded. "She drives a really nice Jag."

"A Jaguar, huh? I've never actually seen it."

"That's 'cause she's never here. Three liter V-six, three-forty horses, supercharger. You should see the color. Dad calls it champagne. She calls it cashmere. Dad says she never drives it fast though. She doesn't let him drive it."

"Huh." Greg rocked in his chair, twice, three times. "Can I ask you something?"

"Yes."

"Who is your mom? You never told me."

Gunnar stared. His fingertips had pressed to his thighs.

"That's okay. You can't answer. I understand," Greg said.

Gunnar's face had reddened. "Why did you go looking in my room?" he said.

Greg let out a nervous laugh. He stopped rocking.

Gunnar relaxed his stance. He glanced out at the grounds and tiptoed over to the screen door to listen to the house. "It's okay. No one's here."

Greg could feel the warmth of red in his own face, threatening to break him out in sweat. "I guess I wanted to make sure you're not getting into any trouble."

"You knew dad before, didn't you?"

"Yes. A long time ago."

"You saw the branding iron, didn't you?"

"Yes. I did." Greg had turned to Gunnar, to look up at him. He had to be careful here. No one knew he recognized the name Double Cross, or even the two Xs. "There were two Xs on it. What are those for? Some other ranch? Karen, your dad, they already have a ranch."

Gunnar smiled. He shook his head, and Greg wasn't sure if it was at Greg's question or at the prospect of a militia running a ranch. Gunnar lost the smile. He said, "Wayne Carver, he says the two Xs stand for a Double Cross—for the two, uh, indigties this area's suffered, from the state government, and from federal government.

"I think he means 'indignities.'"

"It's like injustice," Gunnar said.

"It can be, yes. Do you believe that?"

"You know what I think? I think it's for show. Like some guy gets a shiny new truck to feel bigger. Or he gets a bigger shotgun when all's he needs is a .22. He's really just a big scared baby."

Greg nodded to that. A silence fell, in which two adult men would have sipped their beers, reflected, and sighed.

"Look, just, don't tell dad I had it, okay?" Gunnar said.

"Okay. Is it some kind of proof of something?"

Gunnar glanced at Greg, then stared at the porch floorboards as if they were words to read. Greg gave Gunnar all the time he needed. He took a couple imaginary sips of beer. He looked out. Beyond the ranch outbuilding, a cloud of sheep gathered and began to sit all along a line like so many dominoes.

"If you don't tell him, I'll tell you something," Gunnar said.

"Okay. Deal. I told you I wouldn't."

"Wayne Carver, he's the one who's been messing with your rental car and that bike of yours."

"I know. But thank you. He's supposed to stop."

"He won't though. He thinks you're up to something. I over-heard him. He says you might not be who you say. Says, they should test you more. See what you're made of. See what your secret is."

Greg forced out a laugh. "See what I'm made of? What does that even mean? Did he really say that?"

"He did. Said it just like that," Gunnar said, and went back to reading the floorboards.

20

So, Wayne wanted to test him. Wayne wanted to get at his secret. Greg got another chill from another horrid thought: What if Wayne did know about the lake? That would be almost as bad as Torres knowing, maybe even worse. His panic was back, building up inside him, pressing at his ribs and squeezing organs and making him consider drastic measures. He drove onward into town. Gunnar had wanted to go along, but Greg said that wasn't a good idea because he had some things to take care of; then Gunnar wanted to know how long he would be, but Greg said for as long as it took, so Gunnar made Greg a peanut butter sandwich in case Greg got hungry. Good kid.

Gunnar should have nothing to do with this. The less Gunnar was seen with him, the better. In town Greg cruised Callum Street, nice and slow, then back through the main drag again, eyeing every shop window. No Donny. No Wayne. Greg didn't know Donny's mobile number; Donny had never offered it. Not knowing what else to do, he entered city hall, which occupied the second floor of the Callum Building and was an insult to its grand exterior—all fake wood paneling and Formica like a set from *The Rockford Files*. It was pretty much vacant. He found the mayor's office. An elderly secretary sat behind a dulling Plexiglas screen that she pushed open as if Greg had come to pay a bill. Greg asked if the mayor was in, not knowing what he was going to say to the man, just going with it. The mayor was on a fishing trip, the secretary said, wouldn't be back for a week at least. Greg asked, was his son with him, "Wayne, was it?" The secretary snickered, said she doubted that very, very much, "Not unless Wayne was aiming to do him in."

Down Callum Street he saw Tam in front of Tam's, leaning on a broom almost like she was waiting for him. He asked her if she'd seen Wayne Carver. You might try his feed store, she said. Greg went over there. It was a 1960s prefab building just beyond one end of town, a big sign reading Carver Farm Supply mounted high on a thick pole as if it was meant to stand along a freeway. The front was dressed up like a chain store with colorful sale banners, but the lettering and phrases were outdated as if recycled year after year. The parking lot was empty. Closed sign on the door, not open on Tuesdays. Greg moved along the tractors for sale out front, using them as cover to eye the store windows. No lights on, no one inside. He even walked around the building, passed the loading dock out back. No one parked there, no pickup truck. Greg, calming down now, told himself this was all a good thing. He really did not know what he would have done if Wayne was here. If it were just him and Wayne, he could have gotten away with just about anything. But then so could have Wayne.

A Jaguar sedan, recent model. Greg had sensed a flash of champagne color in the corner of his eye, then jerked his head to see the parked car as he passed. He was cutting through a quaint old tree-lined block on the nice side of town, the houses set back and surrounded by mighty hedges from about a hundred years ago when Pineburg looked to be going places. The white house had ornate woodwork decorating the eaves and windows and manicured shrubs up to the windows. It had a white picket fence, recently painted. The Jaguar was parked inside the carriage house next to the home and the door was still open, the only reason Greg had a glimpse of that gleaming color. Cashmere, Gunnar said she called it.

He took his foot off the gas and coasted a few houses further, then turned at the next street and rolled to a stop, parked. Turned off the engine. He pulled on a hoody from the back seat that he hadn't been seen wearing. He had a bucket hat and he put that on, and sunglasses.

Karen Callum. The only player he had not considered, not really.

The street had dissecting alleys open to backyards. Greg made his way down the alley, eyeing the houses. The first, second, and third looked dark and empty, and he imagined elderly people in them or that each was long vacant after an estate sale and one day would be turned into a bed and breakfast by some city-dwelling inheritor as soon as the area started to pick up. It was the same on the other side, with no toys in yards or signs of decay such as turkeys, pit bulls, and the requisite rusting fridge or car engine. This block was like a museum. The house he wanted had that picket fence out back as well, also newly painted, the back yard ringed by more manicured hedges and fruit trees. He stood in the lane, using a hedge for cover. The windows of this house looked dim too.

The fence had a gate. He stepped sideways over to it. He pushed it open, making sure it didn't squeak.

He moved through the yard, acting natural, prepared to say he admired the house and wondered if it was for sale, even if he ran into Karen—what a coincidence.

Something flew by him, then another little something, buzzing and humming. A hummingbird floated before him, then two and three, and they zipped away one after the other. He couldn't help smiling at that and noticed the porch had more than one hanging hummingbird feeder. He stepped around, eyeing the dim windows, and caught contours of a living room, a kitchen and, at one corner, what could be a den.

He stopped, frozen.

He'd seen shapes moving, like the color of that Jag but brighter, flushed, glowing.

Two people naked, on a chaise lounge. Kissing, caressing, laughing.

It was two women. Karen Callum was one. He couldn't mistake her dark flowing hair, those curves. Her lover had clipped hair and was shorter, thicker, more bulk than curves. He couldn't stop staring. His feet moved him to the side, just behind a hedge. Their lovemaking looked at first glance almost violent in its fury and pace, like flailing, but then he saw its purpose. Caring. Devotion. Tenderness. Like they were painting each other as murals. They turned his way. He ducked. When he peeked again, into a corner of the window, they had turned again, into another position. And he had the sense that they would not have seen him anyway, such was their blind passion.

He ran off.

21

Greg's phone rang again. Someone was calling him again. The screen read Unknown Caller. He kept eying his screen for a voicemail but whoever it was would not leave one. This was not helping his mood, not helping him think. After seeing Karen Callum and her lover, he had gotten back in his car, pulled off his hoody, drove over near Callum Street, parked, got out, and walked. Just walked. He wandered side streets, hands shoved into his pockets, kicking at gravel. He needed to think things out. Break it down.

He should have known about Karen Callum; he had such good gaydar. The question was, what would Donny do? If Donny knew, the result might be the same: If Karen came out and owned who she was for the world, Donny might not be needed anymore as Charlie Adler. And Donny-Charlie could lose face all around, since the XX crew surely belonged to that dwindling minority who still thought gays an abnormality, an unknown entity, and so a menace. This could all drive Donny even farther from him, make Donny realize that their own secret was his last leverage, for someone. That someone could be the authorities. Greg doubted it. That someone could still be Wayne, however. So he had to find out what Donny knew without giving it away.

His phone rang again. Unknown Caller, no message. This was the third time in about ten minutes. It could be Karen. But how would she have his number? Then he realized it could even be

Emily. Was that why he didn't want to answer? Because they were breaking up. There, he had thought it—he had never let himself think it before. But it was true.

He had a sudden urge to call Emily. He owed her a call even if he couldn't tell her much, but now his phone coverage wavered. To get it back, he picked up the pace and found himself on a side street of ramshackle old bungalows and mobile homes, the lane marred with cracks and potholes patched with dirt or gravel.

Up ahead, he saw the three dealer teens, Jamie, Rory and April. He saw Gunnar. The three stood around Gunnar. Surrounded him. Gunnar had that same rigid stance as on the porch.

Greg hurried over.

Gunnar saw Greg and eased up, but the three stood between Greg and Gunnar. They had their loose clothing on—baggy jeans, oversized hoodies, cocked caps.

One of the boys stepped forward, keeping his hands inside his hoody pockets. He had a tribal tattoo on his neck, Greg now saw. "We're just talking, just talking is all," the boy said.

"What's your name?" Greg said.

"Jamie."

"Everything all right?" Greg said to Gunnar.

Gunnar went to speak, but the other boy stepped forward, Rory.

"Why don't you three just leave him alone, all right?" Greg said to Rory.

"Who the fuck you anyways?" April said to Greg. "We saw you fucking looking at us—"

A shout: "All of you! Halt right there!"

It came from behind Greg. Greg whipped around.

Wayne Carver charged out from a cross street. Slung across his back was a hunting rifle, with a scope.

Jamie and Rory backed up, and April slotted in behind them.

Gunnar moved to the side, his eyes shifting between Greg and Wayne coming at them all.

Wayne kept coming. He pulled off his cap and stuffed it in his front pocket, kept coming.

"What you gonna do, huh? What?" Rory said to Wayne. "Think you're so fucking big with your gun, just makes you a bigger pussy."

Wayne charged at Rory, passing Greg.

"Don't! Stop!" Greg shouted.

Wayne stopped and pivoted as if only now noticing Greg.

"They're kids. They just need help," Greg said.

"You can't do fuckin' nuthin' anyways," Rory said. "What are you gonna do?"

Wayne turned and lunged at Rory and punched Rory hard across the bridge of his nose. Rory landed on his back, striking the rim of a pothole. Blood gushed out his nose.

Wayne kicked Rory across the head, in the gut.

Jamie and April ran off. Wayne stood tall over Rory. He let Rory pull himself up. Rory fled, following after Jamie and April. April turned to pull Rory along as if Wayne was still charging them all.

Wayne turned to Greg and Gunnar, panting like snorts from a bull.

Gunnar looked to Greg. His eyes told Greg to get going.

Greg held his ground.

Wayne got in Greg's face, bringing a reek like that bull's snort.

"Those aren't no kids, not anymore," Wayne said. "They're animals."

"You're just making it worse on them."

"You, you're just a goddamn tourist. What do you know? We're just playing you. Charlie Adler is. We all are." Wayne waved at air. Greg flinched. "And you know what? You're on your last legs."

Before Greg could answer Wayne turned to Gunnar, said, "You okay, son?"

"Yes. Thank you," Gunnar said.

"I won't tell your father. Just stay away from them, you hear? They're doing meth and who knows what."

"Yes, sir."

Wayne turned back to Greg, snickered at him, and marched off the way he came, clenching his rifle strap.

Greg and Gunnar watched him disappear.

Greg's phone buzzed again. He let it ring. It stopped. "People really need to leave messages," he muttered.

Gunnar was staring at Greg. He had the wide eyes of someone under great stress. Of someone far older.

"I hate it here. I hate him," he said.

Greg hated himself for just standing there. Sure, he had held his ground, but hadn't he come into town to confront Wayne? Wasn't that really what he was after? But he hadn't expected Gunnar to be there. He didn't want the kid implicated in any way. Something about the way Gunnar said he hated it here, his lips curling and shrinking as if wilted by a great heat, reminded Greg of Leeann Holt. It had tortured Gunnar just to say the words. Another thing Greg noticed: Gunnar didn't seem to have much of Donny's swagger or sense of humor or any of Donny, really. Greg tried not to think about what that could mean, of what shape Leeann was in now, wherever she was. All he knew was that he had to help counteract the force of Wayne and the obstinacy in Donny. Adults were only outsized expressions of who they were and what they were doing as kids. So where would that leave Gunnar ten or twenty years from now if Greg didn't do something to deal with Donny, to shield Gunnar, and to protect his own secret.

He thought it for the first time: He would kill Wayne Carver if that was what it took.

He got back to Callum Street and found his car where he had parked it, in the corner of a secluded parking lot, shaded by trees. He got in.

His passenger door flew open.

FBI Agent Rich Torres dropped into the passenger seat, slammed the door shut. He looked like a local in worn work clothes, a beard that had to be fake, and an old cap.

Greg almost wanted to laugh. He gasped, blurted, "What are you doing here?"

"You kidding me? Who the fuck you think you are, going around my back?" Torres' mouth had scrunched up in a scowl, and his face bore deep lines like scars. He kept one hand fisted. "I've been calling and calling you."

A rush to Greg's head told him to hate the sharper tone of Torres' voice. To spite it. But he took a moment, sighed, and let the heat disperse. "How long have you been here?" he said.

"Long enough to know a lot more than you," Torres said.

"No one said I couldn't go on a trip," Greg said, avoiding eye contact. He shook his head, looking out the window at the wind whipping through the few tall treetops.

"I should just arrest you," Torres said through clenched teeth. "What I should do."

Maybe he deserved Torres' full wrath. Donny probably did. But the last thing Gunnar needed was a state-assigned home. So Greg said nothing, just sat there. Obstinacy enveloped him, covering him like an extra layer between skin and muscle.

Torres eyed him. "Well? Say what you're going to say. Say it."

"All right. Who's to say that a guy can't start over?"

"Oh, so you think you can help Donny? That's why you came here?" Torres blew through his closed lips, sounding like a balloon losing air. "Man. I thought you were kind of a pussy, but I never thought you were this much." He shrugged and added in a calmer voice, "It doesn't matter, whatever you're thinking. You're in now. You don't have a choice. You had a choice before."

"I know where I am."

"Do you?"

Again Greg didn't answer.

Torres leaned forward and looked out each window, at what Greg wasn't sure—all Greg saw were knotty trees, a parking lot needing paving, and an empty road leading to empty shops. The heat in his head was gone, replaced by a chill in his gut.

Torres spoke with staccato precision:

"In a few minutes, you'll see a blue pickup roll by. A Chevy, the rear fender dented. Follow it, but not too close."

And he jumped out.

22

Greg had frozen up, like a lever had been pulled that locked up the gears inside him. Fear had done it to him. All this time, he had let himself believe he had been on his own. Now he saw that he'd only been on a very short leash. That's what he was—a dog. A small and not ferocious or heroic dog no matter how hard he tried. A Chihuahua. Pomeranian. And like that sorry little excitable dog, Greg could not think straight now. His brain was a pea.

He had followed the blue Chevy pickup out of town with Torres sitting in the truck's passenger seat in his disguise. They had driven off the main route, down a long gravel lane that skirted one hill, turned into a dirt road, and ran between two more hills before ending at scrubby woods. Inside the trees stood a mobile home patched together with rusting aluminum siding, gray plywood, and flapping tarpaper—like an old quilt. The yard was strewn with debris, engine parts, and the requisite dead fridge, this one on its side.

The fear in his pea brain making him fret over just how much Torres knew about him and Donny.

Greg was standing inside the mobile home. He watched from a window as his rental car was driven away back down the lane, slowly to avoid stirring up dust.

"The car can't stay here. You'll get it back," Torres said to him, to his back.

Greg pulled the dense curtains shut and made himself turn back around. He saw laptops, surveillance gear, papers, and files running the length of two fold-up tables down the middle of the mobile home. It had a bathroom and a fridge, but the rest of it was basically dedicated office space. A war room.

A bulletin board had stakeout photos of Donny, Wayne, Gunnar, and Greg. All looked to be taken in Pineburg in the last couple of days.

Torres had pulled off his farmer beard. He stood with his arms folded, letting Greg take it all in. "Have a seat," he said.

Greg didn't sit. Why sit? He just felt foolish now, like a guy being used by a girl to make another guy she really liked jealous.

Torres went over to the fridge and produced two tall 22-ounce Portland beers—Lompoc Special Draft. "Look, just sit down," he said.

Greg sat at the long table. Torres put files and photos, documents and newspaper clippings in front of him. They included: a state report on how poor Pineburgers have gotten poorer since the long downturn in logging; a business article about the Callum family expanding its vast land holdings; an impact study from a reputable, impartial science think tank that showed how removing the dam owned by Callum Utility Company would give disadvantaged farmers more water and Native American fisherman more salmon while restoring the habitat, which would also offset any negligible impact from controlled flooding; and an FBI dossier on the Double Cross Militia that illustrated instances, the dam removal most importantly, where militia members worked behind the scenes to exploit populist anger, though who exactly was leading these efforts was not confirmed.

Greg took his time, returning to some documents to re-read them, and Torres let him. He got Greg another beer and some beef jerky. Over an hour passed. Torres sat across from Greg, tapping on a laptop.

"Why isn't this more publicized?" Greg said finally. "Story is clear enough and big enough for some enterprising investigative reporter."

"First things first," Torres said, shutting the laptop, checking Greg's beer. "I can tell you there are a couple reporters of national stature—no offense—who are waiting to pull the trigger. But we've asked for embargo. First things first."

"Why don't you just bring in some of the Double Cross for questions? That'll scare them."

Torres shook his head, took a drink of his beer. "This isn't a sprint. Slow and steady wins this one. Besides, guys like Wayne Carver don't scare. He only reacts, attacks."

"Yeah, he does. Like some goddamn forest boar."

Torres had a folder in his left hand. He opened it and passed a photo to Greg. A bloated, purplish, and bloodied face stared into the camera. A second photo showed the body, stripped down to underwear and in similar condition. One eye was swollen shut, but the other glared at the camera as if to say, take a good look—this is your proof. Greg thought it was a girl—from the long black hair and soft dark skin that was untouched. Contours were hard to make out. It was as if someone had stuffed rocks under her skin.

"You know Tam. Tam's Tavern? This is her daughter. Melanie. Native American girl."

"Wayne did that," Greg said.

"You got it."

"Does Tam know about you?"

"Let's just say she's aware of us. Probably the only one in town who is, on account of her daughter. No use even bothering the so-called mayor. Basically been fishing ever since the local PD went away. Voters took away so much funding anyway, so what do any of us expect? It's practically an unincorporated area."

"You get what you pay for."

"And be treated as you want others to be treated."

Greg and Torres took a drink at the same time. Torres stared at Greg.

"What?" Greg said.

Torres produced another photo. This one showed three sets of buttocks. They were men, judging from their narrow hips. Their pants were down and their hands held up their shirts. Each butt was branded with the two Xs—one X on each cheek, the bright red, blistering brands glistening in the flash from the photo. In a cartoon, this could have been funny. Like this, it was pathetic and a nauseating display of the human condition to Greg. We had advanced so far, and yet human nature was still unchanged—man was always so close to treating his fellow man like cattle. First comes the brand, then the slaughter.

Then it hit Greg. "This was the trick," he blurted.

"Come again."

"Donny mentioned Wayne and the boys playing a trick on some outsiders. Donny wasn't happy about it at all. Freaking out about it, in fact. It's one big reason he's so edgy, I'm guessing."

Torres shifted in his seat, and it hit Greg again. He recalled Torres at the Cascadia Congress: Greg had asked him to sit, but Torres wouldn't. And he recalled Torres scratching at his rear. "Wait—you were one of them?" Greg said.

Torres' mouth had scrunched up again, but he nodded. "Need to see it? How about I pull my pants down?" He stood. "You need to see it."

"No." Greg said. "So, let me get this straight: You were willing to hold off on pursuing criminals who branded your rear end?"

153

"They only used propane to heat it up, didn't get it near hot enough to do lasting damage. Luckily. Look: I'm not holding off on anything. What do you expect? We weren't even sure who they were and still aren't. Guessing isn't busting."

"You want a bigger result," Greg said. "That's why."

"It's part of it. Do you go with the glorified felony battery or something much bigger? Things have to tie together. It's what we do."

"That makes sense," Greg said.

"Does it?" Torres took a step toward Greg. "Or are you just trying to fuck with me?"

"No, not all. I—"

"It sounds like you are. It sounds like you're a fucking know-it-all."

"I'm sorry. I can't imagine. Does it hurt?"

"Not anymore. The itching was worse than anything."

Greg finished off his beer, to give Torres a moment. Torres paced the room, stopping at docs on the bulletin board and looking out windows, keeping to the darkest shadows in the room. And Greg figured it out. Torres wanted these guys so bad. He wanted all he could get on them. Revenge was all about patience, Greg had read somewhere. Was it Machiavelli?

"This isn't about my ass," Torres said finally. "All right? Let me lay this out for you." After his pacing, he had ended up in a dim corner of the room; Greg could only make out his silhouette. "They could hit anything. County offices. State Capital. A federal building. Reservation property. Anything. So, you keep listening. If they talk about going on a trip, hunting, anything."

"I'm not really close to any of them," Greg said. "Except maybe Donny, but he says he's trying to stay clear."

"You'll get closer. You'll get there very soon."

"Hold on. Are you deputizing me or something?"

"FBI doesn't deputize. FBI turns informants."

"And I have no say in it."

Torres shook his head. "I told you. Not anymore."

"But, I told you I didn't want to. I was up front about it. It's a free country, right? I can visit whatever town I want."

"Sure you can. And I got free speech. So I'm speaking to you now: We can always go and look into you, too."

There it was, the moment Greg had feared. Leverage. He hoped Torres only meant his dream of a Cascadia, but how could he be sure?

He didn't force it. He shook his head. "So that's it? I'm your informant."

"That's it. You wouldn't like the alternative."

Greg said nothing. What could he say? He had been running right toward it all along.

"You can make it your own. At least ask for a per diem, something," Torres said.

Greg fell silent a while. Let Torres wait. "I want a per diem," he said finally.

"Done."

"And I want the kid Gunnar clear of this."

In his dim corner, Torres fell silent now, his silhouette facing Greg. Greg stared back, making him answer.

"Okay, the kid is clear," Torres said. "Or at least, he will be."

Greg nodded. He stared at all the documents and laptops and photos in this war room built to fight what Donny had lent his fake name to. His paranoia crept back in, prickling at him like a line of ants running up his ankle, up his pant leg, thigh. Torres seemed to know so much. What else had they learned? And now Torres watched him from his shadows, probably learning more just from the way Greg was acting, simply by the way his temple muscles were working.

"And, Donny?" Greg said. "How much do you know about us?"

"I guess I don't know what you mean there," Torres said.

"I just mean, I think Donny senses that I can help him. That I'm here for more than I appear to be. If that's possible." Greg hadn't dialed it back so much as forced an angle. It was as if his subconscious was speaking for him, anticipating how he should play it. His angle would have to keep Donny motivated to say nothing about what they had done. "Donny did mention the possibility, in his way," Greg added. "But he's smart. He keeps it in terms of only me alone helping him. There's still something there between us. Less like suspicion, more like trust in my outsider status. Does that make sense?"

Torres didn't answer at first. Greg looked to the darkness but could barely see Torres' silhouette. It was as if Torres, the wall, and the shadow had fused into one.

"Only Donny can help himself," Torres said eventually, stepping forward from the shadow—first his face, then a shoulder, then limb by limb. "Identity theft, fraud, these are federal crimes. But they don't have to be the end-all."

"That's something," Greg said. "So, what's next?"

"What's next depends on how smart he is. That or dumb. Same goes for you."

23

Torres had told Greg to get back in town, mingle, act normal, and wait for his signal. They gave him his car back. Torres never said where Greg could or could not go. Greg went to the white house in town. He waited there. He didn't ring the doorbell. He sat on the front porch in a nice new rocking Adirondack chair, spotless white, a decoration. He didn't even know if he would answer Torres' signal. He had to think about options, angles, his own leverage—anything he had that no one else did. Everyone else had that, something in their back pocket. He only had the anti-thing, his secret that could destroy him.

The garage door was closed. Was the Jaguar in there? He couldn't hear anyone inside the house. He wondered if he was the only one who knew about Karen Callum. Torres had never brought it up, had barely mentioned her. Donny had to sense it, had to fear his disposable status.

A late-model SUV pulled up the driveway, the same color as Karen Callum's Jaguar. It stopped a few car lengths from Greg's car. Hanging back. It kept idling. At the wheel sat what appeared to be a woman with short hair and a face that was full but in an attractive way. She eyed Greg. She had music on, a female country singer; it sounded like a faint muffle but was probably real loud inside the SUV, the level of loudness that you sang to.

Footsteps, from inside the house. Karen Callum came out the front door. She locked the door behind her. She had a bag over one shoulder. She passed Greg. She stopped on the edge of the steps. Turned to him. Her expression was so cold and blank, she might as well have been looking at the chair alone, wondering where else she could put it on the porch.

"You all right there?" she said.

He nodded. He wondered how long she had known he was there. She had probably watched him walk up the path and find the steps. Expected him to ring the bell. Imagined him coming in, telling her something only he knew. She probably expected to pay him off somehow.

Inside the SUV, the music had stopped. A window was probably partway rolled down by now. Karen might even have called her, told her there was a guy on the porch, but it was okay, nothing she could not handle.

"I'm okay," Greg decided to add.

"How did you know about this house?"

"Found it by accident. Noticed your Jag," he said. He fought an urge to rock in the chair. That would be overdoing it.

"You can't find Donny? Can't get in the other house?"

"No, that's not it. Gunnar is there. He would let me in."

She nodded, and she shifted on one leg to keep the bag from pulling her down.

"You want to come in? You can have a key? I don't give a rip."

"No."

"Okay. Then have a good one," she said and turned, heading down the steps.

Something about the way she'd said this got to Greg. He said, raising his voice, "You know, I don't get to see you much around here."

Karen stopped on the last step. She seemed to take a breath, just a half second, and turned to face him, a smile spreading across her face. "Well, that is so kind of you. I am out in the country a lot. The whole land agent rigmarole. Sure got a fine network of places to stay, though."

"You should write a book on that."

"Like you do? Will do. Say, a travel guide-type book? That's a good idea, Greg."

Karen was still smiling but holding it as if she was posing for a photo. Like the former rodeo princess she probably was. The sturdiness of it impressed Greg and made him want to kick himself. Of course, strong women were the linchpins for everything—all women were, for that matter, and this one was carrying the heavy water of one local legend named Loren Callum. He couldn't even begrudge her. She was a product of her environment and living up to her full potential. He was the creep. He was the one sitting on her front porch.

But he held his own smile. "I know, right? But I was thinking more like a how-to: How to get good and rich doing what you do."

Karen eyed him for a long beat. Her smile had lodged in place as if her jaw had stuck. "Hey, I know what. Maybe you could help me write it," she said.

The SUV rolled closer, the tires crunching at gravel.

Greg stopped smiling, and Karen did too.

"Yeah. Sure, I could," he said. "I'm ready when you are."

"I'll tell you," she said. "I'll tell you when."

"No one cares, you know."

"What?"

"That you're a lesbian."

Karen said nothing. She took a deep breath. She turned to the SUV and held up a hand as if to say, just wait there a minute.

"No one has anything against it," Greg said. "Against you. It's not even an issue anymore."

She looked him in the eye and held it. "Maybe not, but they used to. He did."

Greg was rocking now. He hadn't realized it. He stopped by planting his feet, pressing down on the chair arms.

"Exactly. Me, I was talking about Portland. A lot of other places in the country. Even around here? You're probably fine too. But who knows? You never know."

"All it takes is one hater," she said.

"That's right. Who knows who knows things? I'm not talking about someone going after you just because they know you prefer women. I'm talking about because *of it*. Just to spite. They out you to get at you for other things."

"I don't know if this is a threat or a warning."

"Maybe I don't know either. But you're smart. You'll know. You know that it's best to keep up appearances—until it isn't. Your father, he probably even had a saying for such situations."

She sniffed. She shook her head.

"Donny could lose face, way worse than you," Greg said. "He might do something drastic in the aftermath. I don't think anyone wants that. I sure don't, not after all me and him have been through."

"It could be broke, though, is that what you're saying? You could do some breaking?"

"All I'm saying is, when people finally figure out how they've been strung along for so long, they are really going to be pissed."

"Is that right?" Karen said.

"Yup. It's only a matter of time. It's called progress. Giving folks a fair shake. Maybe that was one of your daddy's sayings too?"

Karen nodded. Her teeth clenched, muscle flexing at her jaw.

"Are you going to get the fuck off my porch?" she said.

"Yes. Don't worry."

"Oh, I'm not. Believe me." Karen backed down the last step with the back of her hair directed at him as if she had eyes in the back of her head, watching him still. She marched down the driveway to the SUV. As she got in, the driver glared at Greg and kept doing so as she maneuvered her rig around and drove Karen Callum and herself away. Her eyes kept on him in her oversized side mirrors.

Greg started rocking in the chair, at a slow, measured pace. He had just argued against his own principles. He had used prejudice, and he had preyed on someone's fear. All to keep himself safe. He had done this before and he hated this about himself. He couldn't get much lower, not without killing someone again. If he could only help someone, for once. But, at least one threat appeared to be under control.

His phone buzzed, making his feet plant again.

He had a text. It was the signal.

24

Don't forget, Donny told himself—he was Charlie Adler now! Charlie Adler wasn't fucking dumb. Ole Charlie thought things out, played people off one another, like you put one scared-ass cat into a box with another. Any kid could throw cats in a box, though. Wayne Carver could do that. Charlie, he was subtler. Charlie Adler, now there was an operator—that's what Karen had called him.

Even an operator had to have a Plan B, and Donny had his. Not even Karen knew about it. He stood in Karen's office, where it was always neat with no papers on the desk or stacks of folders, no cute notes or drawings around. It was like the museum version of a famous person's office and not much different looking than when daddy Loren was alive. It still had the foot-high bronze statue of a horse and the Pendleton Indian blanket draped over the back of the leather hide sofa with the CR brand of Callum Ranch.

Most important: It had the old man's iron safe, big and black and pinstriped with gold paint and a plaque that read Callum, like something right out of the Old West. "From the robber-baron era," Karen had called it, when men "did what they wanted." Karen had told Donny he was from an age like that. This was the closest she had ever come to saying she loved him. She had done a lot for him, but it was all on daddy's orders, Donny suspected. Old

Loren had said, "A women, no matter her private inclinations, had to have a man in front of her for credibility." Locals probably didn't give a rip who she loved, but her daddy did and his ghost alone was worth a thousand Pineburgers. She should have considered getting closer to him, though. Try him out. But she just didn't roll that way. She never did put out. Daddy would've liked it if they'd married. But she just didn't listen—the only order of daddy Loren's that she had never heeded.

Her loss, Donny thought. He knelt before the safe and tried the combination written on his palm. The door opened, and Donny, careful not to touch anything, made sure all the documents were still there. Karen had copies of land deeds for the farms and properties she was acquiring, all squared away, alphabetically, in a file holder right inside the main compartment. Donny had wondered why she kept copies here, and it made him suspect she too had considered taking off at a moment's notice. The other clue? She had cash money in there, right inside its own bank pouch.

Donny had been checking the safe almost daily now, like some rock star constantly eyeing his hit songs on the charts. The more he rode this horse, the more he had riding on it. He checked whenever she was out, whenever Gunnar was out in his room, even when Greg Simmons was here at the house, in the fancy guest bed or out on the back porch.

No one was home right now. He wondered where Greg had gone after the rally. He had stayed away from the house. Was he sulking? He was probably somewhere in town. Maybe he was in Tam's Tavern again, where he could get some sympathy—Wayne had reported that Greg liked to go in there. Donny didn't blame him. Pineburg wasn't especially welcoming to a guy like Greg. He might as well be Native American. But Greg wasn't making it any easier either. He was pushing it, pushing Donny to change his game, and Donny was beginning to wonder exactly what for. Sure, Greg wanted him to keep his mouth shut about what happened at the lake. But, could Greg really help him? There could be more to it. Donny saw that. Maybe Greg wasn't really going to write a book with him in it about why society had forced him to be the way he had been. Maybe others were controlling Greg. Donny didn't want to think what that could mean. One thing was damn clear though after all these years: Greg just didn't seem as smart as Donny always thought he was. Maybe this was because Donny had made himself into something better than that teen preppy kid-Greg who had talked him into doing stupid shit. Still, if Greg kept this up, with his damn prodding, Donny—the real Donny—just might have to do something about that all the same.

He closed the safe. He tiptoed out, even though no one was home. Made his way back to the safety of his study. He so wanted to celebrate the continued existence of this, his preferred Plan B. A couple lines of meth or even sweet lady cocaine would do, but he killed the need by setting out that FBI man's business card on his desk. He sat at the desk. Eying the card. This was the other Plan B. A way out.

He did a line of meth anyway, got a whiskey going, and heard the banjoes in his head playing Dueling Plan Bs. It didn't help. Nothing could make that card quit staring back at him. Seducing him. Could he fall into the hairy arms of the Fed-cops with their tough love and so-called mercy? It was the one step he had never taken, never considered taking. But now the thought of it was practically wearing a silky pink teddy and pulling him into bed, which bothered him, because Karen's safe with all its goodies should be doing that to him, giving him that woody. Teddies will go and trick a man, he knew that much.

He picked up his phone, made sure caller ID was off, and dialed the number on the card:

"You've reached Special Agent Richard Torres of the FBI. Please leave a detailed—"

"No," Donny blurted, hung up. It was too soon. Too risky. There had to be a better way than making this damn phone call. Had to be a better way than that safe, even. He would be that better way. He would be the safe and the phone call and the goddamn solution all rolled into one. That's the way a man did it.

He made a fist and went to bang it on the desk, but his hand went limp on the desktop.

He slid the card back into his pocket.

25

Donny was just itching for a little pick-me-up. He sat in his booth—the one they kept saved just for him—and imagined waitresses wearing gun belts bearing shot glasses and booze bottles in holsters. If only. The Rooster Lair didn't have hot women, and what was the point of having a private club if you didn't have that much? Of course, the issue was where to get the women. Maybe they had tried in days long past. But they all flee to San Francisco, Seattle, and even Portland in the end. Who could blame them? This dump had a Confederate flag on one wall and a commemorative brass plaque dedicated to the Jefferson States of all things. The lights were too bright so that you could see all the nicks and marks in everything and make out that most of the tabletops were Formica. That alone rubbed him the wrong way— didn't they know most of this great state was built on real wood? At least they didn't have their Double Cross banners waving, or make up silly uniforms with armbands that they would wear only in here like some kind of drag queens. Though that was sure to come, Donny thought.

He'd always thought the Rooster Lair was one sorry excuse for a secret lodge, never once was impressed. But he always had to make a showing before they had their meeting, like some rodeo star has to shake hands with the sponsors in the green room. He sipped his beer. Everyone left him alone. Only Wayne Carver eyed him from over at the Golden Tee game, where he liked to stand because it gave him a commanding view of the room. Wayne was drinking root beer, which he liked room temperature, and that creeped out Donny just as much as the rest of it.

Donny was feeling antsy, sure, and he should be, considering what he would have to do next. He was doing his part, just as Loren Callum had told him. Loren had done it and so would he, if he wanted to stay with Karen. He was more than her straw man. He was her bedrock.

Of course, no one had bothered to ask Karen what she wanted. Maybe that was one reason she was the way she was? The thought made him shrink up inside, his organs gone all tiny.

He looked up from his beer. Greg Simmons was standing over him.

Donny's surprise made him blink and shake his head, and for once he was not faking it. Something was up with Greg. His arms were cocked out and his thighs pressed against the table as if he was going to keep Donny there if he tried anything.

"How you find this place?" Donny said, not smiling nor frowning. Even keel. Never show surprise or cover it up with tricks.

"Not from you," Greg said.

He had said it a little too loud. This was not good. Donny showed half a smile. "Where you been?"

"I went for a drive," Greg added, "Trying to sort this crap out in my head."

Donny wondered just how Greg found this place. People did know about it. Probably be weird if Greg didn't find it eventually. The trick now though was getting Greg's ass out of here before the big show began. "Have a seat, feller," he said to Greg.

Greg didn't take a seat. Didn't answer. He was taking a good long look around the room. Wayne had turned from Golden Tee and was watching them, but the rest kept doing their drinking and talking.

"Come on, have a drink," Donny added.

Greg glared down at Donny, a look Donny had never seen. It pinched up Greg's eyes and made his Adam's apple sit high in his throat, like he was about to cough it up and spit it into Donny's face.

"You don't even give a shit whether your land floods—about the Callums' land flooding," Greg said. "Getting rid of the dam could actually help the other farms, not to mention the town. Help those beloved fellow ranchers like Wayne over there spoke so highly of. But if they're kept starved of water, like they are now, you can go buy more of their land."

Greg had hit the bulls-eye, and you couldn't argue with such a score. Luckily, he was speaking lower.

Donny gave half a nod. "Karen can, yes. That's what she does. I told you."

"You didn't tell me it's not just about crops, ranches. Or even the dam. A lot of those hurting properties she buys have wells on them. Some of the wells are drying out. No groundwater. Aquifers dead. But, when the dam is removed? They might do just fine. The flooding could even help replenish faraway groundwater if done right. But no one wants to know about it. Meanwhile, Karen Callum will have more land for whatever she wants." Greg's whisper was more like a hissing snake. "See, there's even a ground well exemption—land owners aren't supposed to overuse their wells, but if it's at a certain amount used for, say, a residential development, then the owner's exempt. She might add to her ranch lands, or make it a dude ranch, or go with a housing tract or even a strip mall. Who the fuck knows. Any way she does it, and when the economy comes back especially, she wins. Locals all lose. And the residential water takes away even more water from farmers, ranchers, all those locals who support her and Wayne Carver, and all of this bullshit."

"Well. Look who's the expert."

"You know all this. Or maybe you don't. Either way, I actually don't think you give a shit."

Donny had to shake his head. "You weren't really listening, were you? If you ever were. I'm just surviving."

"At Karen Callum's side. As Charlie Adler."

"I was, yes. Then you come along."

"Hell, you might even inherit it all."

Donny laughed. "You believe that, you do not know Karen Callum very well."

"Oh, I think I know her better than you think. Better than you even."

Donny's back straightened up. "What's that supposed to mean?"

"I just mean. Anything else you want to tell me? Anything that's worrying you? If there is, you should tell me now."

"I told you what you need to know."

"Good. Okay. Then, you ready to talk about this? About what you should really do or should be doing? Before your friend Wayne goes and takes it too far. I'm not talking about playing a role. Acting like someone's mascot. I'm talking about doing."

Now Donny was hissing: "You should shut up with that talk, that's what you should do. This is not the place."

"No? Then where is?"

"I'm just another property of Callums. And only because I have a purpose, for now—"

"Until Karen Callum is done with you? Decides on her own way of doing things? Comes out . . . with it?" Greg cocked his head back, swallowing back the words he wanted to say.

Wayne had come halfway over—Donny could make out his big head from the corner of his eye. Wayne stood watching from a table where Casey, Damon, and others sat.

"Look. This is not good timing," Donny said to Greg. "There's a big meeting. The annual powwow."

"What, going to go appoint Wayne Carver the Grand Poobah?"

Greg was being a fool. He sounded like he was the one doing meth. Donny had to handle this, or at least make it look like something it wasn't. He stood, set a hand on Greg's shoulder. "Come with me. Now. Don't say no. Just come along. Okay?"

He walked Greg toward the front door, and on the way he threw an arm around Greg, pushed at him, and laughed. Greg let out a fake laugh—atta boy, Greg, not such a fool after all. Donny kept them going right for the front door and kept on laughing as he pushed them on through the front door and out. And didn't look back.

He walked Greg to his car and stood Greg at the driver's door, Greg planting his feet like he wasn't moving until he heard something he needed to hear. Donny stared at the ground a moment, and when he looked up he had on his dead serious face, with one eye scrunched up as if really trying hard to see Greg wasn't being stupid. He took a look around. He set a hand on each of Greg's shoulders. He whispered, "Listen. Will you? I'm the one keeping these guys in check. The only one. In there? That's only the tip of the iceberg. There's lots more of them out in the wide open, believe me. Guys who don't even venture into the big town of Pineburg. Yet. They're just laying in wait."

"Lying in wait," Greg muttered.

"What?"

"Nothing."

"Good," Donny said. "Any questions?"

Greg had lowered his head.

"What is it?" Donny said.

"What about Gunnar?" Greg said. "How long can you protect him?"

Donny felt his stomach muscles twinge up, wrenching at his rib bones. Nice move, Greggy. "I'll protect him. Don't you worry."

"Even when he starts doing meth?"

Donny blurted a laugh. "What? Come on." The twinge had hit right in the marrow. Donny was done with this. He had to be done. He put a hand on Greg's shoulder. "I'll meet you at the house later, okay?" he said, and opened Greg's car door for him. "Okay?"

"Maybe," Greg said. "I don't know. I just don't."

26

To find Donny, Greg had pushed through the front door of the place, bringing a rush of warm air that was laden with the sourness of sweat-steeped clothes and grease of fried food. The space was no bigger than Tam's but packed, mostly with faces Greg had seen at the rally and near to Wayne. They had to be Double Cross militia regulars. All their camouflage gear had come out, all their favorites they had surely been warned not to wear at the rally. There were guys in camo smocks, camo vests, pants and shorts, and floppy hats, in all patterns ranging from modern US Army desert to SS forest sniper, from Vietnam era jungle to the hunters' shrub-tree look. A few had guns on but most did not. They probably had a hefty gun cabinet somewhere in here where there used to be a coat rack.

Wayne Carver stood over in the corner playing a Golden Tee video game. Seeing him, Greg felt a jolt of anger and fear that blurred his view and narrowed his focus down to a point as if he was peering through a traffic cone. He fought it by taking stock, looking around, widening his focus. To the left of the bar, he saw a doorway to the back, double doors. A banquet room? The way to the former grange hall? Torres had told him to look for that.

Torres had told him how to get here. Torres had driven him in the blue Chevy pickup to a different parking lot back in town where his rental car was parked. He left Greg there. Minutes later, Greg drove out Old Redpine Road, according to his map, and passed over a small wooden bridge. It was dusk. With his map on his steering wheel, he found the turnoff for the gravel road. This was about six miles out of town. His phone had no coverage. The road was long, and winding, and ended in a tight little canyon. Here stood a strange building, like two or three disparate homes pushed together. One end was a log cabin and the other was stucco. All of it was slapdash. He slowed to a stop among the parked pickups and cars. A sign stood between the parking lot and building: Private Clubhouse—No Trespassing. Torres had called the place the Rooster Lair, which was the Double Cross' name for it. In front of Torres, he acted protective of Donny, but the truth was that he wasn't sure. He wasn't sure about anything. Donny was keeping things from him, and what was next? All he knew was, Torres' opportune little exhibition had made him mad at everything and ready for anything, which was surely what Torres had wanted.

Faces turned, but no one stopped Greg. He located Donny in a booth, off by his own. He stood over Donny. Donny only looked disappointed at first as if he'd been expecting his food to come. Greg had tried to push it, see what Donny would do, but he held off when it came to Karen and what he had seen. Donny kept his cool. He walked Greg outside to his car, asked him to meet at the house later. Greg was hoping Donny would cave and bring him along to the big meeting, but Greg still had another way of getting there.

He drove away. He found the other side road Torres had shown him. It was dark now, so Greg could only hope he had the right way. It led him slightly uphill, to the old leaning barn Torres told him about. Greg parked inside the barn, continued on foot up a short but steep hill of uneven terrain, jogging along and working his way around rocks and crevices, his sweat splashing at his wrists. The hill evened out at the top, and a pungent, earthy smell told him that he was in a cow field. He heard groaning and moo-ing in the dark, could see their dark shapes like so many boulders. The boulders moved. One cow jogged after him, and another. He kept going. At the edge of the plateau he came to a fence, short and maybe electrified.

The cow hooves clopped and shuffled, and they neared, at his back. He touched the fence. Nothing happened. He climbed over and pressed on, heading downhill.

Halfway down he stopped and crouched at a bush. He could see the rear side of the Rooster Lair at the bottom of the hill. Behind it, closer to him, stood a one-room hall like one of those few grange halls still left in the farthest reaches of Portland's sub-urbs. His eyes had adjusted, but the square hall with its tarred-up siding was darker than all, like a void. He saw Double Cross regu-lars filing in, taking the few outside steps that separated the hall from the Rooster Lair.

Once the flow had stopped, Greg waited a minute, counting off the seconds.

He made his way down, stopping a couple times to make sure no one was outside on watch. He approached the hall from the side and found an open window. He could see in through a break in what looked like two homemade Double Cross flags doing double-duty as curtains. He saw men sitting on rows of benches, like pews, and a small low stage. With all that camo crammed together, it looked like a small forest right in the middle of the room. Without the Double Cross decoration and camo, it might have only been some odd men's-only church from the pio-neer days since the interior was so bland with its planks for floor and wood paneling for walls. The window was cracked open an inch—Greg pushed it open another inch, a millimeter at a time, and could hear better. The men chatted, boasted, bantered.

Wannabe guards flanked the stage, which almost made Greg chuckle considering the fact that the real danger was he, here outside.

Wayne Carver was there now, taking a seat up front, dead center.

Bland country rock began blaring from a boom box. A man in camo stood and introduced their main speaker, their patron, their leader.

The man he introduced was not Wayne Carver. It was Charlie Adler.

27

Donny was shaking and couldn't stop it. That twinge in his marrow had turned into an unrelenting tremble. It had started as he watched Greg's rental car drive away. So he headed back inside the Rooster Lair and marched straight to the bathroom, locked the door.

Who knew what Greg was up to? How could Donny know? If he asked he'd be giving himself away and showing that he was spooked. And Greg probably knew that. Greg always brought more to the table, more than trying to keep Donny's mouth shut about what they'd done.

Donny wiped down the Formica sink countertop so it was good and dry. He set out two lines of meth. He hadn't planned to do it—he had no problem getting fired up for what he was about to do; he was a natural, people said—but ole Greg, he had left Donny shaking. Just shaking. Maybe Greg still was one of the smartest guys he had ever met after all. That was why he had put so much trust in Greg before.

He snorted up the last of the lines and felt it burn high up his nose then his sinuses, like fucking sawdust and pins, fuck it. He stared at the mirror, right into it, stared until things blurred and it was like he was looking at a movie of himself and his face rather than a mirror image. A screen test, they called it. He made a blank face. Even then he could see the faint line of his dimples.

God bless those dimples, Donny Jepson Wilkie. He tried a subtle
smile, just the curly ends of his mouth, and those dimples deep-
ened and lengthened until he got a big grin going of his white and
shiny teeth. It looked like a grimace if he looked at it too long, but
he only had to flex his muscles and dimples until he had something special going again. Again and again and again and again.

Knock knock knock. Someone was banging on the door.

"Yee-ep!" he shouted, letting that grin show through in his
voice.

"You good in there?" said that whiny voice. It was Wayne
Carver.

"Yep. Coming," Donny said, wiping down the counter and
keeping the damn good grin going. He was going to need it and
he would use it.

He bolted out of the bathroom on his toes. He sensed something and turned to see that he'd passed right by Wayne, who was
leaning against the wall in shadow.

"He gone? He better be gone," Wayne said.

"Sure. I got rid of him. No harm done," Donny said and kept
on going before Wayne could question or answer with one of his
smart-ass remarks.

Attached to the rear of the Rooster Lair was the main hall, an older
building. It had been a grange hall at one point, but it was probably a church before that even though it didn't have high ceilings
or a steeple. About half the length of a little old-fashioned school
gym, the place was. Its wood exterior was almost black from all
those years of oil and tar that preserved the siding. You could
barely even see it from the front of the Rooster Lair, which suited
Donny just fine. It was simple inside, with only rows of benches
and a stage, which suited Donny too. The focus was on the speaker
in a room like this. The man with a plan! Wayne and the boys had

strung up their homemade Double Cross flags and banners on the walls and over the windows, since no one could see them in here, and Casey and Damon were helping the other so-called tough guys stand guard at either side of the stage. It was all a little too close to the Neo-Nazi scene in some dumb thriller movie or even a comedy movie, but what the hell did Donny care? He wasn't the one playing dress up. He wasn't the one doing what he was told.

Their eyes were all on him, about thirty guys including a few he'd never met, they were so off the grid. The seats almost full. Donny took his time coming up the middle aisle, nodding at some dudes and high-fiving others. Wayne had skirted the benches and moved at his pace, practically in step with him, like some mad pig predator eyeing its kill, Donny thought, but then Donny saw that Wayne was grinning too at all these Double Cross diehards.

Donny stood off to the side of the stage, flushed all warm now with the feeling of wide smiles on him and wishing some others would quit talking. Luckily someone had a boom box going, some of that slick and pompous country music that was giving country a bad name, but it had enough beat in it that he started doing his little jig, just on his toes, not too much, just enough to let them see he was fired up and he sure did love it here with them. Wouldn't be anywhere else, no sir!

Man, just what would he do without that meth? Coffee and drink and pot even just didn't cut it at times like this, whiskey no way.

A small farmer-looking feller shouted, "Let's get to it now!" A couple other guys hollered something, and then a couple more were shouting, urging him up, "You get to steppin!" and it was like they were all on meth with him, they'd all done it just for him. Wayne was pivoting in his seat, twisting his neck either to quiet them or let himself be amazed, and Donny decided it was only pure amazement.

Donny leapt onto the stage to wild applause and cheers. It roared on, with beers raised in toast. Wayne stood to quiet them, doing a fake knife across his throat with his hand and grimacing at them, at each one, eye to eye until they stopped.

Quiet now. Donny stood front and center. Looking out. Nodding. Guys nodding back. His feet planted farther apart than normal. Stability. They liked that. No time for dancing now. This place wasn't big enough for a microphone, but Donny would've liked one. Props were no good.

He stopped eyeing, stopped the nodding. He let his focus blur and took them all in. He said: "You saw it yesterday. I saw you saw it. I really think we're on to something here, don't you?"

The crowd burst into hoots and hollers. Donny let them go a while. When they calmed again, he said: "We are not the first who were on the right path. No, we are not. We know there is a long line of heroes who stood up. We will do them proud. We're not going to be ignored. We're not going to be stopped. The first? You know who they are. There once was a little movement like ours, and they called it the American Revolution." A few hollers. "And, and, years later, when that revolution had become all corrupted, there rose up some real brave men to fight back . . ."

And Donny went on, blah blah blah, telling them just what they wanted to hear. He hadn't practiced this much or knew what to talk about exactly, but he damn well knew what to stroke. He spoke to them about a Civil War battlefield in the 1860s, hearing mock-heroic fiddling music in his head as he did so. He told them about waves of eager but poorly equipped Confederate troops charging with the Dixie flag.

He didn't tell them the way he really saw it: Those boys were mowed down as their Confederate generals watched from a hilltop and ordered more, more, more of them to be sent to their death.

He didn't tell them what he really thought: Those dead Johnny Rebs were nothing but suckers and raw fuel for men hunting medals and offices and chests of gold.

He had their attention, had their shiny, perky eyes on him. He moved on: "And, many years later, 1941 it was, we rose up south of here, near this very land right here—and they called it the Jefferson State!"

The crowd cheered, fucking roared.

Donny was hearing silly, good-timey bluegrass music now in his head. He didn't tell them the truth as he knew it. In November of 1941, those Jefferson Stater secessionist yokels—let's just call them what they were—had showed up near the southern border of Oregon and tried to block the interstate highway up from California. They bore guns, touted flags, and had their own slogans, but they were also drinking a shit ton and were certainly almost too drunk to stand. Soon enough, Oregon State Police troopers swooped in and persuaded them to go on home, which they did, without a fight. One vomited on himself. The sucker.

Meanwhile, Donny was telling his crowd: "They showed the powers that be, right then and there, that we're the ones showing them now! Screw us over? Knock us down? Again and again, we stood up again and again, and again we stand up to fight . . ."

Blah blah blah. Giving them what they needed from him.

Now country rock music twanged in his head, from the 1980s—those very tunes Greg had talked him out of listening to when he got into Portland. He told his rapt crowd about the infamous and legendary Posse Comitatus gang and how they stood tall, though Donny knew they were nothing more than bigots and kooks holding meetings similar to Double Cross' but with crosses and sheriff badges and actual swastikas and Nazi salutes, sure as shit, because if you were going to ride that steer, you might as well break a record. On a small town Main Street, the Posse Comitatus had shot and killed two federal marshals. Dumb mother suckers. They weren't even suckers. They were just baby children crying out for attention, wailing for mommy's teat.

It reminded Donny of a bumper sticker he'd seen on a car traveling through Pineburg, probably from Portland: Tea Parties Are for Little Girls and Their Imaginary Friends.

He was practically laughing now as he went on, boasting of how "someone around these parts" just the other day went and stood up to some outsider snoopers over at the old gas station, and for that, those snooping snoopers were good and branded for life. He couldn't help himself.

He could have raved on about other recent heroes, such as that self-appointed rebel grazer of an Arizona rancher-racist who recognizes no authority but that which he himself appoints, or any version of those one-man loser militias who gun down innocent cops while calling themselves patriots. He had to leave something to these boys' imaginations, such as they had them. Each needed a patriot terrorist to call their own. And the boys were going nuts now, standing and pumping fists and high-fiving each other all over; one fat guy actually rose up and ran around the perimeter of the benches like a born-again in a revival tent. Wayne and about five others only nodded, amen—you could bet those were the ones that were there on the spot, Donny thought.

Suckers all, but at least they were his suckers. For now.

And then in a flash—of hope, he hoped, he saw in his head Wayne and his armed Double Cross regulars holing up on the Pineburg Dam like it was the Alamo. Fed officials watch from afar, with Donny at their side because he had made that one very smart phone call to the FBI. And at that scene, Donny pretends to be shocked, just plain shocked at how far Wayne Carver had taken things. If only he could've known. Who could've known?

Looking back, he could see it, sure. There were signs. And he could admit he hadn't helped matters, confessing it with a hand on his heart. But he had simply been honoring the word of Loren Callum for the love of his daughter, Karen. Blah, blah, blah, and blah and blah and blah . . .

"This town was a goner when I got here," Donny said to his boys in the hall. "Folks were just begging for someone to save them, some who've been here since the pioneer days. Then we began to stand up. You are the only ones who can help this poor town. This whole region. This whole state. You! You do it for these sad, frustrated, hard-working folks. You give them hope. And so we will show them there is in word and in deed a right and good way out of this . . ."

The crowd showed Donny frozen and strained faces, some on the verge of tears. So he went for it: "You know, there was this great lady, named Ayn Rand she was, who once said that if we are not understood in our greatness, and the bureaucrats and the lazy and the niggling little rule makers go try and stop us, then we should go leave them be, and go on to make our own world. Well, friends, I am here to lead you there, and I am here to stay . . ."

By the time Donny finished it off, he was shouting and pumping fists right back at them and hooting and hollering too. Out of the corner of his eye, he noticed Wayne still sitting. Wayne nodded, just once. Donny only hoped it was an amen.

28

Greg had heard it all, Donny's whole bullshit speech.

At the end, as the boys inside hooted and hollered and high-fived Donny, Greg thought he heard a door swing open somewhere. He was done anyway, done with this shit charade. He backed away and quickly made his way up the hill, his lungs pumping. Marched straight through the gang of cows who parted for him. He found his car and sped along until he was back on the dirt and gravel side road that jostled him with a clamor like bullets shredding the car.

He imagined Donny boasting to him how he had fed those Double Cross fools the lines they wanted to hear, but substituting "blah blah blah" as he laughed about it.

Donny had pretended to be their leader. Donny had pretended to be his friend. Donny was out for no one but himself. He could sell out Greg at any time. Blame the whole murder on him, even.

Greg certainly couldn't kill Donny now, even if he had the guts. Torres was watching them both.

He should have been banging his fist on the steering wheel. But it only made him think of Leeann Holt. Again. He thought of that photo of her and of those cracking bends and folds that he had tried to straighten out.

He braked to a sliding stop before Torres' ramshackle secret mobile home, bringing flying rocks and a cloud of dust. Torres stood in the open doorway breathing in the dust.

Greg pushed by him, found a chair inside, and sulked a while. Then, ranting, he told Torres about all that he'd seen and heard. Torres nodded along as if checking off a list.

"Oh, he's good, your Donny, I'll give him that," Torres said. "Telling them they're saviors like that. Even trotted out the old Ayn Rand horseshit—pretty highbrow horseshit for this crowd, but I guess it depends on what lines you choose."

"It's a scam. He's a phony," Greg said.

"Come again?"

"He's bluffing them."

"Oh, I don't know. You heard him. Sounds cut and dried to me."

"It's not. He's pretending. He doesn't believe it at all."

"We all pretend somehow. Doesn't take away from the fact that he appears to be leading them. You just heard it. It's a fact. If he's not, who is? A speech like that is big. The challenge now is finding proof of any direct orders."

"You won't find it. And I won't do it for you. He's stalling. If push came to shove, they got no leader. He'd be out of there. It'll be you he's scamming next, just you wait, making you do things you shouldn't have ever done." Greg banged his fist on the table.

"Whoa. Easy. Let's talk it out. How do you know that?"

"I know. I just do."

Torres was silent a moment. "All right, let's just say he is. The question then becomes, what kind of phony is he?"

As they spoke, Greg noticed the two pairs of headphones sitting out over on the desk. They were wired to computers, but the monitors were dimmed. So that someone like Greg couldn't see the screen? He didn't need to see the screen. If this was some 1970s conspiracy film, it would be large reel-to-reel tape recorders with a blanket thrown over them.

"Hello? I'm over here," Torres added.

Greg could feel the sick grin on his face as if someone had pried his mouth open with rubber-gloved fingers. The grin only spread as the realization grasped him.

"You know exactly what Donny said," Greg said.

"Yeah, you just told me. What's wrong with you?"

"No. I never told you about the Ayn Rand horseshit. You're the one who mentioned it."

Torres didn't nod. He didn't shake his head either.

"You heard that speech just now," Greg said. "Didn't you?"

Only now did Torres glance at the headphones. He pursed his lips. He nodded. "Okay, yes. I did hear. Right now, they're back inside the Rooster Lair getting drunk. Some dumbshit just threw up near our bug. Believe me, you don't want to hear that with headphones."

"I wondered why I didn't have to wear a wire—or whatever you call it," Greg said.

He stood. Anger had won the battle in his head, strutting on a stage wearing medals, lugging the bloodied and shredded corpse of poor incredulity. Never had a chance.

He turned from Torres, clenching another fist. He should kick at a table, bash a laptop over his knee, something.

They had him all along. He was theirs the whole time.

He kicked at a chair, sending it clattering against the wall.

Torres waited till it tipped over and lay still. "You want to know why," he said.

"I want to know, why me?"

"We needed someone to be there. Understand? To see it. We only have bits and pieces. I won't lie to you. The Rooster Lair is bugged, but the Callum house and Wayne's are not. We couldn't have them all. Legal minefield. You have to pick your battles."

"I'm a battle. That's what you're saying."

"In a way, yes. This actually protects you, you know. No one can say you were an accomplice to any of this."

Was this a threat? Greg didn't especially give a shit at the moment. "An informant being a witness, you mean. Something you can actually use in court."

"Now you are surmising. So just hold on, and sit down."

"No."

"Don't be this way. Think about it. We were able to pull off the Rooster Lair tonight. Because of that, I was able to show you what we're dealing with. What you're dealing with."

"You realize I'm fucking him over again," Greg shouted. "You do realize that. What he'll do."

"Wait. What do you mean, again?" Torres said.

As soon as Greg shouted it he knew it was unsafe, a slip from the past, a safe pried open by rage. Reason reanimated in his brain, to fix it. "I mean, is this even legal?" he went on, throwing it back at Torres. "Oh, they'd just love this back there at that crazy-ass secession powwow, fits right in with their batshit conspiracy theories, their one world order circle jerk-offs."

He stepped over to the wall and its shadows to hide whatever might be showing on his face.

"Hold on right there," Torres said. "First thing? You need to quit seeing them as bush-league amateurs. Do that, you underestimate them. They're crafty. Will not give up. Eventually, it all leads right back to Oklahoma City, to our preventing something like that."

"You mean Wayne. That's who we're really talking about."

"I mean whoever's in a position to be charged responsible for this."

Greg wandered off to a corner, deep in thought. At first, he wanted to deflect Torres from his and Donny's true relationship, from their secret. But there was more to this. He had seen the clues. He had been holding it in his hand and staring at it—and on and off for years, really.

He walked over to Torres. "I'm just thinking here. How did you really know about Donny and me being friends? It wasn't some database. No one knew about us much. I didn't want too many people knowing I was hanging out with some goofy cowboy kid from the sticks."

Torres made his face blank, blanker than some poker player. He could've been dead. He was good. Maybe he'd once been a Marine guarding embassies, Greg thought.

Torres held the stare.

"Stall all you want," Greg said. "I'll keep asking. She is Gunnar's mother, isn't she?"

Torres kept the mask on. "Who?"

"You know who: Leeann Holt. Used to be Donny's girl."

Torres didn't shake his head.

"Where is she?" Greg said.

Torres straightened up with his shoulders level, equidistant from Greg's, forming a perfect square between them. "I can't tell you that. Confidentiality issue."

"Hers or yours?"

"Both. It's the rules. My rules."

Greg made for the door.

"Wait—where you going?" Torres said.

Greg opened the door, stepped out.

"Just, wait," Torres said, but softer.

Greg stopped in the doorway. "Where is she? Just tell me where she is."

"You can't go. Not now."

"I have to. I have to get away from this."

Torres told him. "You go, you have to come right back," he added.

"I don't have to do anything," Greg said, closed the front door behind him and made for his car.

29

Greg drove right through the night. Torres had let him drive off. Torres had let him leave town. Greg didn't want to think about how easy it had been. Too easy. Just like it had been coming here in the first place. Then again, what could Torres do about it, really? Arrest him?

Greg drove without stopping, right over the mountains. He had so much in his head. He thought about Gunnar, about timing, and the last time he and Leeann had been together. They had gone to a park, for a picnic of their own under a shady tree. He had dumped her in the last place she expected, in a safe place. What was he thinking? Who the hell did he think he was? She should have at least slapped him before she ran off.

Before dawn, he ended up on a street in an older neighborhood on the east side of Portland, close to 82nd Avenue and that solitary hill called Rocky Butte. He was nodding off, yet he still felt a wince of shame, of sheer awkwardness. Humility. He was like the alcoholic forcing himself to return to past friends and relationships and make amends. He parked on a stretch of street near a corner, under a big tree; the closest house had foot-high weeds for a front yard. He slept in his car for a couple hours, then kept low in his seat as the few neighbors passed driving off for work.

He looked at the photo of Leeann Holt at seventeen, all defiant and sexy, too cool for school. Torres had told him the address, and he remembered this street now. The houses small and the same design, most of them, many with flaking paint, blinding spotlights, and chain-link fences separating yards. Overgrown yards. A few were spotless and defiantly so with power-washed driveways and new siding. The housing bubble had been kinder to other Portland streets, bringing more houses like these back to life for a brief time, but not every street could be a winner. Half the houses still had either For Rent or Foreclosure signs. The house of Leeann Holt's parents stood only a few houses down. It had a Foreclosure sign. It was a dull white, the tone of a primer that had never been painted over, and the weeds had won in the flowerbeds.

Sometime between leaving Pineburg and waking and staring at the Holt house, whether through fatigue or the certainty of his reasoning, Greg had become convinced that Gunnar was his biological son. The parts that didn't fit Donny matched him. The fuller face. The build.

He slept some more, in fits and starts. At about nine a.m., he pulled up to the house and walked up the driveway to the front door. There was a peephole, so he stood front and center. He pressed the doorbell but heard only a dog bark inside a neighbor's garage. He knocked. He waited.

The door cracked open. He saw her face. It still had soft lines but had sagged, framed by thinning hair.

"No way. Leeann? Leeann Holt?" he said. He'd practiced this.

"Well, fuck me," Leeann said, her voice croaky like she had just woken up, but Greg guessed it was always like that.

He didn't know what to say now.

"Well, come on, come on in," Leeann said, waving her hand down low as if for a dog, Greg thought. Once inside, he saw her eyes were veined and glazed with worry. She wore sweats, and she seemed shorter than Greg remembered, but it was probably just the furry slippers giving her no lift. He thought she looked ten years older than he did and wondered if he would've recognized her if he hadn't come looking for her.

"Can you wait in here?" she said.

"Sure." She left him in the living room. It was the room of an elderly couple with heavy floral drapes and marred colonial-style furniture. He hoped her parents weren't going to come rolling in—he had made a point never to meet them and didn't want to start now. He had only been in this house when the parents had gone for the weekend, and when they were home Leeann had always had he—and Donny—pick her up outside, up on the corner, or at the nearest 7-Eleven.

He had planned to start by telling her just what he thought of Torres using her to get at Donny, but now, in the moment, he decided to play it cool, see what happened. Always the reporter. The observer. Armed with more info, he would act.

He tiptoed around. In the kitchen he saw two packed bags sitting at the back door. He peeked back down the hall and, craning his neck and using the reflections of a hallway mirror, saw Leeann in a bedroom sitting at a vanity. She put up her hair, then let it down. She trimmed her bangs. She tried on alt-rock 1950s glasses like a singer in the B-52s would wear. She put on red lipstick. She stood at the mirror and squeezed up her face, and then loosened it in a reproduction of her sultry teenage smile.

She got up, vanished. Greg pulled back into the living room. The living room had no photos, he realized. That was what was missing.

Leeann entered wearing a look that was nearing passé over ten years ago but always survived—alt-rock, rockabilly, or country punk, some called it. It was Bettie Page meets Joan Jett, and Leeann's lipstick only magnified the creases invading her lips. Greg had always liked the look even though it was one a girl often held onto for too long. His own look had a similar persistence, he realized, so who was he to get picky?

He smiled for her.

"Don't worry," she said. "They don't live here no more. Why there's no photos." Her voice had somehow turned more hoarse than when she'd opened the door.

"I'm not worried."

"Fuck you aren't. You think I'd let you in here if they were?"

Greg shook his head rapidly, mocking fear, and they burst out laughing. It made Leeann cough and cough, sounding like BBs bouncing off glass, and she turned away to finish the job all that smoking had bestowed on her. He waited it out.

"Greg Simmons. Man, oh man. Twenty years gone."

"Look at us," Greg said, opening his arms, which showed off his faux-vintage shirt—a plaid like on a tin of Scottish cookies. "Like the original band members."

Leeann laughed again and cut the cough short by clearing her throat, which Greg welcomed under the circumstances. And yet, as he eyed her, he saw that she still had it. There was just enough of what brought on the older guys and made Greg and Donny obsess over her. Back then it was the promise of something bolder, an edgier and more exciting world out there. Now? More like a lady working at the post office or deli who you just know has a story or two to tell, and you'd like her to tell just you. Greg wondered if anyone else saw this or if he was just applying his take from twenty years ago. Maybe others just saw a somewhat worn-out woman who'd probably worked too long at some tavern.

"You're some kind of reporter?" she said. "Heard one time you were at the New York Times or some shit."

"I was, sort of. I was a stringer, technically. I was in the newsroom a few times. So, yeah, I was."

One of her eyes narrowed. "Apparently you still are, 'cause you went and found me."

"At your parents' house. Not that hard."

"I'm not living here that long."

"Where are they? I don't want to get busted." Greg added a smile.

"It's only dad left. He's in assisted living. He thinks my name is Alan."

"Oh. I'm sorry."

Leeann shrugged. She eyed him a second, tapping her foot. Then she said, "Donny Wilkie faked his death. What you want to know, right? He paid some creepy-ass fuckers in Mexico to make it fake and then he went and snuck right back in the country like some illegal."

"I know."

"You do?"

"Were you with him then?"

Leeann snorted a laugh. "Fucking A right, I was. Right beside his ass. We shoulda stayed in Mexico. I woulda."

Greg felt a pang in his chest, like indigestion. Was it jealousy? It embarrassed him, so he got out his next words as even and reporter-like as he could. "Were you two married then?"

She nodded. "Then we were." She eyed him again, smirking. "Well, I can see this is giving you a big woody. Yep. A big ole woody."

"No, it is not. You expect me not to want to know?"

"That there's a good question, isn't it?" Leeann turned away and started pacing the room, really wearing out the rug. Greg figured she was gauging what all she should tell him. He wondered why she was telling him anything. Maybe she had never even talked to Torres directly. It could just have been a quick phone call to the FBI, a cheap tip-off. But what had she said? He wanted to believe that she never knew about him and Donny at that lake. Donny had promised he had never told her, but how could he be sure? If need be, he would have to press her on it. He might even have to believe her.

She had stopped at a window, looking out but not too close, like someone afraid of watchers. Greg said, "You're cooperating with them. I know you are."

Leeann whipped around to face him. "Them?"

"The FBI. An agent named Rich Torres."

Leeann let out a big sigh. It produced a cough and rattled more BBs. She passed by him and dropped onto the sofa, slumping, her palms up at her sides. He sat next to her. He said nothing, and he waited, ready to be listening. She pulled off her glasses and set them on the end table.

"I didn't go to that Torres guy. He found me. How you think I'm able to stay here? Parents never let me," she said. "I'll get nothing from them," she added. "I always knew that."

"What did you tell Torres?"

"Wow, you make it sound like you're the one who did something wrong." She perked up, the marbly glaze of her eyes like cracked ice. "What exactly did happen way back then between you and Donny? Huh? You went your own ways real quick, or at least you did. Maybe you made a move on Donny—the guy was pretty fucking hot."

"Why you being such a bitch?" Greg blurted. The words had come out before he could stop them. He didn't regret it, only that he'd said it in the voice of his seventeen-year-old self.

"Fuck you. You don't even know," she said.

She was trying to turn this thing around, stay in control like she always used to be, or so it had seemed back then.

"And Gunnar?" Greg said. "What about him?"

Leeann bolted up and lunged. She slapped Greg hard against the jaw. It stung like hot oil.

"I wanted a kid with you," she growled. "Asshole."

"'A' kid?"

"The kid I aborted. The kid that's not Gunnar."

"So, Gunnar was from Donny?"

"Yes. Gunnar is from Donny."

Greg slumped, as the reality sunk in.

"Dumbfuck," she added.

Minutes later, they stood at opposite corners of the room, Leeann back by the window and Greg near the door. Greg had shot up and intended to stomp out the door and keep on going, but he hadn't. She was daring him to leave, ready to watch from the window and make sure he was leaving for good. That's what Greg told himself. So why give it to her?

The window light suited her, bringing back the softness of her face that always had, ironically, made her seem even harder to him. Those gentle contours always hinted at something tougher, like silk over steel.

She watched him watching her.

"I gave Gunnar up," she said. "What, you don't see how I could? Lots of people can't. Fuck them. Sure, Donny slept around but he was actually kind to me, and he was real good to Gunnar, I can tell you that."

He hadn't been kind to her? He almost said it but swallowed the question back down. Of course he hadn't been. "You could've protected Gunnar," he said.

"Screw you. You don't know half the shit that went on." Leeann's chin quivered. She glared at her feet, fists at her sides.

195

Greg took a step forward, and another.

She glared at him, her eyes moist. "No one wants to know about the mom who gives up custody. Give that baby away? How can a woman do that? A mother?" The tears ran down her face, and she let out a little grunt of pain.

She cried, and it sounded strangled like she struggled to breathe.

Greg headed for the kitchen.

"Stop," she said.

"I was going to get you a glass of water."

"No, just come here."

Greg came back over, and she took him by the hand. Her hand was hot, like just out of the shower. She sat him back on the sofa.

"You know where Oakridge is?" she said.

"Kind of. It used to be a logging town."

"Used to be is right. I was living in a trailer, but I couldn't even keep that heated. In goddamn Oakridge. You got no idea."

"I have some idea."

She shook her head. "I wanted to get farther from Donny, not too far that maybe I couldn't get to Gunnar if I had to. I could save up. In the beginning there was work. Then it just dried up. Knew this one girl who got me on at a chicken farm in the valley. Used to hitchhike, bus if I could afford it. I fuckin' plucked more fuckin' chickens."

She showed Greg a sad smile, which forced the same out of him.

"Know where Rich Torres' boys found me? Washing my clothes in the river. Right near where I'd take a crap in the woods. People are living in the woods nowadays. Regular people. Their great-great grandparents hadn't been worse off."

"You could have looked me up," Greg said.

"Look you up? Ah, and how was I supposed to do that? Facebook?"

She had turned into the bitch again, and yet he still held her hand. They eyed each other. She wiped at a cheek with the back of her other hand. The corners of her mouth turned up, and her eyes widened and brightened.

"Besides, Greggy Simmons, why would I go put myself through all that again?"

Greg leaned closer. Leeann's smile faded, leaving a defiant gaze. Defying him to kiss her, make love to her. Hit her. Kill her? Greg resisted as if an iron bar ran right up through the earth and through him, keeping him grounded. Right now he understood her no more than when he had tried so many years ago. Yet it made him want to try again.

She let go and stood and faced away from him, head to one side, seeming to search for composure like a singer ready to go onstage. And she said: "Look, tell you what, can you just give me a ride downtown? My ole car's about shot to shit."

30

"I'm going to have to tell Donny I saw you," Greg said as he drove on. "He'll know somehow."

"Yeah? Have fun with that," Leeann said.

They shared an uneasy chuckle that sounded more like small dogs being kicked.

Greg was driving Leeann downtown. Rain streamed down the windows of his rental car. He had taken Sandy Boulevard, and they sat waiting at stop light after stoplight. From the sound of Leeann's laugh-cough, Greg had expected her to have a cigarette every five minutes or at least wear a coat that smelled like cigarettes, but she had neither.

"I woulda taken Burnside in," she said as about the tenth streetlight in a row caught them.

"That's even more lights," Greg said. "Should've just taken the Banfield."

Another stoplight. Two bicyclists waited next to them, unfazed by the rain. Greg wished he was out there with them, keeping it simple like he had for so long.

He took the Burnside Bridge. "Good choice," Leeann said.

"Thanks."

Greg's phone buzzed. He slid his phone out of his pocket. Unknown caller, it read. Again. He let it buzz, again.

He could feel her studying his face as he drove over the bridge, the pink US Bank tower and that neon Old Town deer sign coming at them.

"What really did happen with you and Donny?" she said. "You didn't just leave him be. Something happened."

"Nothing happened. He didn't tell you much, did he?"

"He wouldn't talk about you two ever. I tried to get him to."

Greg gave a little shrug as if just thinking about it for the first time. "We just turned out different, I guess," he muttered.

He hadn't asked her where she was going, though he knew there was a county assistance office down near one of the food-cart blocks. As he navigated the one-way streets that delivered them into the heart of downtown, he winced a little inside imagining one of his bike-riding Cascadian cohorts spotting him driving an actual car or asking him if Leeann was his oldest sister or even mother. Leeann would probably kick whomever that was right in the spokes.

He could feel her watching him again. Could she feel him wince, or something deeper?

"I've been going to the Main Library," she said. "In case you were wondering."

"Where you are going is your business."

"I'm looking into going back to school."

"Oh? That's great. I'll get you closer."

He drove around the rear of the library, across from where the Max trains did their U-turns, and pulled to a stop, having to double park. Leeann moved to get out.

He pulled on her elbow. "I'm going to give you a phone number," he said. "It's my, well, basically she's looking like my ex-girlfriend the way things are going. She's a good girl. She gives a crap. If you need anything."

Leeann was biting her lip.

"What?" Greg said.

"My phone, it broke."

"I'll get you one of those pay-as-you go ones. There's a phone store around the corner."

"Okay."

"But you will call her if you need her, right?"

She nodded. "How long is it for? Until you get back?"

He hadn't expected this question, especially since she'd said it like a child would, her voice higher and without a guard up or a joke attached. "That's right," he said. "I want to help you. Okay? I will help you."

"And Gunnar too?"

"Yes. I promise."

Back at his apartment, Greg made half an attempt at tidying his room after stuffing more clothes into his bag on the bed. He had called Emily on the way over, and she had taken it well considering he had not called her for days and now here he was showing up to pack more clothes and leave the dirty ones in a pile. She heard his request to help out an old friend well, too—as he knew she would. She was always ready to help anyone, dropping everything. She said it was in her family, in her Midwestern pioneer genes. That's what the women did. So this was not some trite charity, wasn't like giving some unknown entity a buck on the street. This was a contract, and Greg had never signed one of those before. Emily knew that more than anyone. Still, why was he really doing it? Because he still felt something for Leeann? He wanted to help? Or because he needed Leeann on his side in case she knew about the lake. This was far cleaner than having to silence her somehow. He really could help someone for once.

Emily showed in the bedroom doorway. Her arms were folded across her chest.

Greg's phone buzzed again.

"Aren't you going to get that?" she said.

"Nope."

"It could be her."

"It's not."

She shrugged.

"Listen, I really appreciate you offering to help," Greg said. "She says she wants to go back to school."

"What, so, this is a trade?" Emily said. "You know what—don't answer that. And stop packing for a second."

"It's a way of helping. Doing something."

"Make the world a better place. Is that it?"

"That's right."

"You're driving back tonight?"

"I was going to."

"You don't have to. It's still your room."

"Thanks, but, I just want to get back."

Greg zipped his bag shut and eyed the room for anything else he'd need. He already had his toiletries. He had told himself not to roam the rest of the apartment, because he didn't want to find evidence of another guy.

She stayed in the doorway. He stood at his bag.

"This is about more than some book, isn't it?" she said. "More than some freaky militia?"

Greg sighed. He nodded. "You know how they say that we can kind of end up doing what we liked when we were young? When we were kids. Becoming what we were, in spirit? If we're lucky, we become that. Well, I'm different. I don't want to become what I was. And I'll do anything to prevent it."

31

Greg had actual newsprint in his hands. It left ink on his fingers. He had forgotten what that smelled like, a mix of oily and sweet. Before he hit I-5 heading south, he'd stopped for a coffee at a new roaster in the Ladd's Addition neighborhood. He rarely drank coffee near evening, but then again he didn't usually expect to be driving into the night. He was sitting in the window on a high stool that didn't feel so steady for such a new coffee shop, his elbows planted on the narrow plank of a counter mounted at the glass. the *Oregonian, Willamette Week, Tribune, Mercury*, all were lying mixed in a rumpled stack at his fingers, so how could he not pick them up? The sections were almost interchangeable these days, smaller format, thinner sheets, the same headlines wanting to be click bait, the subheads wanting to be apps. Used to be, you could tell the Big O just by the far superior headlines let alone the tone, but now it was just another brand shouting for attention. He skimmed the sections, barely reading, just like he did online. He was sorry to see papers go, but who needed them when he got the same on a tablet without the ink on his fingers? It made him flinch inside, and he buried the notion under his thoughts of Emily and Leeann and Pineburg piling up like all this newsprint.

Of course Emily had wanted to know more. Of course he would never tell her. He could not damage her with this. He had to keep this contained. They had hugged in the doorway, shared another joke about him driving a car, and he left. She didn't ask him when he'd be back or watch him from the doorway like she always did. He did not ask her if she was seeing anyone, or if she wanted to. She had to know she was an angel for offering to help if Leeann called, and he could only assume she would put Leeann up in his room if Leeann would accept that. Which left him where? He didn't want to think about that.

He put down the "Living" section with stories he'd already seen two days ago online and picked up another section, the *Oregonian* again. Metro news. Another five-year plan for Old Town, more startups coming, another drunk-driver hit-and-run off Powell, multiple injuries and one on life support. Statewide news section now. He scanned on, reaching the briefs.

BODY FOUND AT REMOTE CASCADES LAKE
Authorities Confirm Homicide Cold Case
SANTIAM JUNCTION, Ore. (AP) — Police agencies are investigating remains of a body found at a remote lake in the higher elevations of the Willamette National Forest. A Linn County Sheriff's Office spokesman said the body is believed to be male and was buried there for many years. However, evidence indicates someone had recently dug up the remains and re-buried them, possibly to hinder evidence gathering. The cause of death has been determined but not released. The investigation is continuing and federal authorities alerted. A county spokesman confirms this is a homicide cold case and says that a strong new lead, based on a tip, could result in more conclusive evidence.

32

Greg drove at a steady speed, but not too fast now. He didn't want to attract attention. He needed to get back to Pineburg, but he wasn't in any hurry to be back there. He had only needed to get out of Portland. Needed to keep moving. It was after dark now. He was back on a secondary mountain highway, driving alone in the darkness, heading over the Cascades.

He was better now. At first he had panicked in that coffee shop, his lungs squeezing flat against his chest, his brain flashing with anxiety like spotlights going off inside it. He'd snatched up the *Mercury* and *Willamette Week* sections in that pile, scanning for the brief story there too as if they weren't weeklies and wouldn't be out again for days—and didn't even print spot news unless there was a damn good news reason. He was just reacting, stupidly, from the synapses charged inside him, practically drooling from it. Of course they wouldn't have it, if at all. The *Tribune* would get around to it eventually if they had room. He grabbed the *Oregonian* section, then stuffed it into a garbage can on the way out as if that was the only one ever printed. His legs propelled him into the car, his foot hit the gas.

His mind racing, barreling as he pushed the speed limits, he had decided to drive east over Mount Hood instead and then south and east. The Associated Press byline meant the story was posted all over—state wire, regional wires, national desk even. It could be picked up by anyone, anytime. The AP wires were always to be feared. They were social media for the establishment, the one newsfeed everyone had to know. Any law authority could know about the story, the case. The Feds had already been alerted, it said. Torres was a Fed. But could Torres ever imagine him doing such a thing?

By the time he had cleared Government Camp and was coming down the other side, he was breathing easier, shaking his head, even chuckling about it. Think about it, Greg. It had happened so long ago. He would be okay. It didn't hurt either that by now he was already driving past the narrow forest road leading to the small, ignored lake south of his new route. He was past that vertical line on the map, in his head.

As he drove on, in the dark, he realized the real threat. The threat was not that this could be a cold case. It had happened so long ago, and no unknown third-party could hardly be expected to connect him to it. The real threat came from whoever might have tipped off the authorities. Maybe that person, or the authorities, or both, were only getting this out to the media to see what certain people might do. A person like him. A person like Donny.

At this point, he was fine just driving the speed limit. It calmed him.

It could have been Donny. Maybe Wayne had found out about it. Karen Callum? Who knew. Sure, it might have been someone innocent, a hiker or even a fisherman not knowing the water held no fish. Even so, Greg was realizing what had to be done. This thing had to be cauterized, to prevent bleeding, infection. No matter what. Torres be damned. Leeann would have to wait.

He cleared the mountains and contours of the pale and rolling central state showed in the moonlight. His eyes kept closing, blinking shut.

A truck came from the other direction, blared a long angry honk his way.

It was past midnight, so late he didn't want to look and see what the time was. It was a Monday now. He could have used that caffeine. Like an idiot, some spooked amateur, he hadn't remembered to take his coffee with him when he'd bolted from that coffee shop clutching the *Oregonian*.

His headlights shined on a turnout ahead, on a blur of a historical marker sign. A rest area, more or less. He turned for it and found himself rolling along an inlet road lined with trees, which opened up to a parking lot, empty. Perfect. He turned his headlights off and, letting his parking lights guide him, coasted into an approximate spot. He turned off the car. Took a deep breath. It was all darkness around, enveloping him. Like he was that security guard under dirt, he thought for a moment and buried the horrid feeling with a laugh at his wordplay. But it was true that he was sitting here inside of nothing. He couldn't see a thing. He rolled down the windows. He heard nothing, not even animals. Was everything deadened here? He listened, kept listening. An occasional faint crack and rasping of branches high above and far away reassured him that something could live in this world he had entered. So he leaned the seat back. He closed his eyes, just for a moment, his eyelids went heavy like lead sheets, and they stayed shut.

At some point, he dreamt . . .

The city of Portland is a labyrinth of dark, rainy, rubble- and debris-strewn streets. Fires burn from the windows of condos and wrecked streetcars. Reckless bicyclists ride with axes and guns. Shots ring out and ricochet, just missing them. Barbed wire rings front yard gardens. On side-street black markets, the gaunt and desperate barter for food. Corpses float down the leaden, oil-tinged Willamette River. Thugs in Sasquatch masks load screaming parents into sewer dungeons and carry away wailing children. A ripped and dingy Cascadia flag flies above it all. On Pioneer Square, Greg's corpse hangs upside down, strung up by his toes along with a line of other dead. And yet Greg can watch all of Cascadia's capital descend into a Dark Age from here, from his limbo state. He can watch the thugs pile up corpses on carts as they laugh and howl. Greg's dead and not dead but can feel himself surely dying inside, a slow, shrinking feeling as if his limbs are curling up taut, as if for sleep.

He woke, but not with a start. His muscles felt loose but firm. His eyes alert. He had energy. He was, oddly, rested. It was near dawn again, the sky purple and ashen, the black tree line silhouette replaced by shades of gray-greens. He yawned, stretched, and he went over his dystopian dream of Portland and Cascadia and felt surprisingly warm inside as if, he imagined, he was a philosopher or mathematician who had finally come to solve a major conundrum after years of trying.

He looked around again. Beyond the parking lot was a clearing lined with trees, the area punctuated by tens and possibly hundreds of gray squares and rectangles and a few gables here and there. This was a cemetery. His harbor was a cemetery. That was what the historical sign was for. These were old tombstones. Why were they here, of all places? Was this connected to some early branch of a pioneer trail that ended up leading nowhere? Had these settlers gone separate ways from the ones he had seen in Portland, in Lone Fir Cemetery? It didn't matter. They all ended up the same, Greg thought. Though it probably hadn't felt that way to these good people at the time, for these ones who had surely chosen wrong when they thought they were creating something new, to last forever. He chuckled at the sick irony of that, his muscles twitching low in his gut then rising up his chest and throat until it became a full-blown laugh. Out loud. Who was going to hear him? They, out there? A deer?

"Deer and dead, they don't talk," he muttered, shaking his head at the thought now. He started up the car, and drove on for Pineburg.

33

"I tried and tried his phone. Makes me so fucking mad," Donny told Wayne, screwing up his face to match that rage he could see inside Wayne. If Wayne wanted him to be like Wayne was, so be it. Though he couldn't match Wayne's awkward demeanor or that odd breath. Sometimes he wondered if Wayne had a bad tooth.

"And what? You tried his phone and what?" Wayne said.

"He's just not answering."

It was early on Monday morning. Donny had another appointment with Wayne, in Wayne's den. Why Wayne always had to have them sit at two sides of that desk with a lamp on, Donny would never know. Wayne's desktop was little wider than a sideboard, like a kid's desk. If Wayne was going to act so damn big, why couldn't he get a big boy desk? Wayne didn't even have anything to show under the lamp this time, and yet he glared into the light on the desk as if imagining the FBI agent's card still there or a tiny version of Greg Simmons, like some voodoo doll Wayne could interrogate with extreme prejudice. Because Wayne wanted to know things.

Wayne still wanted to know why Greg had come to town.

Wayne wanted to know why Greg was talking to people.

Wayne wanted to know when Greg was leaving.

Wayne wanted to know why Greg couldn't be located now.

"I have to assume he went back to Portland," Donny added. "Can't say I blame him."

Wayne grunted.

"I thought you wanted him gone," Donny said.

"Not this kind of gone. Who knows who he's getting with," Wayne said.

"Oh yeah? So how come nothing's happened? You're the one keeps telling me that we're good."

"Maybe we are. But, what do we do? In case someone is watching us. You're the one keeps telling me that someone's coming to get us."

This was the risky part, right here. Giving that speech in the Rooster Lair had apparently not given Wayne enough of that Donny-juice that Wayne needed. Donny knew Wayne was wanting to push things, so Donny had to be ready to show that he could go there. But just how far to take it? Wayne wanted less talk, more do, and preferably before his daddy the mayor got back. The upshot: If Wayne went for broke, Donny would just have to make it work for himself.

"Well, we go for it, that's what we do," Donny said. "Do something inspiring. Don't hurt anyone. Just, you know, throw them off."

Wayne fell silent. He leaned back, out of the light and into the darkness of his den. Donny let the man think. Maybe he was coming to his senses. But then he saw that Wayne was smirking, simpering, practically leering at him. The sicko said: "We need to show them whose dam it really is. They can choke on their relicensing. It's our dam. It's our water."

"It's the Callum's, technically."

"So we defend them. We defend it. And we go down with it if need be."

This was not going for it. This was idiocy. Wayne really was sick in the head. "No, we do not," Donny said. "That is what we don't need. I was thinking more like, we hold another public rally, put you out in front again. Let the rough stuff fade away. Really let you rile things up onstage, but with sugar on top. You know? I'm telling ya, you were so damn good strutting your stuff up there—"

"So you can stay hidden. That's what you mean." Wayne grinned now.

"What, you don't like being in front?"

Wayne dropped the grin with a sloshing sound, half his face seeming to sink into his jowls. He glared. "Going for it means going for it . . . Donny."

"Don't call me that. I'm going to pretend you did not just call me that." Donny leaned into the light, glaring back. "Now you listen to me: Going for it, balls out or whatever, it means what I say it means. I promised Mister Loren Callum that."

Donny didn't like to invoke the name of the grand old man, but it was the one thing that always shut Wayne up. Wayne had always tried his hardest to suck up to Callum. The good man had given more notice to his cows. And yet, Wayne still respected the name. Donny wondered if there was something inside Wayne that wanted to be neglected, if only to make him meaner on the outside.

Wayne's shoulders had drooped. He had his head down, shadowed, his heavy brow shrouding his face like the bill on a hat.

Donny reached into his gut and pulled out, kicking and screaming, a smile that he slapped on from earlobe to earlobe. He held his arms out.

"Wayne? Hey, come on ole boy. Look at me."

Wayne looked up, showing Donny big yellow teeth. He lunged, came around the desk. He grasped at Donny's hip fat, squeezing it, clamping down, twisting. Goddamn, it was like fire—like what getting branded must feel like. Donny groaned.

"You listen to me," Wayne said, breathing his weird stank all over him. "Why should I trust you? Don't even really know who the hell you are, what you done before you got here. Not really. But you want us to support you and vice versa? Support the Callums like we always done, so long as it's about more than that money he—his dear daughter—given us? Sure you do. So, we are going to go for it. We are going to show them. And this time, you're going to be right there with us. Right out in front. Waving our flag. Front and center. Giving us all the goddamn orders so everyone knows it too."

Wayne let go, but the burn stayed. Donny hunched over, squinting from the pain. He blacked out a moment, saw stars. When he came to, Wayne had left the room.

Donny stood up to leave, wondering just where in the hell Wayne got that freaky move. Then he remembered—he'd seen Wayne do that with sheep and even cattle.

Wayne came back in, holding an ice pack. He threw it on the desk for Donny, and it lay there shining under the light.

34

Greg's phone buzzed. He pulled his phone out of his pocket. Unknown caller, it read. Again. He let it buzz, again.

That same Monday morning, Greg sat on the back porch of the Callum house. He was waiting for Donny to come back. He was still stinging from the new reality but coming around. Everyone was a true threat now, he knew. But they could all be kept in check. Even Wayne Carver. Possibly even Karen Callum. Above them all, Donny was the real true threat and always had been. Karen might push Donny toward revealing the secret, and Wayne could suck it out of Donny eventually, but only Donny could release the secret. He could release it right to Torres even. Maybe he already had?

Now he had to consider disposing of Donny. Why beat around the bush about it? He would be doing everyone a favor. But could he do it without Torres knowing? He thought it out calmly, reasonably. There were ways. He could pretend to make another trip to Portland as his alibi. He could use Emily, Leeann, call ahead, tell them he was there. He let himself think about doing the deed, keeping it there in his head, imagining things, like a person does when preparing a meal and holding a just-sharpened butcher knife in their hand. People don't let themselves think about things like that too long. They put the knife away back in the drawer, move on. But not Greg. He held the blade out in front of him, watching the sharpened edge gleam. He mulled it over good and long, the blood and gristle dangling, glistening, all wet and greasy. He could practically lick that sharp edge.

He had to do it cleanly, not like it had happened to that security guard all those years ago. He had to do it in a way that prevented it from ever returning. He blamed Donny for making him come around to think this way. This went all the way back to when they'd first met. He had used Donny, thought he was just a bumpkin. Donny could have stopped that real quick. Why hadn't Donny just punched him in the stomach when he'd first seen him? This would all have made more sense if Donny had stayed violent and not become manipulative like Greg himself had acted all those years ago. Way back when, it was Greg calling the shots and gullible Donny Wilkie going along. Then it had changed in a moment, that moment. He could admit that he had come looking for this, but it didn't make things any easier. Finding Leeann like that had only reminded him of the way he had left her. Of what a dick he had been. And then he had the idiotic gall to think Gunnar was his child.

And Donny still wasn't home. This gave Greg more time to think. Maybe he could ask Donny to take him out shooting. Or they could go on a hike, without anyone knowing. It could even be at the dam. Make it look like Donny was up to no good for the XX gang. Maybe even make Donny write a suicide note saying he had done the security guard all by himself.

He was just going to have to make it work. Do it clean. If he could only have believed Donny when he claimed he had never told anyone about the lake. He could have helped Donny then.

Greg's phone rang. Unknown caller. It had to be Torres.

He ignored it. He had to think.

35

Donny sat inside the old diner in the near dark. Just enough daylight got in somehow through narrow gaps in the boarded-up windows and a couple moldy skylights. He needed to hunker down a little after experiencing Wayne like that.

Wayne was a freak. There was no reigning him in. The guy only understood force. The other thing that Wayne told him after being so damn kind as to get him that ice pack was that he, Donny, was to refrain from ever going into the old diner again. It was Wayne's favorite place as a kid. How did Wayne even know that he came in here? Well, fuck Wayne. Wayne wasn't going to tell him what to do. No one had, not since Greg had all those years ago. So call it the start of Donny fighting Wayne with force instead of stroking him like some spooked alpaca.

Fuck the lot of them. He sat in a booth, grinning out into the room as if ogling after a hot new waitress. His meal was out in front of him, such a fine special today. It was two fat lines of meth, fifth of CW Irwin bourbon, tall can of Oly. Now he could finally relax. Take his time with his meal.

He was all spread out, feet up on the bench opposite. Had his phone out. He had newspapers out, too, *Bend Bulletin* and the *Oregonian*, bought them like he always did when picking up beers in the morning, along with pork rinds and Jo Joes from the deli case and hand sanitizer so that he didn't look an alky, more like a guy going fishing maybe.

He had out that card from the FBI man. He had decided it was finally time, and once he had decided on something, it was like it was already reckoned with. He was going to cooperate, tell the man things, and make it work for him. The old win-win. Only question was, how far back should he take it? To Wayne, to Karen Callum? Back to Old Man Callum? Or, and this was the real kick-ass kicker, would it, could it, reach all the way back to one Greg Simmons and what Greg Simmons had "told him" he had done at the lake one time? If it got that far. If maybe Greg Simmons went telling some things about him that he would have to counter. His word against Greg's. But, only if he had to. He would take it step-by-step, reward FBI guy with prizes as FBI guy rewarded him. "Quid pro quo," Loren Callum used to call this. He doubted he would even have to lie about the lake though. It was going too far back. The only thing that he had ever feared was if someone else, some third party, found out about it. That was when he was fucked and Greg was fucked. That was when he would have to come up with something new, no win-wins or quid pro quos, but something like clearing out and starting over. Mexico, part two.

In the meantime, though, it was just: Call that FBI guy. Make contact. The baby steps. To get him in the right frame, he was going to have a little snort first, dance around a little, and fire right the fuck up for running his sneak play, take it in for the touchdown, the big win. He had the *Bend Bulletin* out in front of him. Pork rinds and Jo Joes were in a plastic bag ready to rock. Things looked natural with the paper out on the table. And the newsprint would cover up stuff real quick if need be. He had to be more careful now, seeing how Wayne knew he liked to go here. Sure, he had an iPad, but he just never got used to reading papers online. He was careful to lay the newspaper page like a little tent so as not to budge the good shit he had underneath and mess it all over. As he did so, a blur of letters and words combined and leapt out at his eyes like 3-D movie titles, boring into his brain:

BODY FOUND AT REMOTE CASCADES LAKE
Authorities Confirm Homicide Cold Case
SANTIAM JUNCTION, Ore. (AP) — Police agencies are investigating remains of a body found at a remote lake in the higher elevations of the Willamette National Forest. . . .

Big and bold and sharp and hot the words were, like a brand. Fucking branded.

He started, shot up as if sitting on a wet seat, and the papers scattered as did the meth, like so much salt. "Fuck!"

He pushed the papers away, off the table onto the floor. "Fuck me!" He pounded the table, but that only made the meth jump and scatter more.

He stood, staring at the mess like it was a dog he'd just shot— by accident; it was an accident. He pivoted around, listening as if anyone could be here. And he realized he was actually listening for sirens outside, for cop cars—it was something he hadn't done in so long. He used to be able to tell them just by the sound of their tires.

He needed that kind of focus now. He crouched down and licked his fingers and wiped up the meth with them and licked it off his fingers, letting the bitter chemical taste burn and numb; and he swept some more off the table with the side of his hand and into his other palm, snorting that up right out of his cupped hand. He grabbed the can of Oly, cracked it open, spun off the cap of his whiskey bottle and took a swig, then the Oly. He did this mechanically, re-hitting each spot until the booth and dirty floor was clean of it, and he didn't give a shit how much dust he snorted up along the way.

He picked up the paper and read the short news article again, about the body "believed to be male . . . buried there for many years," about how someone recently dug up the remains and re-buried them, about the investigation continuing with "federal authorities alerted," and about how a "strong new lead, based on a tip, could result in more conclusive evidence."

He found the same news in the *Oregonian*. It was a news-wire item. AP meant Associated Press. The AP was everywhere, that underground spring running under and through all, like an aquifer—the published news being only the well on the surface, becoming a river, then rapids, waterfall. There could be so much more behind this, and he could never know what till it was too late. He had been here before, in this position.

He felt ten feet tall anyway, stomping around the diner, wanting to punch shit. He kicked at a bar stool, hit it so hard it flung up and did a three-sixty, almost landed back on its feet if one of the legs hadn't broke. He got the newspapers balled up in a pile. He lit them with his lighter and danced around it, letting the smoke char in his nose.

Once the flames were at their highest, he threw in the FBI man's card.

He watched it all burn, stomping in place, his hips shifting back and forth, blood pumping. Then he started dancing, and dancing, and danced on top of the embers till they were all out and good and black, practically ground right into the linoleum floor.

Well, that was that, he thought as he grabbed the CW Irwin in one hand and the Oly can and plastic bag in the other, found the back door, and instead of cracking the door open like he usually did, just went and kicked the fucker open, the bone-white daylight blasting him as he jumped into his king cab.

36

After noon, Greg saw Donny on the back porch where he himself had been half the morning. Greg had gone for a walk; he hadn't been able to sit still for another minute, not even after driving and sleeping in his car the past two nights. Donny was slumped in a porch chair. Gunnar was back from wherever he had gone, too—he was out in the open field where the sheep usually gathered. Gunnar had a small rifle and was shooting targets pinned to stacked blocks of hay. Finding the two here freaked Greg out as much as anything. They had all been on the same property today but had never run into each other. These vast lands out here were like that.

As Greg walked up, Donny raised a hand as if he was pushing back an imaginary cowboy hat. "Well, lookee. You're back," he said, sitting up.

Greg took a chair. "I am."

They watched Gunnar. He took his time aiming, getting the right stance, the shot itself almost an afterthought. On the little table between them, Donny had a carafe of coffee and two mugs as if he knew Greg would return. He also had a bottle of Oregon bourbon out—Donny didn't drink it, didn't offer it. They drank the coffee instead, in silence. Greg eyed Donny when Donny was watching Gunnar out there, and Greg could tell Donny was

doing the same to him. They were like mirror images. Greg broke
their copycat state by telling Donny that he had gone to Portland.
He used Emily as an excuse and the breakup. Emily needed to
see that he was okay, he needed clothes, and frankly he had been
frustrated as hell in Pineburg. He didn't come here to see Donny
fuck himself up again and certainly didn't want to be a part of it.
Then, on a whim, he said, he had ended up trying Leeann Holt's
parents back in Portland—and found Leeann there. He couldn't
help it. All this bringing up the past had sent him there. It seemed
the best way to cover himself, just let the falsified story reveal
itself. He and Leeann had caught up, he told Donny. She only
had kind words for Donny. At this point, Donny nodded along,
but his hands hung off the chair arms, ropey and bony like some
tired old farmer's. He said he didn't blame Greg for looking her
up. And they sat a while longer, sipping the coffee that was now
cold. A slight breeze brought over the dry, earthy smell of those
hay bales but, oddly, none of the gunpowder.

"You all right?" Greg said to Donny.

"Sure I am. Why?"

"You look like something's wrong. Anything wrong?"

Donny shrugged. "You don't look so great yourself. Long
drive?"

"Always is. Think you're almost here when you get out of the
mountains, then it's a whole 'nother slog."

"What you do? Listen to the radio? Play music on your
phone?"

"All of that, sure. News is always good. I forget to check the
news otherwise."

Donny sat up, smiling. "Me too. Never get used to all this
news on my iPad. There's too much. Too hard to concentrate on
one thing. You know?"

"Totally."

"Though I know this one trucker, he mounts his tablet right on his steering wheel, reads the latest news that way. You ever do it?"

"Sounds like a good idea." Greg added a smile.

Both had glanced at the whiskey bottle.

"You do it on the way in?" Donny said.

"What's that?"

"Read the news like that?"

"No. Oh, no. Too dangerous—"

"What you like to read? Local stuff? Or I bet you're a *New York Times* guy."

"Sure, sometimes. the *Guardian* also. Locally? *Oregonian* still too, even the *Tribune*."

A pop rang out. Both started. Greg's cup tumbled to the planks, Donny's chair skipped with a crack.

It was Gunnar out there with a new target. He got off a couple more shots. They laughed at each other, mirror grimaces.

"I think I broke my chair," Donny said. "Don't tell Karen," he added in a whisper.

"I won't if you won't," Greg added. "My cup's cracked."

They sat in silence a moment, watching Gunnar reload and pop off a few more.

"I have to say, you kinda had me on edge there, feller," Donny said eventually. "A guy like you doesn't leave his bike behind for nothing."

"I had to. It's safe in your garage."

"Sure is."

"There's another part to this, Donny. I had to make sure Leeann didn't know anything."

"Of course, she didn't. Doesn't. I'd never tell her. I told you."

They eyed each other.

"I have to make sure you don't tell anyone," Greg said.

"Sure. And I could say the same about you."

"Yes, you could." They looked away, now unable to eye each other. Greg saw the bottle. "Mind if I do?"

"Knock yourself out, cowboy. See if you can catch up." Donny handed him his cup.

Greg poured a five count, took a sip. Donny watched him, nodding.

"She's Gunnar's mom," Greg said. "She made sure I knew that."

"Yep. But we cut each other off a long time ago."

"She's had a rough time of it."

Donny opened his mouth to speak, but he didn't. Again he looked away from Greg and now from Gunnar. He was looking out in the direction of the dam, Greg noticed.

"There's another thing," Greg said. "I went back to the spot."

Donny's head whipped around. Greg paused so Donny could comment, but he got nothing.

"The first time I came here, I stopped there on the way and I dug it up," Greg added.

Torres had told him the house wasn't bugged. To be double sure, Greg would only let himself say this outside on the porch.

They glared at each other, their hands grasping at the chair arms. Greg felt all tight and numb inside, a clash of sadness and defiance.

"Then I covered it back up again," he said.

Donny nodded. He kept grasping at the chair arms as if they had oil on them and he couldn't get a tight hold. One of his eyelids twitched.

Greg threw back his whiskey and set down the cup.

"Why you telling me this?" Donny said.

"I want you to know. Also, I wanted to see how you would react."

Donny stared. He shook his head. He stared at the porch planks a long time. Greg gave him all the time he needed. He picked up his cup and poured another. Donny still had not rebounded. Greg took his cup to the railing and watched Gunnar. Gunnar was staring back at them with his rifle barrel pointed down, good and safe. It was too far for Greg to make out Gunnar's face, his mood. He held up a hand. Gunnar held up his free hand. Greg sensed Donny. He turned back around.

Donny was gazing up at him, his eyes sunken. He looked paler and a little shrunken.

"The Double Cross, they . . ." he began to say but fell silent, his lips clamped together, his chin a quivering knot.

The Double Cross, meaning Wayne, Greg guessed. Greg leaned his rear against the railing. He'd give Donny a second.

"The Double Cross," Donny said, "they're looking to show that they won't back down. That they're not just a bunch of yayhoos."

"What are they going to do?"

"Another prank." Donny shook his head at that as if he'd accidentally made a joke. "I can't believe it."

"You say it like they're going egging."

"It's not. It's suicide," Donny said.

"When are they going to do it?"

"Soon. Tonight."

"Tonight?"

"If they get their shit together. Even if they don't, they'll still go and do it," Donny said. He was peering at Greg, studying his face. He added, "Here's the deal. I'm thinking about going to the authorities, telling them everything I know."

Greg kept his face a grim mask. He let his eyebrows raise a little. The trick with Donny and any guy like him was, Greg had to go easy. Donny had to think that what Greg needed him to do was actually his own idea, fully and without doubt. "I'm not going to tell you to go to the authorities," Greg said. "It has to be your decision. But, I think you should think long and hard before you do it."

"This time around," Donny said.

"This time around what?"

"It has to be my decision."

Donny had meant this to smart. He might as well have reached over and slapped Greg across the jaw. Greg's eyeballs had heated up. "I get it, Donny," he muttered. "I get it."

"Do you? The fuck you do. You really don't know the name Charlie Adler, do you? It was the first fake ID you ever gave me. So I guess the name really stuck with me."

"Look, I . . ." Greg stared at the planks now. His thoughts scrambled and the good Oregon whiskey wasn't helping. He glanced back at the field. Gunnar had picked up his gear and was trudging over to them. Greg had to act fast. He turned back to Donny, put on half a smile.

"We really have to get beyond all that, you and me. Why don't we do something together? Just me and you. A hike or something, go for a float."

"Anything but snowboarding. That right?" Donny smiled.

Greg smiled. "That's right. Plus, gives you a good alibi in case The Double Cross do something stupid. Who we kidding? It's Wayne we're talking about."

Donny nodded at that. "Why would I need an alibi? Who'm I telling it to?"

"Everyone needs one. To anyone who's listening. There has to be good camping around here."

"You fucking hate camping," Donny said with a grumpy little rumble in his throat.

Greg held up a finger. "No, see, that's where you're wrong. I used to hate camping. But I keep telling you—I'm not that guy you used to know."

37

Leeann Holt was back in the Main Library again. She finally got an Internet terminal after waiting forty minutes. Hers was on the end of a long table of terminals with people passing by and some brushing by her like she was just a chair back. She'd been coming here more. The truth was, being in her parents' foreclosed home was beginning to freak her the fuck out. That damn house was dim and damp and drafty and cold in the rooms where she wasn't, like the parts of her half-empty bed when she stretched out, trying to get back to sleep, feeling for someone who wasn't there.

Her dad used to tell her he wished she would've gone out for sports because she would have been good at them. He also used to tell her she should have played an instrument because she would have been good at that considering how much she listened to music—junk music, he called it, but music just the same. She should have taken more math classes because the world needed more lady scientists, he said, emphasizing the lady part as if that was the real goal. Her mother telling dad she'd become a lady in her own good time. She wasn't going to become no fucking lady. She was going to become anything they weren't, she had told herself again and again. They were two half-drunks drinking cheap jug wine from the time they got home till well after she would sneak out. Lounging around in their robes, his stubble graying, her expanding chins drooping over the years as they complained about everything, everyone, like two convicts thrown together in a cell but with no plan to escape. They weren't good or bad, her dear mom and dad, just trapped in a world they thought was beneath them.

She was too fucking cool for school. She had showed them.

She had told the truth to Greg Simmons about going back to school. If the people around her here in this library could do it— your homeless, your general poor, immigrants with no English— then she could do it just the same. She had dreamed about it for so long.

The room had high ceilings and columns built into the walls and tall windows bringing in golden light from the trees outside even though it was cloudy out. Why hadn't she come here years ago? She wanted to shout it to everyone, to the librarian lady who was a little too much like her mother with her screwed-up, unsure eyes.

She needed people, she had finally realized. Independence was overrated, that was for sure. She had always said she was too proud to depend on help; but the truth, she could admit, was that she hadn't wanted to know if she could live up to the help or not. Do it right. Make them proud.

The other thing was that she had about twenty dollars left. That was it. The food she'd bought was almost gone in the house, and the house itself was going to the bank in a day or two—the bank wouldn't say when, just that someone would be showing up so be ready.

She thought about contacting that FBI agent Torres, but what could he do? She had no more information he needed. Greg had been in contact with the man.

She hunkered down and peered at the screen, at the web page that read Portland Community College: Admissions and

"Welcome back, LnHolt. You're admitted! To enroll in classes, click here . . ."

A heat filled her chest and clogged it right up, and she had to sigh to make it go away. She always got to this point. And stopped. It was becoming automatic like some damn lock.

How was she going to go to school if she had nowhere to live?

She clicked over to Facebook and entered the name Gunnar Adler, which brought up Gunnar's Facebook Profile. There was no info to click on, not even friends or a town—his daddy obviously teaching him a thing or two about privacy. But there was a photo of a somewhat serious and thoughtful boy in paintball gear, holding his paint gun downward to be safe and his shoulders straightened—the whole thing like one of those Civil War photos you could recreate in the carnival. She wondered if he had meant it that way, if he was smart and creative like that. His face looked more thoughtful too, a bit longer than Donny's and more set. He had none of Donny's dimples, and his eyes were more rich than intense. She could see how Greg Simmons could make that dumbass mistake he made. She probably shouldn't have slapped him for that. It was only twenty years late. And yet he wanted to help her, didn't he? So he said.

Leeann had to take three busses to make it back to her parents' house. When she got there, she found a letter taped to the front door from some people representing the bank. It had lots of codes and numbers and long sentences in small print, but the gist of it was that she was not at home (no shit) and that they would be back soon to take over the house. She assumed they wanted her signature so they could break in. Well, fuck them. They could go right ahead and break in.

She thought about going to visit her dad, but since he'd been calling her names like Alan and Maria and Hugo, she just didn't see the goddamn point. She marched through the house, grabbed her few loose things and whatever food she could carry, and stuffed all that into her bags by the back door. She heaved those into the back of her car and got in and turned the key, the car coughing and barely starting up, the battery hardly juicing, and the electrics whining and dragging everything down. She drove off, thinking, she would have to think carefully about where she was going to park once she stopped. It might be there a while. She might be. She only hoped it was close to the library.

They called it pride, but it was more like shit when you swallowed it. Your taste buds never got used to it. At the food bank in Old Town, she waited in a line that stretched around the block. She had found it simply by following people who had that look she knew from the people living in the forest—casual but alert at the same time, trying to hide the fear. She had been standing over two hours. Some were like her, heads down, their clothes not too dirty nor smelling while others had been out a long time and probably knew little else anymore. Some were passed out or hawking shit, but the people like Leeann ignored them. Then it started raining, and she still had another hour to go she guessed since the entrance was around the corner, still two sides of the building away. All she had was a chain link fence to lean on.

Raining. She didn't even have her old plastic raincoat with her. A rush of shame and sadness had crept up from her cold toes, filling every crevice. She buried her chin in her clavicle as her tears rolled down under her hoodie and down her chest.

"Aw, it's all right, honey," someone said to her. It was a man. "Come on over here, I'll fix that for ya."

She stepped away from the voice, and then she was marching away to somewhere, to anywhere but here. She pulled out the little phone Greg got her—cute little thing, like some Japanese teen tourist would have, they had joked, and at least that made her smile. She ducked into a doorway, but it reeked vinegary like fresh piss so she stomped on through puddles and found another doorway that faced away from the street. She reached in her pocket, unfolded the piece of paper Greg had given her.

She called the number. Emily was the girl's name. This Emily answered and asked her where she was in a pleasant little voice, not too flustered or put out. Leeann had crossed the street to a small plaza of grimy red bricks and grotesque shrubs. Some skate kid had told her this was "Paranoid Park," and that's what she told Emily.

"O'Bryant Square," Emily said. "It might take me a minute, but it won't be long. Hang tight."

"Okay."

Leeann stayed on her bench for a good hour, but it was nice just sitting there thinking someone knew she was there. Even if the girl didn't come. Leeann wouldn't blame her if she didn't. This crappy square was the kind that the homeless, junkies, and skateboarders flocked to. Something smelled like a giant loogie, spit, or both, and few things made her want to puke like that. Her forest near Oakridge was better; at least the shit had a chance to soak into the ground. Her eyes kept shutting. She let them . . .

"Leeann? Are you Leeann Holt?"

Leeann's eyes popped open. She saw a petite thing with short hair and she was pulling it off, too. She had on a quarter-length coat that was double-breasted with big buttons.

"Cute coat, honey," Leeann said.

Leeann let this Emily take her to a nearby coffee joint that had more bicycles out front in its own bike spaces than cars parked down the whole street. It was full of trendy people but was the closest place. This impressed Leeann—most girls like Emily would never take someone like Leeann to their own territory.

"My car might be broke for good, I'm thinking. I got it parked near the library, but it won't start," Leeann told Emily.

They sat in a corner by a window for privacy. Leeann told Emily how she didn't need anything, not yet. The car could sit a while, fuck it. She just wanted to check in. That old pride again. It always came back just when Leeann needed help most. But Emily rode it out. Checking in was no problem, she said, in a genuine way, like she was talking to her own mother.

By the end of their coffees, they were laughing and joking.

"I can't even get a credit card without a credit card," Leeann was saying. "I mean, why's a bank want me to run up their credit card so bad if they're so concerned I can't pay it?"

Emily had laughed at that and asked Leeann how hard it had been. Leeann told her, "Honey, know how many goddamn McJobs I tried to get? It's like I'm one of those illegals."

Emily smiled and then set her big eyes right on Leeann. She placed her little hand on Leeann's wrist. "You can stay at my place," she said, and she didn't add "if you want" or "if you need to" like everyone always did.

"Damn, that's sweet of you, honey—Greg was right. But, no. I just wanted someone to talk to."

And Emily's eyes teared right up. She touched at them with her pinky.

Leeann gave her a second. They sat there with their hands wrapped around their coffees. "Tell me about it," she said.

"Why? No. My problems aren't really . . . problems."

"Not like I got. It's okay. You go right ahead."

"Well, I feel bad," Emily told her. "This guy Judd, he wants to see me all the time. Greg doesn't even know. Neither of them do." The tears rolled down.

Leeann touched Emily's hand around her coffee mug and held it there a while, a whole lot of warm going on. They didn't need to say anything, not like guys always did.

"Hey, I should be the one crying," Leeann said finally. "I tell ya, that one job, I fuckin' plucked more fuckin' chickens."

Emily snorted a cute little laugh, and a smile broke out. That a girl.

"Me too!" she said. "Back in Iowa I did. People don't know that here, but it's true. I don't keep it from them. But they'd just think I was joking if I did."

"Well, I know you're not, girl. I know."

38

That afternoon, Greg holed up in Tam's Tavern. He nursed an iced tea as Tam eyed him from behind the bar, and he eyed her back while she helped the few customers—a booth of four men who looked retired or at least out of work long enough to appear so. Tam hadn't talked to Greg much, and he told himself she was just busy. What more could she say? Offer him more iced tea? Especially if she was on to him. Neither of them was supposed to talk about the obvious.

It was time for him to do the job as Torres had laid out—either get Donny to come in on possibly some kind of witness protection deal or help Torres do his job so well that Donny got the full wrath of the Feds along with the rest of them. But Greg had his own route, his third way—make sure Donny never spoke about what had ended at the lake. He had to be ready, get his duckies in a row. So, camping it was. Donny had said he was up for it. Possibly tomorrow. Greg made himself ready to go any second. Before coming back into town, he had mounted his rack and bike back on the trunk and stowed all his bags in the car. He couldn't lose his nerve. He should confront Donny once they were alone, see what he did. Then be prepared to do it. For that, he would have to get a weapon, something that he could later say was Donny's. He thought about Gunnar's rifle, but he didn't want to implicate him. When he was back at the Callum house, he would have to find a weapon that was Donny's and somehow sneak it along.

The only question was: Should he tell Torres about the Double Cross planning another "prank," as Donny called it? Either way, it could throw his plans into even more chaos.

The four men left. Tam disappeared into the back, leaving Greg alone at the bar. Stewing. Afterward, he told himself that he would have to make up the best lie he had ever declared and stick to it, rehearsing it over and over before coming back in from the woods but not waiting too long before the blood dried.

A grim thought clawed at him, at his gut: In the aftermath, who would look after Gunnar and even Leeann? It wasn't like this place was going to be much better off. This town had to get its act together.

When Tam came back out, the words spilled out of his mouth like too much iced tea:

"Why isn't anyone doing anything about it?"

"Come again?" Tam said.

"About the dam? About all of it? Why aren't you?"

Tam set down her towel, folded it, and lowered it into her bleach bucket. She faced him with arms folded across her chest. "When you say 'you,' who do you mean exactly?"

"You. Native Americans. American Indians. However you say it."

"'American,' I usually say. What do you expect me, us, to do? Hold some creepy fucking pep rally with guns? Harder to do when you don't have Callums or Adler as a sponsor."

"No. Of course not. Hold a protest, something. Try to get the press here."

"Kid, you haven't been here long. We've been doing that for years. Decades. No one gives a shit about fish except the people who give a shit about fish—and live off fish. So, scour the Internet and you'll find this and that about our efforts here, but you won't read about the crowds that come out and certainly not about TV cameras."

"I didn't know."

"You got your own business to worry about. The water issue will come out. Here's a fact in the West: Private little utilities can control irrigation and make deals for irrigation and buy up land that's not irrigated. Not to mention power generation. If the conditions are right—or wrong, as it were. But the real issue they want us to believe? That the dam's too important to their business, and they create all the business here, giving people jobs, however meager, so they're too big to fail. They'd pull everyone down with them."

"This is what I'm saying," Greg said. "It doesn't look like people can get pulled down much further."

"That's a good point."

"But, it's not yours to make."

"Our main focus has been the salmon," Tam said. "It's much broader than that though. It's about our legacy, our right. I shouldn't have to say that every time, though I do."

"But you're not big enough."

"There just aren't many of my people here. Our time might have passed. Not like in other areas. Take the Klamath for example. But even they have a hard time of it. They've been promised help for decades, practically a century. And so have we. Until most of us went and left. I left."

"Yet you came back?"

Tam rolled her eyes as if fighting the urge to make a self-disparaging joke.

Greg held his iced tea with both hands, studying the ice melting. He wanted to bring up her daughter, but Torres had forbidden him to talk, and he'd already said enough.

Tam eyed him a moment, giving him the slightest nod, like a little salute. "Excuse me, I got things to do," she said. "Thanks for bringing it up though—I mean it," she added and went into the back.

Greg stared into his ice tea, which had reduced to slivers of ice drowning in an inch of watery amber. A squashed lemon wedge. There are people whose driving ambition is to control others, he thought, and there are people whose driving ambition is to resist the control of others. The problem is, Greg knew, the resisting often becomes the controlling but even worse. The country kid's fear of becoming a farmhand reliant on a rich rancher turns that kid into a cunning robber baron. The city kid's fear of being an overeducated slave in a corporate cubicle turns him into a corrupt broker or politician. This played out in a million other varieties, scenarios, tragedies—

The front door burst open with a flash of light. Torres bolted inside and in three long steps reached Greg at the bar. He grabbed Greg under each arm, hauled him through the swinging door into the kitchen. Greg tried to shake it off. Torres tightened his grip and had Greg off the ground, his toes dragging like a toddler's. Torres pushed him out a back door.

Torres' blue Chevy pickup pulled up. Driving it was Field Agent Mitchum, who Greg had met at Torres' secret roost. Mitchum was a stout little man with a square head, like a wrestling coach, and crow's feet, Greg imagined, from a life of stakeouts and vigilant teamwork. Mitchum pivoted around, checking all directions. Torres pushed Greg around to the passenger side, threw him in, locked the door. He came around to the drivers' side and drove them away.

Torres drove with bursts of speed like a man who wants to break the speed limit but knows there's radar. He parked them in a small parking lot behind the town's tiny library. Greg and Torres said nothing the whole ride. Greg could practically hear Torres' teeth gnashing. Mitchum had made his way over and stood a block up on Callum Street watching out for any incoming persons of interest or anyone trailing them, all the while looking like a bored guy waiting for a bus.

The blood had drained from Greg's face, he could feel it. It all rushed to his heart in a panic. He had ignored what Donny had told him, was really telling him. Donny had tipped him off about the Double Cross, but he had been too wrapped up in planning his own way out. Greg sat up straight and tried to match Torres' and Mitchum's hard looks as if he were ready for action too.

"What do you got?" Torres began, "you have something—"

"Donny thinks that they're going to pull another prank," Greg blurted as if he couldn't wait to tell Torres.

"A prank? When?"

"Tonight, it looks like."

"This night, tonight?" Torres pulled out his phone.

Greg grabbed Torres' wrist. Torres glared at him.

"I have to tell you something," Greg said.

Torres was still glaring, but then he sighed and lowered his phone to the dashboard. He nodded; he would let Greg have his say. Greg let go of his wrist.

"It's about when Donny and I were teens," Greg said.

"All right. You got one minute."

"Donny was this real bumpkin. I was the only one who didn't make fun of him, okay, not to his face anyway. He was funny. He had a way. Chicks dug him. Sure, he had a screw loose even then, but that's kinda cool when you're eighteen, and you want the world fucked up."

"Country in the city. Got it. Look, I'm not your dad—"

"Just listen. We did speed, coke. Even did crank when we couldn't get those—what they call meth now. And, we did a couple break-ins, little mom and pop stores."

"I don't think you should tell me this."

"I do. Because the thing was, it was all me. It was my idea. I led him to all of it."

"And then you quit. Right? You stopped and he didn't. So some are smarter than others." Torres reached for his phone.

"Wait. Okay? Just, wait. Later, when we weren't getting along so well? We . . . were going to break into this hobby shop near my house. I knew where they kept the money. Donny really wanted to do it, way more than me. You see, before that, around that time, something . . . had happened to him."

"Nothing just happens."

"This did. It was like someone else had taken over his body. His mind."

"I think that's called the late teens. Growing up. And look who had something to do with it."

"I admit that. I told you. But, this was different. It was like a switch had turned on, you know?"

"It happens. I could see how that can happen. Go on. What do I need to know?"

"I told him I would be there. We were going to do this hobby shop, middle of the night. I hated the owner guy. This one was my idea too."

"Don't tell me. Donny's first arrest. Breaking and entering? Like I said. You got smart."

"I never showed up. I was the one—and then I didn't get his back."

Torres sighed. "Okay, fine, you screwed him over. That what you want to hear? And tell me something else: Why is your bike back on your car? You going somewhere?"

Greg's chest burned and seemed to expand like a balloon, pressing at his ribs. "You don't understand!" he shouted. Hot tears spilled out, ran down his cheeks. "Afterward? With his one fucking phone call? He calls me. Me."

"And?"

Greg turned away from Torres. He could take Torres' pity or disgust, but he could never give away that he wasn't telling the whole truth. He wondered what was worse: Accidentally killing a man or having the cunning to cover it up. Donny had done the deed, sure, but Greg had schemed to make the murder vanish forever. He had expunged all trace of a human being. And now he was aiming to do it again.

"I didn't pick up the phone," Greg said. "Not even Donny knows that. I got questioned about it briefly. I said that I hardly knew Donny. Said, he was new in town. I didn't really know him no matter what he says. He was a little bit of a hanger-on, if not a stalker, I told people. My alibi was always easy. I was a good student. I was the one going to Dartmouth."

"All right, look. We make choices. You made yours. Donny Wilkie's obviously gotten over it. Has he ever brought it up?"

"No. I thought he would for sure, but he hasn't. We ran into each other after that, right after he got out, and I thought he was going to fucking kill me, considering. He probably should have. I told him that I couldn't get out of the house and that he should've waited for me. This being before cell phones."

"What did he say?"

"He said he didn't need me to do it. He said he understood me looking out for myself."

"He definitely learned from it, in his way."

"That's what he had said: 'I learned a lot from all this.' But none of it was doing him any favors down the road."

"Well. There you go," Torres said.

"But, it's more than that. The thing is, I don't believe him. We might be going camping, tomorrow. That's why I got my bike, my bags. I'm freaked out though. I think, maybe he's going to use it . . . to make something happen."

"You think? I'm not seeing it. Besides, the Double Cross will need him."

"I don't think he wants that. I told you. It's all bullshitting."

"Well, he might not have a choice."

Greg shook his head, playing the innocent. He held up his hands in frustration.

"Look, okay," Torres added, "so maybe you're the cause of Donny in the big scheme of things. I get it. All I care about is what are you going to do about it?"

"I'm going to show them. Donny, Leeann Holt, even Gunnar. Show them how I've changed. How a person can change."

Torres stared a moment as if waiting for more, but Greg was finished. He had said what he needed to. It was done and doled out. Even he didn't know how much of it was true.

"Okay. We're good? Then good luck," Torres said and grabbed his phone. He dialed and turned away, talking on the phone in coded language and acronyms that only emphasized to Greg how on his own he was.

Torres hung up and his face looked drawn, deflated. "This prank of theirs? It has to be something to do with Pineburg Dam. Am I right?"

"I don't know. Donny didn't say."

Torres added a snort of annoyance. "And you didn't fucking ask."

"What about Donny?" Greg said.

"Word is, he's supposed to be there this time. Running the show."

"What?" Greg straightened up.

"A leader needing to show he's a leader and all that." Torres added a grunt. "So much for your campfire."

The situation had just changed and drastically. But one thing still didn't gibe. Why was Torres not riled and ready? Torres should have kicked him out of the truck already. Why would Torres even take the time to listen to Greg's story with all that was going down?

"Shouldn't you be all fired up?" Greg said.

Torres sighed.

"Well? Shouldn't you?" Greg added.

Torres paused a moment, staring out the window. "There's a meeting coming late next month—a town-hall type event here, about the dam. All the players will be in town. State, fed, the main interests. Whole delegation. It's been secret, a real tight lid. I was the field scout. I probably shouldn't tell you that, but, fuck it."

"So, Wayne and company couldn't have known. That's good, right? They're in the dark . . ." Greg let his words trail off. The way Torres shifted his lips back and forth like he needed to spit already told Greg the answer. The Double Cross was forcing Torres' hand without even knowing it. Torres wouldn't get to play the hero this way. By foiling their prank now, he wouldn't be preventing anything but a bunch of yahoos whose ideological platform seemed to be the proliferation of nasty practical jokes. Then the truth hit Greg. He said:

"Ah, I get it now. You want them to know about the meeting."

"What are you talking about?" Torres said.

"You know exactly what I mean—you wanted them to know so that they would make a play for it. And you could be the one who stops them."

"You got no idea what I want."

"I have some idea. I can see it on your face. And I sure as hell am not doing it—I'm not leaking that info, if that's what you're trying to get me to do."

"Shut up, just shut it," Torres, said. His phones buzzed, rang. He picked up, listened, and started up the pickup. "I'm on it," he said into the phone. "Be ready to rock."

He drove off with Greg still in the pickup. He slammed on the brakes with a squeal.

"Get out," he shouted at Greg. "Get the hell out."

39

Greg was in a dilemma—a vice, more like. If he went to the dam, he could be seen as Torres' man all along and Donny would know it. Donny would feel betrayed, again. That alone could make him spill the beans about the lake. The game had changed. If Torres had it right, Donny was only stalling by telling Greg they would go camping. He wouldn't be able to get at Donny, to get him to react, kill him, whatever he had to do.

The Callum house was his only chance.

It was getting dark by the time he got there, quiet all around except for his bike rack rattling on his trunk. He pulled up with his lights off.

He just didn't buy it that Donny would hang himself like Torres was saying. The guy had gone so far as to fake his own death to stay alive and keep living. He would never let himself be caught at the dam.

The garage door was open, no cars. Greg poked around outside. He found Donny's pickup parked around the side of the house. The house had a couple lights on somewhere deep inside, giving the front windows a glow only, like a train set home illuminated from some small light bulb behind.

Greg went inside. A light was on in Donny's study, the door open. Greg walked toward it. He heard drawers opening and closing and someone stomping around as if looking for something.

He heard Donny's voice, frantic like Greg hadn't heard it for years, if ever: "You there? Goddamn it, I told you I'll be there. Any sec. I'm in my truck right now hauling ass, what the fuck you think?"

Greg entered, but with one foot only, like a cat testing out a perch.

Donny had hung up. He had one eye on Greg. He smoked from a glass pipe, really sucking it down. Papers were strewn about the den. Drawers hung open. Meth paraphernalia lay out on Donny's desk. A mirror held lines of coarse white powder.

Donny blew out smoke with a pop. "Yes, that's meth. Oh, so scary. You all watch too much *Breaking Bad* or whatever. But you know what? There are people who do benefit from it."

"Until they don't." Greg moved inside the room, but kept close to the door.

"I'm practical," Donny said. "I usually snort or ingest it, keep things even keel. But tonight? It's a special night."

"You're supposed to be there," Greg said. "At the dam. You were talking to Wayne about it just now, I heard."

"Yeah? And you were supposed to meet me that night," Donny said. His hands grasped at air as pincers that needed to itch, scratch, pull. "Said you fucking would. You said robbing that hobby shop was the best deal ever 'cause the owner was a dick."

"Donny. Come on. I was seventeen."

"Eighteen. I was still seventeen. You were going to score us the coke too, remember? From Leeann."

"Here we go," Greg said.

"Here we go," Donny sneered, mocking Greg. He stomped in a circle, and who knew what the meth was doing inside him. How do you convince a child that his puppy needs to be put to sleep?

Donny stomped his way over to the window. "Know what?" he said, his back to Greg. "I shoulda killed you instead of that old tin badge."

244

"Who?"

"Don't give me that bullshit."

"You shouldn't say that," Greg said. "You don't mean that."

Or should he say it? This place could be bugged too, like the Rooster Lair. Torres said it wasn't, but who knew? If it were, Donny would be doing all Greg's work for him.

"You got no idea what I mean." Donny twitched, stole peeks out the window. "I saw you coming just now—saw you this whole time since you came here. Know that? So don't think I didn't. I let you in here. Let you play around. I did."

Something about the way Donny said that, with that know-it-all tone, reminded Greg of someone Greg had known. Someone he had left behind. Then he realized: It was himself. Something about the horrid thought made Greg bound into the center of the room, his legs and arms surging with mad energy. "Oh, right, just like you let Wayne in. Am I right? Or did he only let you play on account of the Callums?"

"Shut up. Just shut the fuck up with that."

Greg was like the one on meth now. He pivoted around the middle of the room, his arms cocked. Bugged or not, there were things that needed to be said. "That big speech? To your followers? You don't believe that bullshit any more than I do."

Donny faced Greg. "Hey, if they're stupid enough. Oh, what, was it going to be so much better in your Cascadia LaLa Land?"

"It's a book. Mine's just a book. But it will be; it will be." Greg was shouting. "So fuck you!"

"And screw Leeann," Donny said. "She gave up Gunnar. She was the one. How could a mother give up custody? After I went and married her and tried to make it work. What did you make work? Words? Some stupid fucking book."

"It's more than that. People believe in it. And good people will find their way to it. Want to know why I'm still here? It's Gunnar.

What do you think he's gonna do when he finds out about all this? Look at you. The great Charlie Adler's a fucking meth-head."

Donny sucked in a gulp of air as if taking a hit. He started to leave the room.

"That's all you got?" Greg said. "You haven't done anything? You regret nothing. You have nothing to hide . . ."

Donny had passed Greg. He turned back. He glared at Greg.

"You did it," Donny said. "You're the one."

"Did what?"

"You tipped them off. There's a news story. All over the place. Someone found the body. Don't look at me like that, like you don't know. At the lake. I'm thinking someone tipped them off, more like. Told the cops. Or is working with them."

"Donny, I . . . You got to help me out here. I don't know what you're taking about—"

A flash of hot pain hit Greg's eye. It shot out the back of his head, yanking him backward.

Donny had punched him, a sucker punch.

40

A small hill of rock formations presided over the entrance road to Pineburg Dam, like some ancient and crumbling castle ruins that the earth had reclaimed as its own. These rock palisades were so dark by night that their silhouette didn't always show against the sky. On this night the profile of a man could barely be seen moving over the hill's crest, between a gap in the rocks. FBI Special Agent Richard Torres jogged over the hill followed by four others—FBI agent Mitchum and three far-flung county sheriffs who'd been shocked awake by the FBI calling them. All wore black Kevlar vests. They scanned the rocks behind them, their path ahead, and the road down before them constantly, like the last soldiers on a lost patrol fearing they'd be outnumbered again.

They jogged along the hillside of the road, keeping to its shadow as they made the turn that would reveal the dam. All were surprised to see no light coming from that direction. The lights to the dam entrance were out—lights any human could get at if they really wanted. The dam itself though, while not large, still had lights on that shown like a stadium at night.

Torres led his men in closer, to take stock. They crouched in the gully of the entrance road. The requisite Off Limits sign lay in the road battered and bent as if hit by sledgehammers. The gate, part of a chain link fence that ran from either side of the entrance, was torn off and trampled. Padlocks had been cut.

Objects caught the light from the dam. Fish. Salmon lay strewn about near the entrance, shiny and slimy, some still flopping.

Torres pulled his Glock and the rest followed suit, Mitchum with an assault rifle, two of the sheriffs with Glocks like Torres', and the other with a shotgun. They crept closer at Torres' hand instructions, stepping around the fish.

Inside the gate, more fish, fish blood, and what looked like a mound of cow shit left a trail along the dam's passageway leading to the dam house, a stout concrete block structure a third of the way in atop the dam and no bigger than a large backyard shed. The dam itself stretched no longer than a couple playing fields. Still, it stood high above the reservoir, higher than a man could jump and survive.

Torres led his men to the busted gate. They walked like crabs now, guns aiming. They glanced at each other as they eyed the mess and made faces from the smell and sureality of it.

They spread out and took up positions along the fencing, aiming through the chain links and sweating from crouching, listening, and breathing through their mouths so they didn't have to smell the fish mess.

One county sheriff kept watch behind them as they focused on the gatehouse about forty yards away. The metal door was dented, partially open. The trail of slime and shit led inside. They heard a couple thumps and banging, and they reset their grips on their aiming guns.

The dam house door flew open, clanging against concrete.

A cow stumbled out.

A cow?

Two locals followed, Casey and Damon. They held a whiskey bottle between them and staggered as if the bottle was the only thing keeping them up. Each had a hunting rifle.

The cow stumbled in a circle, its tail and side quarters bumping at the passageway fence, not sure where to go. On the cow's hind quarters: X X.

Casey and Damon looked out, saw Torres and his men. The two froze. Three more Double Cross regulars stumbled out of the dam house, laughing and drinking. One carried a Double Cross flag.

Torres had dropped to his stomach for cover as had his men behind him.

He didn't have to yell a warning. Casey and Damon dropped their rifles. They got down and lay with hands up. Seeing them, the cow lowered itself down. The other three Double Cross regulars already lay prostrate.

"Don't shoot, don't shoot. Oh, god. Please don't shoot," one muttered.

Torres came in closer, onto the passageway, aiming at Casey and Damon.

Damon vomited.

Torres crouched over Casey. "Wayne Carver!" he shouted. "Where is he? Charles Adler? Where is he?"

41

A warm thickness spread down the side of Greg's throbbing face. He touched it. Blood.

Greg looked up, squinting. A blur of a shadow stood over him. It became Donny. Donny's eyes had softened. He bent down and grabbed Greg by the hand.

"I thought it was you . . . I thought you were the one who might of did it," Greg muttered.

"Come on," Donny said, his voice gentler.

They heard a grunt.

Wayne Carver stood in the doorway of the study. He aimed a rifle at them.

Was Greg really seeing this? The gun was black and stocky but with a long skinny barrel. Wayne wore tan combat boots, desert camo fatigues, and a Kevlar vest, looking like he just stepped off a military transport craft; all that was missing was the helmet.

"I knew it," Wayne said. His eyes had locked on Donny.

Donny was still crouched, but his hands had raised. Greg's arms went up.

"Little lover's quarrel we got here?" Wayne said.

Donny cracked a smile for Wayne but it stretched thin. "Hey, come on, feller. I'm just playing Greg here. Just in case."

Wayne stepped closer, his eyes darkening. "In case of what?"

"What about the dam?" Donny said. "Why aren't you there?"

Wayne laughed. "Now, that there's me playing you. I wasn't there either. I only wanted to see if you'd really show. I guess I got my answer." He aimed the barrel at Greg. "Get up, your back up straight. Turn around. Let me have the back of your head."

Greg did so. He was on his knees, his back to Wayne and that skinny barrel. Was this a test, some joke? Greg couldn't believe this was happening. His logic wouldn't let it. He eyed Donny.

Donny lunged at Wayne. Wayne swung the butt of his rifle. It hit Donny's stomach with a thwack, like a meat tenderizer on a steak.

Air launched out Donny's mouth with a whoosh and he dropped, stunned, his eyes wide.

"Turn around!" Wayne shouted at Greg.

Greg did it. He felt the barrel's mouth, millimeters from his skin, prickling up the hairs of his neck. "Listen," he said, "you have to listen to me—"

A crack—a blast. Red mist and a roundish object flew over Greg's head and hit the desk. It looked like a deflated gym ball dunked in berry jam.

It was most of Wayne's head.

Greg jerked to the side. The rest of Wayne's body thudded at the floor, almost on top of him.

Greg's eyes found the doorway. Gunnar stood there, his stance rigid, still aiming his rifle at Wayne's body.

Donny and Greg stayed in a crouch. Gunnar couldn't stop staring, aiming at Wayne.

"Shit, boy," Donny said.

Gunnar saw his father now, eyes wide too as if he'd only just now discovered him here. He released his stance, mechanically. He stood the rifle against the wall. He sat in a chair, leaning forward. He wore his dark paintball gear.

Donny scrambled over and hugged Gunnar. Gunnar hugged him back, squeezing, his fingers white from it.

Donny turned back to Greg. "Listen to me. I did it. Okay? I did this," he said.

"No," Greg said.

"No, dad," Gunnar said.

"Be quiet. Please, be quiet," Donny said in the tone of someone who just needed to think. He said to Greg, "I did it. I did it before. You know I did. That one time I did. So I did it again."

Greg nodded. Okay. He would have demanded the same to save a son.

Donny kissed Gunnar on the forehead and stood facing the room. He looked around. He looked to Greg. "Take care of him?" he said.

"Of course."

Gunnar was crying. Donny went back to his son and held him.

"Turn yourself in," Greg said to Donny's back. "Right now. I'll help you. It wasn't your fault. You couldn't control it. You can give them information."

Donny turned back to Greg, eyeing him up and down as if recognizing Greg wasn't what he thought. "That's what I was going to do," Donny said. "Then you come along."

"You still can. You can."

"Just don't say anything about you and me, what we done. That it?"

"What do you think?"

"But what if they know? What if they already know? Huh? They could use that against us? Between us." Donny's face had gone pale with urgency, with anxiety, and a stream of drool and sweat and tears shone on him like someone had rubbed his face with an oil.

Donny had a point, Greg had to admit. "Just don't say anything," he heard himself say, his voice calming, in monotone. "You don't know what they're talking about. You know how to do that. You know how better than anyone."

Donny stood again, between Greg and the doorway. "Sure. And I learned it all from you," he said. He backed up to the doorway. Gunnar was watching him, his eyes stuck on his dad, pleading with his dad to look at him. Donny kept his eyes on Greg. "Want this house?" he said. "Karen'll take you in. She just won't love you. You're not her type."

Donny turned and headed out the door and down the hallway.

Greg moved to run after, but Gunnar in the room made him stop. He checked himself. Oddly, he had no blood on him except for a few specks. The trajectory must have gone right over his head. Maybe he had some on his back.

"You don't have any on you," Gunnar muttered.

A back door slammed shut.

A handkerchief stuck out of Wayne's back pocket, a blue plume. Not knowing what else to do, Greg yanked it out and used it to wipe down Gunnar's rifle as Gunnar sat there stunned, staring at the body. Greg grabbed Gunnar by the shoulder.

"Come on. We have to go. We have to go now."

42

Greg's eye ached and swelled and he told himself to get ice when he could. The bleeding had already stopped; the gash was just broken skin, and the bruise would be far worse. He could drive, no problem. Gunnar directed him to a junction, to an old gas station that had been closed for years. Gunnar disappeared around the back, somehow made it inside and opened the garage. Greg drove in, parked. Gunnar had a flashlight. He led Greg into the office where the moonlight through the windows let them see so he clicked off his light. Gunnar led them to a desk and two chairs, holding Greg's hand and calling out objects Greg should avoid hitting. They sat in silence a few minutes. Gunnar sobbed a little, and Greg held him by the shoulder.

Gunnar wiped at his eyes. He told Greg everything he knew. This gas station was where Donny had hid out when he first came to town many years ago. Gunnar knew it like his own bedroom. He could get in from the back way or from the roof. There was even a cellar and a gas lamp if they needed it. It was safe. Outside was also where the Double Cross had ambushed the three men from the Feds and state. Suddenly Greg wasn't feeling so safe, but Gunnar said it was the best place to be because no one—not even Double Cross—would be stupid enough to come back to the scene of a crime. That didn't stop Greg from crouching at the windows and peering out. His stomach ached with hunger.

Gunnar produced a package of beef jerky for Greg. Gunnar had other emergency goods stowed away, he said. He even had a pay-as-you-go phone that couldn't be traced, though the signal was no good here.

"I know where dad went," Gunnar said.

He laid it all out, proving his hypothesis as if explaining a science experiment at school.

"You sure he's heading there? You gotta be sure, buddy."

"I'm sure. He's my dad." Gunnar added, now reciting his own instruction manual, "When you are on the run and on the move, you must become a creature of habit or you will not make it." Greg imagined Donny drilling a young Gunnar with such lines. Words to flee by.

"Stealth helps too," Greg said. "I'll have to leave the bicycle here and the rack with it. They know me by my bike." He had to; otherwise, he might as well fly Cascadia flags from the car and airbrush headshots of himself on the doors.

"It's safe here," Gunnar said. "I like your bike."

Greg pressed fifty dollars in Gunnar's hand. "Don't look at me like that," Greg said. "You'll need this to get by. I know someone—Tam, of Tam's tavern. Can you get to her?" Gunnar nodded. "It's a good thing you have that phone," Greg added. "Call her when you get a signal."

Gunnar nodded. "I have my own ways back into town. No one will know."

"Good. Now, once Tam says it's okay to come, remain there with her and stay put. She won't let anyone get near you, not even any Feds. She'll keep you out of sight. I know she will. All right? Anyone does ask, you were there with her the whole time. You were nowhere near your house tonight."

"No, I mean, right," Gunnar said. He fought more sobs, and Greg felt a pang of guilt leaving Gunnar in this situation. How many times had Donny put his son on the spot like this? And now here he was playing the role of Donny.

Greg's phone rang. Unknown caller. It had to be Torres. He let it ring.

"Can you tell me something?" Gunnar said. "What was dad talking about? About what you two did one time, years ago?"

Greg looked into Gunnar's eyes. He held him by the shoulders. "It was nothing. We did a couple break-ins when we were young. He was always scared someone would find out. You can imagine how it must have bothered him back then. He was your age."

"Yes," Gunnar said. "All right, time to go. You have to go. I'll be okay."

"Good man."

Greg pulled over, gathered dirty wet snow from the side of the road, dumped it into a plastic bag he had, and put the cold bag over his swelling eye. He began to feel safer as he drove on. He was up in the Cascades and taking all secondary highways back to Portland. He and Donny had a few things working in their favor, he realized. He hoped. Torres would have to deal with the Pineburg Dam incident, since that was his turf; meanwhile, there was a murder at the Callum place. Greg imagined Torres and his agent Mitchum pulling up to the Callum house and finding a corpse in the den—the body of one Wayne Carver, the public leader of a would-be militia group at war with the Feds. They would also see that Donny had taken off only with what he needed to live on the lam. Maybe there was a safe in the house too, or a secret stash now emptied? Whatever they discovered, it would require eyes and legs and Torres could only leave so much to his county colleagues. He and Donny had some time on their side.

The sun came up over the Willamette Valley, painting the fields purple along Highway 99. Less than an hour from Portland. Greg's phone rang again. Unknown caller. He turned it off. And felt less safe. Could his phone give him away? Was that even legal? He wondered if Torres would defy the rules again to locate Donny—and now Greg himself.

By eight in the morning, Greg sat in a doorway about five blocks from Emily's apartment—his home. He had a beanie-style stocking cap on and could have been a homeless guy to the casual observer. His car was parked on a side street. He had another bag of ice on his face.

Emily walked up and sat next to him. Right on time. She was always that. Another reason he didn't deserve her. She had on a stocking cap like his but with a ball on top. In better times, they would've chuckled about it.

"Are you okay?" Emily said.

"Yes." He pulled away the ice to show her the little bandage. He'd live.

"Did you deserve it?"

"Depends. Anyone come by your place asking for me?"

"No. Who is anyone?" Emily said.

"They'll probably look like they're in the FBI."

Emily didn't seem to wince, but she hugged herself as if cold.

"Actually, they are the FBI," Greg said. "If they come, just tell them exactly what happened. You saw me, right here, and I told you tell to them this."

"Okay." After a silence, Emily said, "Does this have anything to do with your Cascadia activities?"

"No. Certainly not. I'm not wanted for anything." As far as he knew. "I'm sorry about this. I'm just trying to help someone."

"I gather that."

"Look. About Leeann. I owe her. I'm sorry," Greg said.

"Quit saying that. Is she in danger?" Emily said.

"Maybe. I don't know."

"Then I know where she is."

Greg hopped on the Number 15 bus and got off minutes away in Central Eastside where bridge overpasses rose over warehouses and train tracks close to the Willamette River. Renamed Produce Row, this area of old brick buildings, narrow loading-dock lanes, and equipment supply stores had been proclaimed the next big thing in Portland ever since a DIY skateboard park sprung up under the Burnside Bridge in the early 1990s. Greg's Cascadia Congress was held here. But the area hadn't fully arrived just yet, and the stretch under the on-ramp to the Morrison Bridge definitely was not there. The street was a patchwork of cracked concrete, asphalt, and exposed cobblestones showing old street-car tracks. The bridge overpass hovered above, a concrete sky. It sheltered a homeless village of tents and tarps, cardboard, and shopping carts that lined one side of the street. Few of the inhabitants were out, Greg saw as he walked along the hovels, and he wondered if they were still inside their structures or already out doing what they had to do to get through another day. The few he asked didn't know of anyone who fit the description of Leeann Holt, but Greg suspected there was an unwritten rule always to say no.

He walked the few blocks south toward the Hawthorne Bridge overpass and the next homeless camp, the river and the I-5 Freeway at his right shoulder and the railroad tracks to his left crisscrossing the river bridges.

"Oh, sorry." He'd bumped into someone coming around a corner.

Leeann?

Her look said the same about him. She had a blanket wrapped around her and wore a baseball cap that was too big, her hair hanging down like greasy strings.

Greg gave her a hug. She hugged him back and grasped at his shoulder blades, holding on. He didn't ask if she was okay—of course she was not.

"Donny's here," he said. "In town. Gunnar told me."

"Donny hit you? What happened?"

"I deserved it."

Leeann held her chin up. She pushed hair out of her face.

"It's all right. Come on." Greg took her arm and led her off.

Leeann shook her arm free and led him along instead, asking him where his car was.

"Where's Gunnar?" she said once they reached the car.

"Safe. I got him safe."

Leeann sighed in relief. "Good. Okay."

Greg's phone rang. He let it. "Torres again," he said to answer Leeann's stare.

"He won't like that," Leeann said. "You sure Gunnar's safe?"

"As sure as I can be. Where you taking me?"

"Years ago, before me and Donny hit Mexico? We had this nice little squat up the river a ways. It's got to be the place."

"That's what Gunnar said too. He told me."

Leeann stopped, glaring at him. "He did, did he?" Then she broke into a smile that was broad and rare, one Greg had not remembered—it seemed like pride, he thought.

Greg delivered Leeann back to Emily, who got Leeann to a budget hotel room and set her up. Greg took off. Emily called Greg back to report: She had left Leeann in the hotel room sitting on the bed, just her and the phone that Greg bought her. She had Leeann's car towed too and paid for it. Leeann had thanked her and told her she should go home. But, Emily told Greg, she couldn't help noticing that Leeann kept staring at her new phone as Emily pulled the door shut. It meant Leeann might call Torres, Greg thought, but what could he do? He just had to hope she wouldn't.

North of the city, Greg walked along the east bank of the Willamette River. Nearby shipyards and their cranes loomed as Greg navigated a void in the riverscape—a low basin that held train tracks, a few abandoned buildings, and rusted, busted moorings that poked up from the water like giant deadly weeds. The punks and skaters called this area Pirate Town. Greg could see the tallest downtown buildings when he looked behind him, which was often. His path was a mix of railway gravel, oily scrubs of grass, and encroaching river mud and rocks, bringing a smell somewhere between algae and motor oil.

He tried to predict Torres' next moves. Torres had to be in Portland soon if not already. Greg could just see him and his agents pulling up to the Holt home to find it confiscated and Leeann gone.

He pushed on, but the ground started to feel softer and wetter so he moved up onto the train tracks, trying not to stumble on the greasy ties.

He wondered if Torres was on to him yet. They had their ways, and Torres wasn't against flanking the rules.

He looked at his phone again. It was already off. He looked at the sky. Who knew what devices they could track? He took his plastic bag, shook and wiped it dry, and set his phone in it, wrapping it tight. He dug a little hole in the gravel, set the phone down inside, and placed a rock over that. And he walked on.

43

At the farthest end of Pirate Town stood an abandoned grain exchange from the days of the robber barons. The two-story stone block of a building looked majestic but was small, like a rural bank or a library branch. Decades of neglect made it look blacked out, bombed out. The sun was about to go down, casting angular yet misshapen shadows down its facade.

Greg approached, peeking in windows and doors. He shouldered a side door, and it opened, delivering him into a minefield of debris and smells he didn't want to know about. The tall ceilings and windows made for more long shadows. It was becoming night inside here already. Gunnar had told him to bring a flashlight, so he'd bought one at a minimart. He clicked it on. Dust and mold covered the overturned tables, chairs, and hard contours of unknown origin, and green-spotted streaks of mold owned the walls like ivy—one of those images that belonged on some blog for majestic buildings in ruins. The floor plan was open, and Greg imagined traders hustling here back in the day. He saw a broad and grand stairway that rose from the far middle of the floor, leading upward. Now he clicked off the flashlight. Gunnar and Leeann had each told him not to use the flashlight if he could help it since it invited trouble and spooked any others holing up here.

He headed up the stairs. The second floor had lower ceilings and fewer and smaller windows, the first floor having served as the showy main entrance hall while this was the grimmer paper-pushing reality of whatever grain exchanging entailed—grain that probably came from areas east of Pineburg, Greg realized. He moved along in the darkness, sliding one toe out in front of the other. He hit a board, a brick, and something soft that tumbled away. A rolled up sleeping bag? Dead rat? Who knew? A window far in a corner brought in some light and a draft. The glass was gone. He made his way over to it and looked out. Beyond the train tracks stood a wooded ridge with a cozy North Portland neighborhood, a horizon of lights as dots, and a tree line as spikes. He looked down. Connected to the outside wall and cascading down the building was an ornate fire escape of black iron, thick and slick and probably far heavier than it needed to be.

Greg turned back to the floor and clicked on his flashlight for a quick scan of the room. A few yards from the open window stood an office that was missing one wall, creating an L-shape that provided both shelter from the open window's draft and a hideout from the stairway. Greg made his way over.

In the corner of the L were a foam bedroll, sleeping bag, back-pack, and small cooler.

It could be Donny.

Greg clicked off his flashlight and stood still, listening. Heard nothing. He sat on the bedroll a long while. His eyes closed once, then twice. He shook himself awake. He rested the back of his head on the backpack. He thought about Torres and imagined FBI whizzes in the Portland's Federal Building somehow locating Greg's phone under the rock. They could ping it or something. Who knew what they could do with technology? He read about the NSA being able to track phones even when they were off. It might have required some authorization Torres had to push and even lie to get, but a man like Torres would probably get it. But at least Greg had a head start, he thought, and his eyes closed again. They kept closing.

Greg's eyes popped open. Morning light streamed in, a blast of rays from more windows than he'd expected in the dark. Squinting, he adjusted to the light and propped himself up, feeling his joints pop and his muscles strain from stiffness.

Donny sat before Greg. He sat on his haunches, perched on his sleeping bag like a yoga instructor, but he wasn't dressed like one, or Charlie Adler for that matter. He had on old coveralls and a cheap fleece pullover over that, all worn and faded so as not to look out of place, Greg thought. He already had a stubble going. He had transformed into a passable homeless guy.

Greg didn't know what to say. His pulse had quickened, but his face still had the numbness of sleep. His eye throbbed, the throb making a straight line down his neck to his heart, which thumped from it. Donny kept staring.

"I figured this was your stuff," Greg said.

"Good thing it was. Street guys don't cotton to squatting." Donny added a smile.

Greg smiled, but it only made his blood race more. "I can't believe I slept this long."

"You been out. Long time. You must have needed it," Donny said, losing the smile.

Greg looked around. Donny had a couple of lines of meth going on a little shaving mirror on top of his cooler. Donny went over and snorted them. He stood and stretched. A pistol was tucked into the front pocket of his coveralls. The gun was small and black, no bigger than a flask, only the end of the butt showing. He could have kept it hidden easily. He wanted to show it.

"You didn't call the cavalry," Donny said.

"Leeann told me you'd be here if anywhere. She wants to help you. And, no, I did not tell anyone."

Donny lifted a half-empty bottle of Old Crow, took a big swig. "Is Gunnar safe?"

Greg nodded. "Only I know where he is."

"Good, good." Donny passed the bottle to Greg. Greg took it and drank, the rim wet from Donny. It burned and gave Greg an instant headache as if skipping right to the hangover. He handed back the bottle and Donny took another swig.

Donny crouched, stretched, and walked the floor, anything but sit comfortably like Greg. He grabbed a chair and turned it backward and sat staring at Greg, but he was looking on through Greg as if asleep with his eyes open. His stubble seemed thicker already.

He threw Greg a sandwich from the cooler. It was peanut butter. Greg ate it.

Donny didn't eat. He paced the room again.

Greg knew he didn't have much time, but he couldn't rush it either. He also wondered how Leeann was holding up in that hotel room. Alone again. She had to be worried about them. It was a fine line. All she had to do was pick up that phone he got her and call Torres.

Donny stretched again. Greg really wished he'd quit fucking stretching. Donny sat on the chair again, eyeing Greg, nodding.

"They don't know you're here," Greg said. "Got no clue. You tricked them."

"Sure. Just like I fooled Wayne." Donny let out a big sigh. It turned into a groan. He paced the room again. He came back and crouched close to Greg's face. "What are you doing, man? Huh?"

"I'm clearing my conscience," Greg said. "No reason to lie."

"Then tell me how you came to Pineburg," Donny said. "Go ahead. I already searched you for a wire. Not even that woke you up. Well?"

"All right. The FBI came to me. They wanted me to inform for them. To act as an informant. They wanted to find out what was going on with the Double Cross. When they first contacted me, they led me to believe you were really dead. Then I got the old bait and switch; oh, guess what—Donny's alive now. Surprised the hell out of me. I think they planned it that way. But I rejected them all the same. Told them no the whole time. I came to town on my own."

Hearing himself confess this out loud, Greg realized just how stupid it was. He was prepared to get Donny's pistol in his mouth, to be thrown out that window, a boot to the balls, anything. Donny just nodded along.

"You had your own reasons," Donny said.

"That's right."

"That fellow Torres involved? The FBI Agent."

"Yes. And he still is. He'll be wanting to know where I am. But you know what? I'm on the run too, in a way."

Donny stopped nodding. "Is that what this is?"

"At first I was hoping I could get you to prove your worth to them, or at least your relative innocence. Lay it all on Wayne. But you kept screwing that up, and I did too, and I didn't know how to tell you. So now I'm telling you."

"Bullshit. You were just making sure I didn't tell anyone about the lake."

"Yes. Of course. That too."

Donny bounced a knee. "And you didn't tip off the cops about it?" he added. "You weren't the one?"

"No. I was thinking maybe you did it. Thought it was some kind of move you were making."

"No. No."

"So, worst case is, someone is putting pressure on us. Or, it's coincidence."

"Hell of a thing, either way," Donny muttered.

They brooded in silence a moment, leaving a void where they might have speculated on who it could be.

"Not a great spot we're sitting in, is it?" Donny said eventually.

"You know what I'd really love?" Greg said. "If you'd come walk with me right to the police. Portland police. FBI can wait. We'll call a good lawyer on the way. Maybe a civil liberties specialist. I think some rules might have been broken."

"Yeah, well, we broke some rules too, ain't we?" Donny pulled back, his eyes to the ground. He shook his head as if he had a bug in his hair, the meth not letting him think.

"And, we'll get you some help," Greg said.

Donny didn't respond. He marched over to the open window and looked out. He looked down. He turned to Greg, the pale light of the window framing him in silhouette.

"You know how you can help me? You tell them that you never saw me."

"You mean, say that I never found you here?"

"That's right. I must have headed the opposite direction." Donny grimaced, his teeth glowing inside his shadow. "He went thatta way."

"It would give you some time. Okay. If that's the way you want it."

"Even with that news story, cold case, whatever, they'll never figure you were in on what went down at the lake."

"How can you be so sure?"

"Because there's me instead," Donny said. "There's always me."

With that, Donny fell silent. His smile dimmed away. His head hung down.

"You know I will look after Gunnar," Greg said.

Donny rushed over crying, the tears rolling so hot off his chin they gave off a little steam. They splashed on his knuckles as he grabbed at his stuff and started to pack it in the backpack.

The problem was, Greg still wasn't sure Donny wouldn't talk. He wanted to grab Donny by the wrists and shake him, talk him out of it. He needed more from Donny. He had to make sure he wouldn't tell. But he played it cool, just showed Donny a shrug, and then he pushed it: "There's something you're not telling me," he said. "I'm guessing a family like the Callums had quite a stash. Karen must have had a safe right in the house. You probably scored."

Donny glared and wailed, a yelped from deep in his gut. "There was one. She took it, took it all. She emptied her fucking safe! It was like the bitch knew somehow . . ."

Greg glared back in horror. She had probably done it sometime after he had confronted her. He, unknowingly, must have woken her up to the threat. "That's terrible," he said.

"I wanted it to be for Gunnar. It was for him. For him!"

"I'll take care of him. I told you. I'm guessing you got a nice new fake ID though. Where is it this time? Alaska, Canada? Mexico again?"

"Yes, yes. Mexico didn't work out so well, but . . ."

Donny stopped packing. He had stopped crying. He pushed himself up from the chair and stood tall.

He laughed at Greg.

"Oh, shit. Man, you're doing it again, aren't you?" Donny said. "That's just what you're doing. You're screwing me again." He came over to Greg and sat down right next to him. "You know what? I'm not going anywhere."

After a few minutes, Donny lay out on the bedroll and stretched his legs. He had twitched into position, scratching at his crotch.

His eyes had slowed to a stop, taking in everything and nothing at once. He was rethinking things, and Greg didn't like it. Now Greg paced the room. He kicked debris out of the way, an old tin box and a parched leather glove. He looked out the open window and saw no threats yet, only the afternoon glistening on the train tracks. He thought it strange that no trains had passed, but he wasn't even sure if this was a working rail line. He went to the other windows and rubbed off dirt but saw nothing to worry him.

"My beard's growing in good," Donny said. "Got a shopping cart, now all's I need is a bunch of cans. No one notices a homeless guy or girl for that matter. I wait it out like that. Then I go."

He jumped up. He fished around in his stuff. He pulled on a soiled and threadbare riding coat and slapped on a grimy, open-crowned cowboy hat. "This is what you think of us. What you thought of me back then. Then came that ole security guard— didn't quite get what you thought you would, did you?"

Greg didn't take the bait. Donny was just stalling now. Holing up here wasn't good for either of them. Donny was slowly losing his marbles. It meant Greg was going to have to shut Donny up. "Every minute you wait? They're going to figure this out."

"You brought all this on me," Donny said.

Greg shouted: "Don't be a fuckin idiot!"

Donny laughed. He danced his goofy country jig. It was barely amusing before. Now it made Greg want to kick out Donny's legs from under him.

"Know what I should go do?" Donny said. "Go bomb the Federal Building, leave a big ole Cascadia flag and a bicycle behind, and blame it all on you. How'd that make you feel?"

Greg could only hold out his hands and sigh. Donny dropped back on his bedroll. Greg paced and paused, paced and paused, listening for sirens or intruders. But of course they wouldn't use sirens, he thought.

He wished he would've tried to get a gun somehow before he came here. But he had no idea how. He paced. He glanced again for Donny's gun. It was still in his belt.

"It's like you're the one on meth," Donny said.

Greg stepped over to him. "I'm telling you everything. What more do you want? They needed someone to be an informant. For prosecution. Maybe they don't have a case."

"Informant? You mean a weasel. Backstabber. A narc."

"Don't forget 'hypocrite.'" Greg huddled with Donny. "Okay, look. I will go with you. How about that? Gunnar's good and safe for now. But you have to listen to me. We have to go now."

Donny stared at his knees, his hands upturned and limp at his sides. "No. I don't believe anyone. They'll just fuck you over. They will. Us."

Greg felt like a father talking to a boy who got beat up at recess. He tried to simplify things. "That pistol you have? At least get rid of that. It's not smart, remember? You told me that. Violence is never smart. You gave violence up yourself. That was your vow."

"Yeah. That I did. I did learn that then, when we did that."

"So," Greg said. He was whispering now, cajoling. "I tell you what. Why don't you just give me your gun?"

Donny scowled. Donny grinned. "Oh, no. No way. I see what you're doing, what you're trying to pull—"

A knocking sound from downstairs, echoing.

Greg tightened up inside, his pulse throbbing. Donny's eyes locked on Greg's, urging him to be still.

Donny tiptoed to the middle of the room, facing the open stairway.

No sound. No response. Greg stood, his jeans making a faint whooshing sound. Donny held a finger to his mouth, shushing Greg.

Inching along, Donny moved to the edge of the open stairway. He pulled his pistol. He crab-crawled on all fours, craning his neck to see. Still no sound.

Donny turned and smiled at Greg. Then, Donny stood. He started down the stairs, taking careful steps. Greg watched Donny descend until only Donny's hat was visible.

Donny's hat froze in place as if hovering.

Greg whispered, "Donny?"

Donny backed up a step, and another, reaching the top of the stairs.

"Stop! Lower the weapon!" A shout. The voice was Torres.

Donny lowered his pistol.

"Now drop it!" shouted another voice.

"Drop the weapon!"

Donny pivoted. He charged back up the stairs and through the room.

He aimed the pistol at Greg's head.

A rush of footsteps sounded, closer, coming up the stairs. The sound stopped. They occupied the stairs now, crouching on them for cover.

Donny aimed at Greg's heart.

"Toss it down!" Torres shouted from the stairs. "If you don't, we're coming up."

Donny, his eyes locked on Greg's, tossed the gun across the floor. It clattered down the stairs.

"Okay, okay," Greg told him, "but now, you have to listen—"

Donny charged to the open window.

Men charged up the stairs in a thunder, aiming weapons— Torres, FBI men, cops.

Donny lunged out the window, looking out. He scrambled outside.

Torres and agents rushed the window. Greg got there first. Three men aimed on Greg.

"Not him!" Torres shouted.

Greg and Torres and others crowded the window, looking out and down.

Donny was hustling down the fire escape, grasping at the iron structure. He slipped on the wet metal and almost fell. The ironwork creaked and shifted.

Donny kept going. The fire escape bolts loosened from the wall, sending down plaster.

Donny held on, riding it out. He was halfway down.

Donny slowed. He glared up at Greg, at Torres. The fire escape shifted again. To steady himself, Donny lowered down to one knee.

The ironwork was loosening free near the window. Greg reached out to hold onto it. Something made him do it. He grasped and pulled and his muscles burned, his knuckles wanting to break through his skin. "Help me!" he shouted at Torres.

Torres leaned out, grabbed on.

Someone was holding Greg's legs to keep him in place, but the iron was pulling his arms from their sockets. The pain surged up his neck, down his back.

Donny saw them helping. He hustled onward, downward.

The fire escape buckled and creaked.

Greg's hands bled, the blood making his hands slip. He let go. Torres let go with a gasp.

Donny raced down, slipping and falling, the ironwork lunging, swaying, shifting. It separated from the wall. He rode it on down, flailing on slippery metal as the ironwork collapsed into itself. It crushed Donny inside as it plummeted down.

It crashed to the ground.

Greg kept staring, unable to move, his hands still clawed as if grasping the iron. Raw, red. The man holding his legs tried to pull him in, but Greg shook him off.

Down below, Donny lay trapped like an insect in a web, his limbs at odd angles. He appeared to be looking straight up at Greg, but he was not seeing. Blood spread out from his wounds.

Eventually, Torres and others appeared below, surrounding the wreckage. Sirens sounded in the distance.

Someone kept a hand on Greg's shoulder, but he stayed at the window. He couldn't help thinking, what he saw now reminded him of the way the security guard lay on the concrete that night so long ago. Blood dripped from Greg's hands, running off the tips of his fingers, and it would splash into nothing, somewhere down there with Donny.

44

Greg wasn't sure why he tried to save Donny, in the end. Was it something like actual compassion, or were his instincts simply kicking in, exploiting an opportunity to show the cops he was the good guy? He might never know.

They were keeping him at Good Samaritan Hospital. He had his own room on a floor across the street from the main building—a floor he suspected most people didn't know about. They treated his hands and bandaged them, but other than that, it was like being made to wait in a hotel room. An FBI woman asked him questions about his time in Pineburg, but most of her probing seemed designed simply to assign him to various times and places as if she was completing a puzzle. He told her: He was there at the Callum House and he saw Donny kill Wayne, right at the very moment he was trying to persuade Donny to turn himself in, to tell the FBI all that he knew, to assist their investigation of the Double Cross. Wayne had come out of nowhere. Donny had hit Greg out of shock, fear. Greg pursued him to Portland anyway, partly to protect Leeann in case Donny came after her. It was stupid of him to do it on his own, but he thought he could still save Donny. These were more answers than the woman needed, but why not get it all out? It was good practice.

Greg got the papers, TV, a tablet to use. The media was developing its own angle, he saw: The ludicrous attempt on the

Pineburg Dam had less to do with a secessionist militia, dam removal, and environmental policy than a long-festering power struggle between one Wayne Carver and the reclusive Charles Adler aka Donny Wilkie. Their feud led Donny Wilkie to kill Wayne Carver and flee to Portland where he died attempting to escape. No stories mentioned Greg. The FBI had been monitoring the movement called the Double Cross and was making arrests, it was reported. Teams from the FBI and other agencies raided an unnamed militia "headquarters"—which had to be the Rooster Lair—along with remote barns. They found weapons and explosives. What had once been a minor rural nuisance but protected by free speech could now be seen as a dangerous homegrown terrorist movement prosecutable under multiple charges of conspiracy. Felony battery charges were also mentioned, but details weren't released. FBI Field Agent Rich Torres got a brief mention for his efforts.

Greg kept asking the FBI assigned to him about Leeann and Emily and Gunnar. The FBI woman eventually assured him that the two women were safe, and that he could speak with them soon. Gunnar was staying with a friend, in Pineburg, and was doing as well as could be expected.

On the third morning in the hospital, they transported Greg—in an unmarked car, without cuffs or cages—to a room in the Federal Building downtown. It was many floors up, a stark space with no windows but no shackle mounts or two-way mirror either. A more discreet briefing room than an interrogation chamber. He sat at the gray Formica-topped table, was left alone.

After a few minutes' wait, Rich Torres came in and sat across from him, Torres wearing casual slacks and a pullover. He glanced at Greg's bandaged hands but didn't ask him how they were; Torres would know that already, of course. Greg said nothing.

He had thought of asking for a lawyer, but he wasn't sure why he would need one just yet, so he held off.

Torres stared at him a moment, but like he was counting to five. Then he sighed. "How you holding up?"

"I'll live."

Torres asked Greg questions that allowed him to repeat the events he had told the FBI woman in the hospital. Then Torres asked him again. And a third time, until it became mechanical for Greg and without discrepancy. Once that was over, Torres gave himself another five-count pause and added a question:

"Was Gunnar there?"

"No. I did not see him."

"Nowhere in the house that you knew of?"

"Not that I knew of. I guess he could have been watching somehow. It's possible."

Torres gave Greg a long, hard look. "Okay," was all he said, and he left.

After about ten minutes, Torres came back in and sat down. He was looser, leaning back, legs spread.

"We're putting all this on Donny," he said. "That includes Wayne Carver's death."

"The papers had it right for once," Greg said. "It's just like I told you."

He straightened, expecting a tirade from Torres despite his casual face. Casual could be a ploy.

"Well, you could thank me," Torres said finally.

Torres' comment confirmed to Greg that no one was listening in. Greg didn't thank him. He had planned to say nothing more, but he could not help himself.

"This must all be such a big disappointment to you," he said. "I am. They are. You wanted them to try something bigger. That's what I thought and still think. I don't blame you. It's what you do. I just wanted to be clear."

Torres held out his hands. "What did you want me to do?"

Greg had no answer for that. He just shrugged.

"How did you locate Donny and me? Did Leeann call you?"

Torres shook his head. "Officially, I can't tell you. But it wasn't Gunnar either."

"I never thought he would," Greg said.

They had a staring contest for a few moments, just like when they'd met that first time in Lone Fir Cemetery.

Torres reached into his jacket, Greg flinched. Torres pulled Greg's phone out and set it on the table. It was still wrapped in the plastic bag but looser and any dirt wiped off. He slid it across to Greg.

Greg stared at it a moment. He didn't even want to know how they'd found it. "What about Karen Callum?" he said.

"There's nothing to connect her. She owns a ranch, a load of property, and a big chunk of a public utility. She buys up the land. That's what she does. Daddy's little girl. The laws don't question it, not until something goes broke."

"Like the water supply for example?"

Torres shrugged. "Tell it to about ten other agencies. That's not our turf. I'm just one guy."

Greg reached for his phone, unwrapped it, pocketed it, and left the plastic on the table. He stood. What else could he say? The world marched on, no matter what he did. Only Cascadia could change that. Someday it might. He would probably be an old man by then if not dead.

"Well? That mean I can go?"

"There is something else," Torres said. "There was a murder—a security guard was killed. Near Mt. Hood. Years ago."

Greg, standing over the table, kept his feet planted. "Uh . . . I guess I'm not following."

"It's been on the wires. Got picked up all over, just briefly, but still. It's a cold case. Reporters like that."

Greg's heart thudded from the strain, and only Torres really knew if it showed. "I don't read the *Oregonian* much anymore," Greg said.

"In any case, it happened about the time you knew Donny. Did you know they picked up Donny for it? It was a couple years after the fact. County detectives were following up, had time on their hands, I guess. His truck had been spotted at the scene. He denied it, of course. Said he had been snowboarding all on his own. Learning how. They couldn't peg it on him, and they never got another lead."

Greg was still standing over the table, over Torres. "Wow. I don't know what to say."

"You know anything about that?"

Greg made his head shake. "I know that he used to snowboard a lot. We hit the mountain a couple times. I was more of a skier though. We would've taken my car. I wasn't the type who wanted to be seen in a pickup, not back then."

Torres sneered. "Too cool for school, that it?" he said.

"I told you. I told you in Pineburg. I went my own way. He went another."

Two weeks later, Greg, his eye blued but swollen no more, packed his last load onto the cargo bike and trailer he had borrowed from a friend so he could finish moving. He had scored his own apartment just north of East Burnside, only ten minutes away. Torres had arranged for him to receive a retainer, which let him put the first month's on the apartment and pay off some bills. For his part, Greg had signed a waiver and confidentiality agreement that prevented him from writing about his direct involvement in Pineburg and afterward: He had technically become an inform-ant after all. He didn't intend to write about it in any case, so why mess things up?

He had gotten lucky. Donny had his chance to pin the secu-rity guard murder on him long ago, yet Donny had not. He never told Greg he had been picked up and questioned years ago. Maybe it was even the real reason he had bolted for Mexico in the first place. He had saved Greg's ass more than Greg ever knew. His luck was a bitter pill. Donny probably never would have revealed their secret, not even today. But Greg had not been able to trust that. As for Torres, he was possibly the only other person in the world who knew about it—if he wanted to. Torres might have even leaked the cold case story, for all Greg knew, just to see how he and Donny would react. Well, the man got his wish.

Greg had saved every bungee cord he had ever owned, and now he used every one of them to secure the last boxes. He was outside Emily's apartment, taking his time, certain she would come out.

Emily skipped out and down the steps and stopped before him, feet together, grinning. She held up a tee shirt that read Republic of Cascadia. They laughed.

"I admit it: I never wore it," she said.

"That's okay. Keep it. Make a pillow out of it."

She gave him a kiss on the cheek.

"Stay in touch. You will, right?"

"I will."

Greg pedaled off on his borrowed ride, finding the bike lane on SE Seventh and giving it all he had for the little hill that would kick him up to Sandy Boulevard. Wishing he had his own bike back. At least he knew his bike was safe. He had talked to Gunnar, who was keeping his bike for him and had taken to riding it around

Pineburg. Gunnar was still staying at Tam's, which was a modest bungalow on the poor side of town, near streets of worn motor homes and clapboard shacks. Tam was going to put Gunnar and a couple other kids to work painting her house; Gunnar got to be their foreman, they joked.

Gunnar had told Greg: After Donny fled, the FBI came by Tam's to ask if Gunnar had seen Donny, but Gunnar and Tam said no. The FBI people had only stayed for five minutes. "It was like they were just running errands or whatever," the way Gunnar put it, with things to check off. They had offered him care and support, but Gunnar said he liked it at Tam's. He told Greg about Tam's daughter Melanie, about what had happened to her: Wayne had tried to love her but "didn't know how," as Tam put it. Wayne had beaten Melanie up so bad that one of her eyes might not ever look right again without surgery, though it worked well enough to get her into the Air Force. She also probably wouldn't have gotten the heck out of Pineburg if Wayne hadn't slapped her around so much, so there was that. That was one big reason why Wayne could never have become police chief and certainly not mayor of anything, ever.

Greg imagined that Gunnar had cried a few times in the past couple weeks, possibly in Tam's arms. He hoped he had. He had told Gunnar he would drive back out and get his bike, and Gunnar was welcome to come along back to Portland. Greg could put him up. Gunnar said he'd think about it. Meanwhile, Karen Callum had told him he could always have his room at the Callum house for as long as he wanted, but Gunnar thought that would be more awkward than ever, especially since Karen's longtime friend Brenda had moved in. The two were nice enough to him, but they were always off doing their own thing. Besides, Tam had told him he could stay as long as he liked. "Maybe when I'm done painting her house," Gunnar said.

And Gunnar and Greg had promised to call each other every week.

Two weeks later, a town-hall type event was held in Pineburg about Pineburg Dam. All the players were there—state, federal, all the agencies and the interested groups, including Karen Callum and her team of lawyers and experts, a true delegation just as Torres said. Even a few TV crews. It went off without a hitch, successfully resolving many tricky water issues for the near future, and got little more press coverage than Wayne Carver's angry speech from a fallow field. The biggest breakthrough came when Karen Callum announced her intention, as main owner of Callum Utility Company, to relinquish the relicensing process and agree to the dam's removal. A solid deal had been struck, it was reported, and one that worked for all.

45

One year later: Greg was walking near his East Burnside apartment with Gunnar, who was pushing along the bicycle Greg had scored for him. Gunnar had been in Portland for almost nine months. His hair was longer. He wore jeans and a hoodie. He had a studio in Greg's building after living with Greg for two months, and he was working as a prep cook at a brewpub. He said he was thinking about going to Community College. He was going to see how well his mom did with it.

"I'm starving," Gunnar said.

"Good deal, buddy. We're doing that Pho place you like."

Leeann Holt stood in their path, farther down the sidewalk. She had on a jacket and skirt and cute hat that made her look younger. Emily had given her some clothes and helped her find new outfits. Leeann had her own place, too—renting Greg's room from Emily.

Greg and Gunnar walked up to her. "I thought you were going to meet us at the Pho place?" Greg said to her.

Leeann was holding back a grin, standing on tiptoes. "I couldn't wait," she said.

"Why? What?" Gunnar said.

"I passed all my classes. Every last one."

Gunnar grinned. Leeann grabbed him and hugged him.

That evening, Greg was typing on his laptop, working on the introduction for the draft of his new book. The words onscreen read:

"The schism between city and country will never be a black-and-white issue. If someone tells you it is, don't ever believe them. They might be trying to hoodwink you for their own ends. Starting over as Cascadia comes with baggage loaded down with past burdens. These must be dealt with for the new society to survive and prosper. Cascadia may never succeed if the urban and rural rupture is allowed to fester, to bleed. There are ways to stanch the wound, but the compromises required will demand real grit . . ."

His trip to find Donny Wilkie had made him realize that he had never included the more far-flung and opposite rural regions of Oregon in his vision for Cascadia simply because they did not fit. He wouldn't have known how to fit them in. Their puzzle pieces were a shape all their own. His wasn't a conscious decision but rather the result of subliminal process of elimination. We tell ourselves what we want to hear. As for the Pineburg area, it was on the border of that unknown, unwanted puzzle. Time would only tell if it would join Cascadia or choose an abyss. In his new book, he offered hard choices. Those regions in Southern and Eastern Oregon so unlike the bioregion of Cascadia could be left to join their own breakaway state, whether it was a new Jefferson State or something worse—a homeland that made a guy like Wayne Carver feel right at home. Whatever is was, it would always border Cascadia and could never be ignored in the future.

Greg also knew: The truth was, he was FBI Field Agent Rich Torres' informant forever. Torres would always have a hold on him. They would. Because Greg could never really know what Torres knew about him and had on him, until it was probably too late. If anything ever came of Cascadia and it threatened the

Feds' interests, they could come to him, make him do what they wanted. Torres could even come acting on his own, the solo operator with leverage. Greg knew this was wild speculation, but it didn't hurt to consider the scenarios. The dead had failed at less and the victors had succeeded at worse. If they ever did ever come for him, he was the best mole they could ever wish for: The true believer.

His doorbell rang.

He went to the front door, checked the peephole, and, shrugging, cracked open the door.

There stood a guy in his twenties in black garb. He had a tough look with a crooked jaw, but Greg wasn't sure how much was for show. He looked familiar to Greg somehow.

"Can you let me in?" the guy said before Greg could get a word out.

"Who are you?" Greg said. "How did you get in the building?"

The guy turned to run.

"Wait," Greg whispered—why he was whispering, he wasn't sure. He had swung his door open wide. The guy turned back.

Minutes later, the two of them were sitting on Greg's sofa in near darkness. The guy had asked Greg to keep his lights off. The guy's name was Luke. Greg had a beer going. Luke had a water. At first Greg had thought this Luke was some kind of anarchist or street kid but he didn't have the smell they often carried, like wet dogs that smoked. Though Luke had once been a street kid, he explained.

"That was, until your book changed my life," Luke said.

"My book?"

"Yes, your book, sir. *Rescuing Cascadia*. You gave me a copy once, outside the Cascadia Congress last year."

Now Greg did remember. This Luke and a girl had been coming to his talks. He had taken them for the usual street anarchists, never serious about anything except nothing. Now this Luke looked ten years older. "Thanks for reading it," Greg said.

"I've done way more than read it," Luke said. "Maybe you don't want to believe this, but . . ."

"What? What is it?"

Luke beamed. "You? You are, to us, the father of the Cascadia movement."

"Us?"

"That's right, us. They are many more of us than you know about. And, we are ready. We are so freaking ready, man. There are more of us every day. We're counting on your support, because the shit's getting serious. It's way past time to fight back, and hard."

Greg could only stare. He moved to speak but nothing, truly nothing, could come out.

Acknowledgments

Special thanks to my brother Dave, a veteran police detective who's always a huge help with those details only cops know, and to Portland State University professor and urban studies and planning expert Ethan Seltzer for clarifying regional land and water use issues. Any missteps made are my own.